THAW
By: A.C. Kabukuru

1

TABLE OF

CONTENTS

Ch. 1 Santa Angeles North Island, 2163 - 5

Ch. 2 A Breakthrough in Amsterdam - 18

Ch. 3 Grave Concerns - 33

Ch. 4 Replicating Conditions - 45

Ch. 5 Curious George - 50

Ch. 6 He's Alive - 64

Ch. 7 Blue Jay - 79

Ch. 8 George Finds Out - 92

Ch. 9 Favors - 108

Ch. 10 Your Own Private Apocalypse - 121

Ch. 11 Thin Ice - 133

Ch. 12 No Atheists in Foxholes - 145

Ch. 13 The Worst Kind of Magic - 155

Ch. 14 The Monte Carlo Theory - 164

Ch. 15 Mistakes were Made - 181

TABLE OF

CONTENTS

Ch. 16 FOMO - 196

Ch. 17 Silence and Darkness Forever - 209

Ch. 18 Low Blows - 223

Ch. 19 New Alliances - 237

Ch. 20 Breaking Points - 251

Ch. 21 Everything's Going to be Different

Now -260

Ch. 22 A Promise is a Prison - 270

Ch. 23 An Ominous Prelude - 280

Ch. 24 Phone Home - 296

Ch. 25 Disavow All Knowledge - 303

Ch. 26 Thanks for Nothing - 311

Ch. 27 R.I.P. - 319

Ch. 28 High Tide - 328

Ch. 29 Poster Boy - 341

Ch. 30 Life is Long - 355

Acknowledgements - 367

Chapter 1

Santa Angeles North Island, 2163

It was dusk on the industrial side of the island, when their experiment, a tall youngish man dressed only in a flapping hospital gown, found himself cold, alone, and hunted. As hard as his pursuers ran, he ran harder. Their hazmat suits slowed them down while he chopped away at the wind resistance with his pumping arms. The fugitive's head was shaved and thick streams of blood trickled down his forearms, not that he seemed to notice, as he gracefully hurdled over stray trash cans and abandoned shopping buggies. The two suits stopped for a moment to catch their breath, and surveyed the land ahead, looking for some advantage that they would desperately need if they were going to catch him. They could not come back without him. One of them carried a gas mask.

The runaway reached a road just as the sun set. The super pollution made for bewildering sunsets. Headlights approached from a distance. He checked behind him for his pursuers, before anxiously fixing his eyes back on the road. The headlights belonged to a lumbering vehicle of epic scale, twice the height and width of a common city bus, marked only by the number 75. He was taken aback by its strangeness. It stopped. A panel slipped open and a ramp silently descended at his feet. He stepped back.

A man's voice in the distance began shouting, "No, no, no, no!" The two uniforms had broken out into a full sprint.

The bald man, clocking the uniforms closing in fast, decided he had to take his chances inside the mystery box. Once inside, he was momentarily blinded by the bright overhead lights. When his eyes adjusted he observed two levels of passengers. They were dressed oddly and some wore surgical masks. He was also a head taller than most of them in his bare feet; only adding to his fish out of water-ness. They were as startled by him as he was of them.

"Ten dollars please. Ten dollars please," chirped a scuffed up box mounted to the wall beside the door. Though the man had never seen such a contraption, it's purpose was abundantly clear.

Exhausted and panting, he felt out of immediate danger for the moment. He clenched his gown closed in the back, sparing the upper deck the sight of his bare ass. He looked out the windows trying to get his bearings. It was dark, but what he could make out wasn't familiar. Was he in a foreign country?

A kind-faced woman approached him gently and advised him, "You need to pay, ki."

He couldn't seem to get enough air and started to wheeze trying to force the oxygen into his restricted capillaries. He understood the woman but he shook his head, and turned toward the front of the bus to address the driver. He wanted to explain. But explain what? Even he didn't know what was going on. But there was no driver at the front, not even a driver's seat. The goddamn thing was driving itself. Then out of the window, in the distance, he saw a familiar structure. It looked like the L.A. Forum, but it couldn't be, it was on the waterfront.

He turned back to the woman and asked her, "Where am I?"

"SANI, Santa Angeles, North Island. You lost, ki?"

What was she talking about? His wheezing was worsening, he began to rub his burning chest in vain, his eyes were bloodshot and bulging. *What's wrong with me?*

A disgruntled laborer shouted from the second story, "If he can't pay, he needs to get off!"

"Yea, I don't want to catch whatever he's got,"

added a lady in the back.

The kind-faced woman took mercy on the wheezing stranger, and reached for her purse. She noticed the blood on his arms and said, "Oh ki, something's nicked ya"

Under the bright lights it was now clear that his blood wasn't red. They were both surprised to see it was a deep purple. She recoiled. The vehicle stopped again and the hatch hissed open. The two uniforms from before boarded the people mover.

They moved through the crowd swiftly toward their target. The sight of people in hazmat suits apprehending a patient in public, threw everyone into a panic. Anyone not already wearing a mask, snatched their scarves or bandanas up over their nose and mouth, and made moves toward the exits. It devolved into a trampling hysteria.

The target pushed backwards through the frantic crowd. The hazmat suits cornered him against the wall, where he slid down to the floor - trapped. One of his pursuers was a young man, with platinum blonde hair and delicate features. He clumsily restrained the subject with plastic zip ties. The other hazmat suit was a darker skinned petite woman, only a little older than her blonde comrade. The chain from a pair of dog tags peaked out of her suit collar.

She crouched down next to the subject and checked his heart rate like she was trained. He was lame from exhaustion and his respiratory episode, otherwise he might've been able to fight them off.

She said, "George, what are you doing? You scared me to death." Then she slipped the gas mask over his struggling face. His breathing started to relax. Kelley hit him in the neck with a hand held tranquilizer, the kind they used during prison riots.

"Who are you?" he asked her, before losing consciousness.

2020

It was after dark and George was trying to get comfortable in the backseat of his 2010 Honda Accord parked on a side street in LA's old Highland Park neighborhood. He looked different with a head of dark wavy hair. He twisted and turned his too-long frame, but his knees just came up too close for comfort. His car was trashed, overrun with plastic water bottles, soda cans and various fast food leavings. He was indulging in his favorite brain melting past time, scrolling through Tik Toks. He sighed and put his phone down against his chest, and tried to close his eyes.

A fist rapped hard against his window. He startled up, but was relieved to find a friendly face. It was an unhoused American man about fifty, heavy set, and wearing too many clothes for the summertime. A bit embarrassed, he reluctantly rolled down his window

"Whatchu doin out here like this G?

"Hey Peaches. Nothing, just got in a fight with Alison."

"What's that got to do with this?"

"I'm just waiting out the storm brother. Women, right?

"Whatchu fightin about?"

George smiled up at Peaches, hanging one hand out of the window and gesturing with it emphatically. "Nothing man. It's stupid. You know when you're arguing and at some point you realize that you're wrong, like totally dumbass wrong, but you've already acted like such an ass - you can't like, she's gonna roast you hard if you fess up to it, right? So you have to like double down on your crazy, really dig your heels in. I've found that a good old fashion storm out is very effective because after a while they just want stuff to go back to normal and they forget about who was right or wrong."

"But you didn't storm out to nowhere, you're out here in your car like a simp."

"Only cause I don't have anywhere to go, but she doesn't know that. She probably thinks I went out to a bar, and I'm chatting it up with a pretty brunette—"

"Listen to yourself, man."

"You're right. I'm going, I'm going. -- Hey, wait a minute—"

"What?"

"I got some bottles and cans and stuff in here, cause I knew I was gonna see you, and I didn't wanna be empty handed."

"Uh huh," said Peaches as George gathered up his recyclables.

"It's not usually like this."

2163 A.G. (Before George)

James P. Getty, a square-jawed mid-level government bureaucrat, waited in the back room of a seedy storefront situated in Mar Vista's backstreets, trying to buy an edge. Franscois was the greasy low life proprietor who traded mostly in duped Chinese technologies. He produced a velvet blue ring-sized box.

"How do I know this is legit?" asked Getty looking over his shoulder.

The salesman opened the box. He handled the merchandise delicately with a pair of tweezers. "Oui, you see the serial number here, and here... is the manufacture date."

Getty held up the box and marveled at its contents' exquisite craftsmanship.

"It's beautiful."

***

Years ago the urban sprawl from Santa Barbara to Los Angeles on down to San Diego had all congealed into a massive gridlocked super city. Municipalities joined forces and tax bases and renamed their newly minted metropolis Santa Angeles.

Between 2110 and 2130 a series of huge earthquakes, like nothing in recorded history, set off a geologic string of events. Fires, floods and cracks in the earth half a mile deep effectively sliced off the west side from Malibu down to La Jolla and inward as far as Inglewood and Bellflower. And just when Angelenos thought they were safe, the latter quakes broke western Santa Angeles in half, creating two islands. Bridges, ferries and underwater trams connected the islands to each other and the mainland.

Many people's homes ended up in Atlantis, the nickname for the underwater neighborhoods at the bottom of the Gulf of Redondo. But others, like many lucky Compton residents, experienced an extreme reversal of fortune. The Comptons beachfront community, as it was rebranded, became a desired get-away destination for Hollywood's up and coming. Native residents built generational wealth by leveraging their properties into lucrative boarding houses. A jitney shuttled stressed out wellness gurus from Calabasas to the Comptons every weekend during the high season.

The split wasn't in the distant past. Many locals had lived through it or been raised during the aftermath and rebuilding. Though there was a lingering PTSD among real Angelenos, California was still the biggest economy in the United States, which was still the biggest economy in the world and a few earthquakes were not gonna keep them down.

***

A self-driving personal pod wrapped in the Health and Human Services logo, pulled up silently to the industrial building on Ettinger Street. The suicide style doors lifted open and out stepped Inspector First Class, J Getty. Wanting one final look, he discreetly pulled the velvet box out and opened it, revealing a beautifully mounted house fly with metal wings that glistened in the sun.

Getty stepped into the Cryonicor lobby. He was late forties, clean shaven, and smelled like fresh cut wood. His gray eyes quickly surveyed his surroundings. A slogan of sorts, "Death is not an event, it's a process" was emblazoned across the wall behind reception. He shook his head in disgust. The lobby was empty, including the reception desk. He made a few quick notes on his glass reader.

"Hello, anybody back there?" he called out to the offices behind reception. There was a mysterious rustle in the back. A minute or two later, a no-nonsense woman emerged. She was dark skinned, wore no makeup and her hair, half-braided, was pulled back neatly. She wasn't wearing her white lab coat, and her fitted scrubs revealed the impressive physique of a retired Navy Seal.

"Samantha Witten? Well, I did not expect to be greeted by you personally."

"Short staffed today. Mr. Getty, what do I owe the pleasure? We don't have an inspection scheduled for months."

"Surprise Inspection, your favorite."

She began walking back into the facility, wordlessly inviting him to join her. She smiled a go-fuck-yourself smile, and said, "I always have time for HHS. Shall we?"

He interrupted her, "—Why are you wearing a stethoscope?"

The question stopped her cold. She forgot she had it on. *Shit.* She took a deep breath and turned on her heel to face him. "You're right. I don't need a stethoscope because all my patients are—"

"Dead?" he offered smugly.

"Only legally. No, I was just helping out in our new hospice wing for our terminally ill members. You should have the paperwork on that."

They kept walking down the hall of the dimly lit and slightly run down facility. It smelled of bleach and formaldehyde. He scrolled through his reader, but came up short. "No, I don't have anything on that."

Witten 1. Getty 0. She smiled her cockiest smile, and led them through a pair of double doors. Witten's high cheekbones, big eyes and arched brows gave her a regal profile. She carried herself with a sure confidence and a smidge of gravitas. "Well check it out when you get back I guess, we got all the permits and approvals from the state. The hospice add-on was a natural continuation for us. It is critical to get our patient's brain frozen right away and having them deanimate naturally on-site is really the best option for them, for the ones lucky enough to see it coming anyway."

Getty was a guy who followed his gut and his nose. No matter what this charlatan was trying to sell him, it didn't pass the smell test, and it pissed him off. He turned up the bass in his voice and said, "You know if I find out, you are doing anything with these frozen stiffs, other than what you are licensed to do, which is **nothing** but keep them on ice—"

Witten cut him off, "—Oh I assure you, everything here is above board and by the book. But, just in case we did want to do research on human subjects, is there an application I could fill out? Because I looked on the portal, and I didn't see one."

Getty could give as good as he got and wasn't intimidated by a snake oil salesman like Dr. Sam Witten. While her back was turned he pulled out the box and released the bug. He said, "Oh we have them. They are right next to the one's for magic carpets."

Dr. Witten had stopped in front of another pair of double doors. "Shall we start with the supplies bay?"

"We'll start where I say to start Ms. Witten."

"It's Doctor Witten."

"Ms. Witten, question one. How do you sleep at night fleecing the grief-stricken?" asked Getty, as he routinely peaked his head through the doors of the supplies bay.

Witten recited, "Cryonics is a service. We freeze the newly deceased to prevent decomposition in the hopes that future medical technology can restore them and give them their lives back. It's not a scam, or some cheap time travel trick for cops and robber movies, it's just hope."

"You are selling something you have no way of knowing if you can deliver. How is that not a scam?"

After the inspection, Witten watched Getty return to his government issue pod through the blinds. Once he drove off, she turned back down the hallway in a hurry. She rolled through the supply bay doors, and walked to the back right wall, to some giant chemical vats. She slid one to the side effortlessly, revealing a secret entrance. She leaned in for the facial security scanner and the door whooshed open. She pulled the containers closed behind her to conceal the entrance.

Chapter 2

A Breakthrough in Amsterdam

Witten returned to her secret lab. A 70 year old subject was laid out on an operating table. He was hooked up to machines that monitored his vitals and seemed to be breathing unassisted. Mr. Kelley Baker and Ms. Priya Cayhill flanked the patient at their consoles. They had been her trusted cryotechs for five and ten years respectively. Though they had no formal medical training, they were unusually bright in their own ways and Witten had managed to mold their skill sets to suit her peculiar needs. They were loyal and they were discreet. In the very back of the room there was a glass tank filled with a pink gel, where a half-thawed George floated face down.

Priya and Kelley looked to Witten expectantly, as she pulled her hazmat suit back on.

"What happened?" asked Priya.

"Surprise inspection."

"He didn't find anything right?" asked Kelley.

"No. But I forgot I had this thing on." She took off her stethoscope, frustrated.

"Oh my god," said Priya, knowing how stupid a mistake that was.

Witten approached the man on the table. "Where were we?"

Kelley stepped up with a heavy hand-held laser gun. "The lower brain functions are active and regulating his breathing. We were just about to take a few years off this old boy."

"Have at it," said Witten. She stepped aside, pleased with their progress.

Priya massaged the man's skin with the pink gel. Kelley switched on his new wave ambient trance music and started going over the body with his laser - rejuvenating muscle mass and stimulating rapid collagen production. An image of the man on a nearby monitor in his late twenties gave Kelley a reference. It was a scanned polaroid, bearing the handwritten message, "this is as I wish to be restored."

"Now you're just showing off," called out Priya over the thumping base.

Kelley, feigning humility, said, "I'm just grateful for the opportunity. You know they won't let you into medical school if you have a felony on your record?" His boyish bravado and hubris amused Witten.

Priya asked, "Are you saying you would rather

be doing anything else?"

"Not at all. The wild wild west of medicine feels like a good fit for an outlaw like me."

The comatose man on the table was ageing backwards before their eyes. His nasolabial folds on the sides of his mouth receded back into his face. His crows feet were retracing their steps right off of his temples. His muscles were firming up in his arms and chest. His jaw was even taking back a more square shape. He looked thirty years younger in minutes.

Witten nodded to Priya who launched the nanobot repair program. The glittering I.V. bag was distributing thousands of tiny machines into his bloodstream. They worked in concert to search out and repair the damage sites caused by the trauma of the cryonic freezing process itself.

This was the third and final round of nanobot deployment on this patient. A hyper-realistic hologram of the patient's brain appeared above Kelley's console. The brain rotated at a slightly tilted angle like the earth. Thousands of green dots represented repaired damage mapped by the nanobots. A few red dots represented irreparable damage, however these were not in neuro-critical areas. This was where the magic was supposed to happen and they all knew it. But nothing was happening, again. Kelley reran the program himself. The results were the same.

Priya reluctantly reported, "There are no signs of higher brain activity."

Witten, "Are you sure?"

"She's right. This guy's an eggplant," said Kelley.

Witten leaned over the man to listen to his chest with her stethoscope. His heart beat loud and clear. "How long has he been in again?"

Priya quickly confirmed on the console the information she knew by heart. "He died fifty years ago. He was a veterinarian. Awe."

Witten checked his pupils with her light pen. No dilatation. She stroked the hair on his head. She pulls out her phone and dictated the following, "Thaw attempt 26. Achieved sustained unassisted heartbeat. Full muscle tone and skin rejuvenation successful. Brain activity could not be revived. Attempt Failed."

Priya's head dropped at this. Witten composed herself on her way out, "He's a lost cause. You know what to do."

"So that's it?" said Priya. Witten turned back to the stubborn cryotech, who continued, "Can't we try a peptide solution or trans-cranial laser therapy? Or maybe the PURP isn't calibrated—"

Witten held her hand up, and declared "Priya it's done. He's been out too long already. I don't like it either. But we have to learn what we can from him, and move on, or else we're never gonna get there. Right?"

Priya's deference to Dr. Witten was almost absolute and had been since she first came to her for help as a preschool teacher with a dying husband on her hands. She had no choice but to trust her mentor even when every fiber in her body disagreed. She swallowed her disappointment and said, "Right."

After Witten left, Kelley and Priya got to work. Kelley attached adhesive pads to the man's head and chest. He gave the nod and Priya threw the switch, sending 600 watts of electricity into the brain dead patient. She looked away. It was an archaic but convenient solution that left no paper trail. As he was electrocuted, he convulsed gruesomely, and finally flatlined.

***

Priya and Kelley wheeled the body bag through the halls of Cryonicor. Kelley kicked off and stepped onto the gurney like a kid riding a cart in a grocery store. His short sleeved scrubs revealed extensive Japanese inspired body art that covered both arms down to the wrists. His bright green eyes reflected the fluorescent lighting. But Priya was despondent and in no mood for his shenanigans, not today.

"Can you not?" she asked.

He dropped down obediently. He was only trying to lighten the mood. "What's up?"

They pushed the body bag through the double doors labeled: TRASH INCINERATOR. Once inside they lined the gurney up to a chute in the wall.

"Sorry. I just got a lot on my mind. Thinking about freezing my eggs," she said, as she opened the hatch. Hydraulics lifted one side of the gurney so the body, neatly and without much ado, slid down the chute.

"Look, I don't *not* get it. You're getting up there, no offense. And you're in the right place. I think it's healthy, it keeps your options open, like everyone does it. You want me to ice my spermies in solidarity? I'll do it." Priya shook her head amused.

"That's not necessary, but thanks," she said, patting his shoulder. As she reached for the big red button, he stopped her.

"Wait! Can I do it? Please?"

"Go ahead," she says.

Minutes later, an eager Getty hopped to when he saw some action at last from his perch across the street. He drew his military issue binoculars to his eyes and focused them in on two young cryotechs exiting out of a side door of the main building on the compound. One carried a bag and the other a small shovel. He quickly lost their sightline as they disappeared behind auxiliary buildings heading toward the back of the property. He sighed, bringing the binoculars back down to his chest. He chewed his toothpick and took solace in the fact that the bug was hard at work.

***

The sun sets over the floating neighborhood known colloquially as The Keys. A dozen modular floating platforms, each containing homes for up to 300 souls, linked up to create a community living half a mile off the mangled Southern California coastline. Seagulls perched upon the makeshift balconies of a housing complex made of stacked up 40 ft. shipping containers. The multi-colored Lego-like boxes bore the logos of foreign companies. The once vibrant community of starter homes had deteriorated in recent years. The balconies were littered with drying laundry and piled up rubbish. Inside the second to top row, far left side unit, Priya Cayhill got home from work.

She was greeted warmly by her only roommate, an obese black cat, named Bear. She promptly fed him, and stripped down for a shower after a long disappointing day. In the shower, the water timer counted down from 45 seconds. So much for conditioning. After her shower, she grabbed a beer and stepped out on her balcony looking back at the mainland. She could hear the nocturnal soundtrack of The Keys; a low-fi mix of crashing waves, obnoxious music, babies crying, and people fighting. Across the water, she saw pods zipping around and people living their lives. She bitterly felt herself missing out on all of it.

She went to her tiny desk, sandwiched between the fridge and a washer-dryer all-in-one. She docked up her reader and logged into her Facebook Legacy account and reloaded her views. Try as she might, she couldn't seem to kick this habit. She typed into the search bar a name. And profiles appeared for the dunzo veterinarian.

His name was Ronald Rogers. Like many, he had lived his whole life on social media. Getting his own profiles at around ten years old and posting regularly until the week of his death. She scrolled through his stories, birthday wishes, vacation pictures and watched him grow up, get married, have a baby, get married again, get his own veterinarian practice, get married again, and retire. She could see everything except his DMs. She played a video from a surprise 50th birthday party; he was giving a toast.

"You guys are crazy! I can't thank you enough really! I see so many faces that have been by my side for decades. And some of those faces are a little too... unageing, it's creepy, you know what I'm saying. What gives with that? But seriously thanks guys, and thanks to all the animals that have enriched my life along the way, big and small (he gooses his latest wife). If you know me, know us, we don't like to live in the past, it's about the future and what's next. So..to the next fifty years, am I right?"

The crowd applauded him vigorously. He seemed beloved, but social media had a way of distorting reality.

Her cursor went back to the search bar. She hesitated and then typed another name: John J. Cayhill.

Warning: You have exceeded your monthly allotted views for this user profile. If you wish to purchase additional views, price per view doubles. Would you like to proceed?

"They really know how to bleed you, don't they," she said to herself.

Too rich for her blood, she logged out of the platform. It had been ten years since John deanimated, and after the day's events she felt no closer to bringing anyone back. Though there were more and more fertility options available all the time, her biological clock was ticking in the back of her mind, growing louder and louder. How long could she wait? She felt herself approaching a crossroads. That night, a dark despair crept over her, a feeling that she might spend her life working on an unfixable problem, and miss its preciousness all together. But whenever the dark feelings would surface she had developed a sort of tick, like a glitch in her programming. Her mind cycled back to the soothing narrative that presumed his reanimation was just around the corner. She returned to her furious research.

***

That night Priya wasn't the only one beginning to feel desperate. Samantha Witten stood in the bathroom of her high rise condo. Like all urban homes, it had a small footprint, less than 450 square feet. But it was elegant and clever, decorated in a Wabi-Sabi style. The spacious second bedroom was Witten's office and home gym. She washed her face thoroughly and inspected the new baby wrinkles beginning to form around her eyes. She pulled eye drops from the cabinet and applied them. She was reasonably sullen, taking in her failure. Failure 26. That's 26 souls perished forever. Lost to the senseless tragedy of mortality. And her new wrinkles reminded her of her own upcoming date with the dark river.

Her wife, Gwen, found her in the bathroom staring solemnly at her reflection. Gwen leaned on the doorway. She was in her satin night robe. Gwen looked about the same age as her partner, she was half-Kenyan and half-Korean raised in Belgium. She spoke with an accent that was impossible to place. She over pronounced her Ts.

"Hey. You okay?" Gwen asked in that just woke up raspy voice.

"Uh, yeah. Sorry if I woke you." She leaned into the mirror again. "Do you think I should get a nano-treatment for these new things around my eyes?"

"What are you talking about? You know you are 75 right? You look great." She smiled at Witten, shaking her head at her wife's insatiable quest for youth. Witten forced a polite smile. Gwen lovingly touched Witten's shoulder and persisted, "What's wrong?"

"Nothing. Just work stuff. We lost one." Witten finished up her skin care regimen, which is as extensive as one would imagine for a 75 year old who looks like a 45 year old retired MMA fighter.

Gwen cocked her head to the side like a puppy. "How did that happen?"

"Busted sensor on a cryostat. We didn't know it was out of liquid nitrogen, body partially decomposed so..."

Gwen pulled Witten to her. She said, "You can't let these things upset you so much. Life extension is one thing, but death is a fact of life. It's a non-negotiable."

At this, Witten released from their embrace, casting her eyes down, unable to meet her wife's gaze. *Says who? She doesn't get it.*

Gwen tried to pull her wife's wayward gaze back to her with widened eyes that demanded acknowledgement. "You coming to bed?"

"I'm not ready to close my eyes yet. I am gonna get a workout in and then I have some work I want to finish. I'll be in my study." She started to head out when Gwen stopped her.

"Samantha, maybe you should talk to someone. I could refer you to one of my colleagues." Dr. Guinevere Kim Witten was a high profile psychologist, who received some celebrity status for her groundbreaking work with combat vets and her follow-up book on the subject. Though Witten's brilliance was exceptional, her obsession with life extension had marginalized her career to say the least. And it wasn't easy being married to the other more famous and respected Dr. Witten.

Witten leaned over and kissed Gwen appreciatively on the forehead. She assured her, "I'll be up in a little bit."

In her study, she was stripped down to her sports bra and joggers rowing hard and steady on a wooden rowing machine. She was lean but extremely toned. She rowed like she was rowing for her life. After an hour on the machine, she stood up and took a swig from her water bottle. Her golden brown sweat drenched skin soaked up the soft lighting. She pulled a lightweight windbreaker on and cracked open a post workout supplement shake.

She sat down at her desk, and activated the docked transparent glass reader with a swipe. She was scrolling through research papers when a notification drew her attention to a new paper: **Medical Miracle in Amsterdam: Scientists Re-**

store Brain Function to "Brain-Dead" Stroke Victims. She sat up straight, put on her detested reading glasses, and began speed reading the article. *Yes, this is it.* She read words like: calcium-boosted neuro receptors, dormant synaptic fibers reanimated, domino effect, chemical etching-

Her cell lit up on her desk. It was China. She understood Mandarin but didn't speak it. She picked up the call and listened, "Yes, I saw it. Those findings had to be unintentional, Jansen wasn't even working on stroke recovery. Right!? Yes. That's exactly what I thought, penicillin all over again. " She was grinning like she just got into her top choice grad program, like she was 22 all over again. She got another call, it was France. "Let me call you back. K?"

Witten switched over the call, and walked out to her balcony overlooking SANI, and skyscrapers that went as far as the eye can see in every direction. She couldn't talk about this stuff inside, not with Gwen just in the other room. "Bonjour. Yes, I've seen it, Julien. Are you thinking what I'm thinking?" The moon was full and ominous. "Of course, that's the hope, but honestly I can't even begin to speculate about the ramifications." She was getting another call, this one was Priya. This one was personal. Whatever the pretext of this call might be, Witten knew the subtext. And it overwhelmed her jubilant mood with a sense of dread. She hesitated to take the call. *Just breathe.*

"Julien, I have another call, let me let you go. Au revoir," she said, clicking over to Priya. "Hey."

Priya was looking at her reader, smiling from ear to ear. "Did you see the Amsterdam article?"

"Yea."

"You know what this could mean?"

Witten rubbed her eyes and said, "There's not enough in the article to retrace his steps exactly."

"I just got offline with a post doc from his lab. He just snipped me Jansen's lab notes."

Damn. Priya is good. Witten could see in Priya from the beginning her dogged determination, her gift for research, networking, problem solving and resourcefulness. Witten needed someone to help her, she couldn't do it all. She had allies scattered around the world, many were doctors like herself, but some were too afraid to leave mainstream medicine and others simply too far away or too much of an alpha themselves to be decent collaborators. Witten needed someone close to her, someone smart, someone invested, someone she could trust, and someone she could control. Witten could teach the science part. Good help was hard to find, even if it did come with ghastly strings attached.

Witten said, "Really?"

Priya said, "What do you think I am doing in those international forums? We're not gonna solve this problem in a vacuum. See you tomorrow." They hung up. Witten looked back up at the

moon unable to resist the excitement of the moment, grave concerns aside.

Chapter 3

Grave Concerns

2163 A.G. (After George)

Some days after George's dramatic capture and sedation on the people mover, he slept soundly in the recovery room. Cameras in the ceiling sent a live feed to monitors in HQ. Witten had direct access to the feed on her cell.

This recovery room looked like what it was, a cleared out work room. There was a stool and one small window with an obstructed view of the Cryonicor campus. The room was bare of creature comforts like television or tablets. It was definitely maybe the worst place imaginable to wake up in.

Upstairs in HQ, Priya was on duty watching the monitors. They had been watching in shifts for days, waiting for their experiment to recover from a case of pneumonia he had caught when he was outside. After they tranq'd him, they put him into a brief medically induced coma so he could recover and get stronger before burdening him with consciousness. But those drugs had worn off and his body was recovering nicely. It was only a matter of time before he woke up.

Priya stared at him a lot, she wondered what he was going to think about the future. *Will he be amazed? Will he feel like he has been reborn? Will he be lonely?* Just then she saw him stirring as his brain activity began jumping. Priya slammed the call button. In a matter of moments, Witten was in the recovery room with George.

His eyes blinked in slow motion, before finally opening. His pupils dilated. The bright room was all blurry mounds, 8-bit marshmallows and light rings. His eyes began to focus and he observed his surroundings... and the person watching him, who was ominously dressed head to toe in a plastic suit and head covering.

"Who are you? Where am I?" he asked, startled, in a low raspy voice, still drowsy from the sedatives.

Back in HQ, Priya's call had also summoned Kelley, Jack, and another man in a suit to watch the monitors. *George speaks!* Their jaws hung slack from their skulls, stupefied by the unbelievable.

In the recovery room, Witten's cautious exterior cracked and a smile spread from cheek to shining cheek across her face. She was in shock herself, struggling to find words for a response. His elevated heart rate on the monitors snapped her out of it.

"Try to remain calm Mr. Gilroy, I'm Dr. Samantha Witten, and I'm here to help you."

"Why are you wearing that thing on your face?" he asked, seeming to regard her with the kind of fear you have for a person who is pointing a gun at you.

She explained, "This is a clean room. I'm wearing this for your protection." She approached him and he recoiled, only to discover his wrists were in mysterious restraints that lit up red when he struggled. "I know. I'm sorry about that. You ran outside before, and we can't have that again. We had to restrain you while you calm down, it's just temporary."

Outside? He searched his memory for a clue to what she was talking about. He half remembered a bad dream, there was a chase, terror, a bus.... What he recalled was only a rough sketch of a moment. "What's going on? Why am I in here?"
"Well, this is a medical facility. And I am playing catch up a little bit here too, so I just need to ask you a couple questions and then I will explain everything we know, OK?"

He started coughing hard. Witten waited patiently for his breathing to normalize before proceeding. "How old are you?"

"30, no wait, 31, yeah."

"Wow. Your speech is so clear, incredible."

"Why is that incredible? Did I have a stroke?"

"No. What year is it?"

"2020," he said, a bit irritated by her elementary questions. She tapped on a mysterious piece of glass. *Is this a bad dream? Wake up George! Come on!*

"What did you do for your last birthday?"

It took him a few moments to recall, then he snapped his fingers. "I know. We rented a sailboat and skipper by the hour, he sailed us and some friends from Marina del Rey to Malibu and back. We swam off the boat. Alison's idea. Big mistake, I almost fucking drowned. No more ocean for me."

The episode he described sounded excessively reckless to the ultra cautious Samantha Witten. She continued, "And this was your 31st birthday, you're sure?"

"Uh... actually, no. Now that I'm thinking about it, it was my 30th birthday, it was kinda special."

"So you're 30, not 31."

"S'weird. I guess, yeah, I'm only 30 but—"

She sees his attention is drifting away. "It's okay. Mr. Gilroy, this is important, have you ever been told you have a congenital heart condition?"

"No. Do I?" He felt his chest and looked under his gown, no scars. Witten looked up at the monitors disturbed by his answers. Back in HQ, they were equally concerned.

"Can I have some water?"

"There is water right there," she pointed to his bedside. He marveled at the paper cup that wasn't soft, wet, or cold. He drank the whole glass in one go.

Witten continued, "One more question, Mr. Gilroy. Have you ever heard of cryonics?"

"No. What is that? Do I have it?"

Witten looked back up to the camera and tapped on her reader. George followed her sight-line and noticed the watcher in the ceiling. *Restraints and cameras and a lady in an alien suit?*

Witten pulled up the stool and sat beside George. "So it seems you have suffered some memory loss, approximately the last 16 months of your life. That's why you are disoriented and you don't know how you got here and can't remember your birthday. You're 31."

George said relieved, "Okay. So it's 2021. What's wrong with me?"

Priya watched the monitors, listening with great anticipation. The moment was at hand when she would get to experience the vicarious euphoria of watching the promise of cryonics register across the face of a person who had actually benefited from it directly.

Witten cleared her throat as she considered her words carefully and continued, "You got sick. You had a procedure. And now you're recovering. But your immune system is extremely vulnerable. That's why I am wearing this thing."

Priya was surprised at Witten's deceit. She shook her head in disappointment tinged with anger.

George asked, "Where is my cell? I want to talk to my Mom."

Witten smiled nervously and glanced again at the cameras. Priya nodded her head emphatically. *Of course he is asking for this, what did you think was gonna happen?*

Witten said, "Later. You need to get some rest. You caught pneumonia from being outside only a few minutes."

Outside? That's right, he was outside before. The half remembered dream was coming into focus. *What was that weird bus about? This is not okay.* A pit in his stomach opened up like an abyss. "Can you take these off?" he asked, testing the waters, holding up his wrists.

The three people watching the monitors all shook their heads NO. But Witten knew she needed to do something here to gain his trust. She released the restraints with a few taps on her glass reader. The peanut gallery raised their hands in disbelief.

He was confused when the restraints appeared to fall off on their own, but he was mostly relieved. This small act of contrition had the intended effect. It eased George's fears a bit. Maybe he wasn't trapped in an episode of Black Mirror.

Witten asked, "How do you feel?"

"Like I have pneumonia I guess. Tired. My head hurts." He coughed again and again.

"Get some rest. I'll be back soon to check on you and we will talk some more."

Too tired to protest, George rolled over on his side and fell back to sleep.

Upstairs in HQ, Witten arrived to face the firing squad. Christian Martinez was the son of Javier Martinez, the founder and director of the Martinez Foundation. He had just flown in from Barbados to witness the second coming of George Gilroy. He was in good spirits.

Martinez greeted Witten warmly, "Incredible Samantha. Much better than last time. My father will be very pleased."

Priya, disgusted by their glad handing, interjected, "We are totally unprepared for this. You never said anything about him not being able to breathe outside."

Martinez tensed up, like his couple friends had started fighting in front of him when he thought they were just getting some beers. Kelley took his cue from the open animosity and wordlessly exited. Priya was taking a rare stand.

Witten, eyeing Martinez, calmly said to Priya, "I'm so sorry, but I could not have foreseen this. I was so focused, WE were so focused, on just bringing him out - I mean we failed so many times before, if I had set up everything for every contingency beforehand, I mean it just didn't make sense."

"That was kind of a shit show, how he just ran out into the streets," added Martinez, sympathizing with the young cryotech.

Witten admitted, "Yeah, I know. Look, this place is designed to keep people out, not keep people in. We're gonna do better now that we have an actual—"

But Priya was not satisfied, "—Yeah okay. So now what? What about him?" she motioned to the man on the monitors and continued, "we have a responsibility to this person, and frankly we have no infrastructure to support this kind of rehab."

Witten snapped, "So what do you want us to do Priya? You want us to take him to an ER, so they can find out?"

Martinez, put his hands up calling for a cease fire, "Ladies, ladies, c'mon. This is a good problem to have, okay? I think Dr. Witten is right, if we turn him over to a hospital we risk being exposed. Let's be strategic about this."

Priya asked Martinez, "Are you going to tell him it's not 2021?"

The financier brought his meaty fist to his nose in contemplation, then looked to Witten, "What do you think?"

Witten cracked her neck and said, "I think his body is under enough stress as it is. Who knows what news like that could do to him. He doesn't even remember being sick or signing up for cryonics at all. How would you feel if you went to bed one day in your normal life and woke up dead a hundred years in the future?" And there it was. She set off a truth bomb. They fell silent, grappling with its smoldering embers.

Jack poked his head in the room. Jack Wagner was a mild mannered administrator. He had trimmed curly hair and giant blue eyes that hid behind some audacious red rimmed glasses. He was dressed in a low-rent shirt and tie. In addition to being Witten's oldest friend, his primary role at Cryonicor had been as a counselor and intake specialist.

"Sorry to interrupt, Priya, your 8AM consultation is here," said Jack uncomfortably.

Priya looked at her wristwatch, "Shit. Human or Pet?"

Jack rechecked his glass reader, "Human."

Martinez and Witten felt saved by the bell. The descentor left to attend to her duties. Martinez was handsome beyond measure, he flashed a knowing million dollar smile at Witten. She was unaffected by his model/professional baseball player looks or his fancy cologne. At the end of the day, they had had a good working relationship for going on twenty years and he was as much a friend as she felt like she had in the world. There weren't many people, outside her subordinates, whom she could be honest with.

"Congratulations by the way," he said after a moment.

"Come on. This is a disaster."

He shook his head, "No. This is proof of concept. You know what this means?" He made the international hand sign for MONEY.

"Good. Cause we are gonna need a lot more of that."

"Keep him alive. The money will take care of itself."

They looked back to the monitors - like proud parents watching their newborn in the hospital nursery through the glass. And what a specimen he was, a regular sleeping beauty. He was their precious little billion dollar guinea pig.

Martinez swatted at an annoying house fly in his orbit.

"What the hell, Sam?"

"You get it?"

"No."

***

Getty sat by himself in the employee only cafeteria. He finished his prayer and began to eat. His food was divided in a bento style box and he ate one type of food at a time clockwise, never mixing them or eating out of order.

This cafeteria serviced several agencies not

just HHS, there was Immigration, FDA, and FBI. They were all cliqued up across the massive cafeteria. He watched the FBI guys getting all agro about whatever. They high fived and laughed obnoxiously loud. Part of him was glad he had been rejected from their training program. They were a bunch of douchebags anyway.

Near him was a table of his fellow HHS employees including several other ranking First Class Inspectors. The short one called CJ and one of his lackeys walked up to Getty who braced himself for another unpleasant encounter.

"By yourself again, huh?"

"I like to eat alone."

"Yeah that must be it. How you liking the job, Inspector First Class?"

"It's fine."

"Yeah, I know this gig probably sounded exciting but a big day for us is closing down a restaurant, right?"

"I've had all the action I need for one lifetime."

"Have you even closed a restaurant yet? No, that's right you haven't. That's second class scutt work. You wouldn't know anything about that, cause you skipped the line."

"I know more about scutt work than you could ever imagine."

"Oh yeah? Seems to me you married your way into this sweet gig... company pod, corner cube, on the golf course by two, hardly seems fair to the rest of us. If you had a clue what you were doing, it'd be one thing, but you don't even know what to look for, much less what you're missing. C'mon, there's no shame in just collecting a pay-check bub."

"Don't call me bub. And I'm working on something big."

"Something big? In the crematoriums and funeral homes sector? Necrophilia? You wish, perv. See you on the links."

Once they had gone, Getty counted down from ten while his pulse steadied - a trick he learned fighting Puerto Ricans in the marine corp. Then he pulled the glass reader out of his satchell and opened the FlyGuy app. He converted the Chinese characters to English and logged on the cloud to download the footage.

Chapter 4

Replicating Conditions

2163 B.G.

The team set to work the next day replicating the conditions of Jansen's success. They poured over hundreds of pages of lab notes from the Amsterdam study. Priya ordered materials, new machines, and strange chemical ingredients to even stranger solutions. But it wasn't easy. She was redirected and told things were out of stock or no longer available. She was messaging morning, noon and night using translator apps to talk to obscure suppliers in 2nd tier countries.

Some of the equipment they could not buy outright. They were told they had to be a medical facility, for the living, not the dead, in order to even open an account with critical suppliers. Kelley came in handy, back channeling deals using shell corporations to get them the items they required.

More than that, they had to teach themselves elements of molecular chemistry and new biotech procedures that Jansen's lab had spent years learning and perfecting. They didn't have the experience or the time frame. They had months to get themselves ready for the next patient who was already thawing in gcl. Once the gel process was over, he would be ready for the reanimation attempt. He would remain viable for only 23 hours. This was their window.

But their next attempt would be on a truly ideal candidate. A programmer named George Gilroy who died in 2021, at the age of thirty one. Even though he had been on ice much longer than most of their patients, his preservation had gone smoother. His scans showed the cryoprotectant, the 'cool-aid' as they called it, had maximum saturation, preserving 98% of his original tissue. The speed of the preservation was also flawless. After legal death his brain was on ice in less than four minutes. It didn't hurt that he was in pristine physical condition when he transitioned. He had been an athlete and had the build of an Olympian. He was pretty big, almost 6'4, broad shouldered and two hundred pounds. He had clearly kept himself in shape during the years after college. When Priya and Kelley first pulled him out of the steel tube and saw him, they joked about pulling Captain America out of his ice crypt.

George had a bad ticker that caught up to him. He didn't get a transplant in time, having ignored his symptoms for months before seeking medical attention. If George had been alive today, their medicine could have created a new heart for him in a lab. At one time a heart condition like his was potentially terminal, but today it was a minor medical problem. George just had the bad luck to be born too soon, like billions before him. Cryonics nobly sought to right these injustices.

Priya studied the history of all of the patients they worked on, looking for any edge or insight she could give their thaw attempt. Unlike Witten, she always got attached. And this time Jansen's success convinced Priya more than ever of their own impending good luck. This intensified her projections of some symbiotic relationship between herself and the dead man in the tank. Sometimes couples or entire families were interred in preservation, clearly sharing values and a plan to reunite in the future. But according to their records, George had no one connected to him in preservation. That made Priya sad. She imagined how John would feel if he woke up and she wasn't there by his side, if he was surrounded by strangers in a strange world. It broke her heart to think about that. His orphan status made her feel even more protective of him.

What Priya and Kelley didn't know was that

this next attempt would be their last shot. Witten was coming to the end of her twenty year funding agreement with the Martinez Foundation, a venture philanthropy firm she had covertly partnered with decades before. Cryonicor made some money off preservations of the newly deceased, but to be honest, that barely kept them in liquid nitrogen. The price was an annual membership during life and a one time payment upon death - for perpetual cryonic suspension. And it wasn't cheap, but it wasn't strictly for the super rich either. There was a non-profit aire to this industry. Most life insurance policies could absorb the costs. But, the real funding came from the Martinez's foundation. They agreed to finance Witten's research for twenty years, and in the event of a successful reanimation, they would throw in a multi-billion dollar kicker to fund the research once it really got going. Witten was using every last penny on attempt 27. A lifetime of research telescoped down to this last buzzer beater.

Being a garden variety narcissist, Witten believed her failure would spell the end for all reanimation research and it would only be good luck if someone picked it up again a hundred years from now. Since she didn't believe in luck, she saw her own ending coming into focus on the horizon. Some fooled themselves into believing that a long life by their standards, 130-40 years, was enough. But it wasn't enough for Witten, she wanted more... much, much more.

When Witten was eight years old her mother was killed in an accident on a people mover on Santa Angeles's westside. It was the first time she was touched by death. And it was terrible. The accident made the news nationwide. Eleven people died in the fiery explosion. Her mother had been on her way home from work at her job as a tech at a drone repair store. But that day she never made it back. Witten waited for her all night long, and it wasn't until noon the next day when the peace troopers came to their apartment with the news.

Witten was small for her age, and interested in the way things worked. She was like her mom that way, mechanically inclined and forever taking small electronics apart and reassembling them. She was curious and bright. She was also the only child of an only child, and after the death of her mother, was sent to live with her maternal grandmother, Arlene, as no other provisions had been made for her, the death being so sudden and all. Miss Arlene, as she preferred to be called, was as blind as she was unfit for the raising of children. And it was there that Witten would be transformed from a precocious child into whatever she was now.

Chapter 5

Curious George

2163 A.G.

Getty initiated the footage download from the cloud. He rubbed his palms together, giddy with anticipation. The operation errored out. He translated the Chinese to English again, the message read:

> Insufficient signal. FlyGuy unable
> to upload files from current location.
> Manual upload required.

"Manual upload?"

He pulled the velvet box out of his satchell and removed the mount, behind it he found a short black cord. *A cord? What the hell?* Getty cut his eyes back to the table of snickering inspectors. He would have to make up a good excuse to show his face back at Cryonicor so soon.

***

Priya rode the elevator from the top floor to the bottom, on her way to meet her 8 AM consultation. It was partially mirrored and partially glass. On a clear day you could see all the way to the water. The busy world of 2163 roared just outside the window pane. But inside the silence was deafening. Priya stared solemnly at her own reflection wondering how she got here.

After John, she had a lot of energy and nowhere to put it. She had always been a good student in school. Witten soon discovered that Priya was a prolific amateur medical researcher, bombarding her with articles, studies, and new drug trials that she thought could help with cryonic reanimation. But experimenting with reanimation was illegal. Witten had let her know, though they weren't experimenting directly on patients, they were working on the obstacles that they would eventually face. Witten didn't lie outright, but she spoke in half truths and let Priya assume whatever her heart desired.

When Witten approached Priya with a job at Cryonicor, she was surprised and initially resisted. She loved her job at the school. But she had to admit, these days she was mainly going

51

through the motions. It felt like nothing mattered anymore. Still, she didn't know if she could stomach the eternal waiting around in store for her at Cryonicor. It sounded like too much for her to bear; having someone so close, and yet so far. But Witten persisted.

One day the doctor told Priya the truth about her secret research. Granted, it was reckless, but Witten was a betting woman. She convinced Priya she could play a direct role in bringing patients back from the ice sleep.

Upon learning this, Priya's eyes were opened. She drank the cryogenic cool aid and her spirit was revived overnight. Witten's secret research gave Priya back a sense of agency and control over her life that she had thought she lost. She quit her teaching job without notice. They agreed it was best to transfer John's tube to their North Dakota facility. It would be easier for Priya to focus. She went to work everyday at Cryonicor, a pay cut by the way, with enthusiasm and curiosity. She thought she had a purpose before helping the kids, but this was a bigger purpose. She felt like she was finally doing what she was meant to do.

***

Mr. and Mrs. Goldstein, were an older upscale couple. She was considerably younger looking than he was, but maybe he hadn't been as diligent with his skin care routine. Priya walked them through a cavernous basement brimming with 9 foot tall steaming steel cryostats. This room was known amongst the Cryonicor staff as *the foxhole.*

"Finally, these are cryostats, we call them tubes. They are twelfth generation. Each tube holds four patients," Priya said routinely, her mind on other things.

Mr. Goodstein asked, "What happens if there's... an earthquake and you lose power?"

Priya answered, "We have two sets of backup generators. Trust me, we take this very seriously. In fact, we store our patients upside down. Because in the unlikely event that there is a temporary interruption in liquid nitrogen refills, the patient's head would be the last thing exposed to room temperature."

Priya was going on 48 hours of no sleep and it showed. Mrs. Goodstein stopped her to ask, "Are you okay? You look like you pulled an all-nighter."

Priya nodded appreciatively, "I am just coming off of a graveyard shift, pun intended." They all smiled at her little joke.

Mrs. Goodstein asked, "How many people do you have in these?"

"We have roughly a thousand people here, and another thousand in our North Dakota facility."

"—Does it hurt?" Mr. Goodstein asked.

"Adam," said Mrs. Goodstein, shushing her

husband's naked emotion.

"What, I can't ask a question? Because you said I'll be dead but not dead-dead so…"

His candor and vulnerability drew Priya out of her wandering thoughts and back to the present. She explained, "When we freeze you, your heart will have stopped on it's own, but your cells are still alive. You're right. From what we can tell, your nervous system is very much down." She smiled empathetically at this beautiful couple and asked gently, "How much time do you have?"

"Couple months maybe," said Mr. Goodstein.

Priya said, "I'm so sorry. That's a pretty cruel ending to a happy marriage if you ask me."

Mrs. Goodstein ran her fingers down one of the frosty tubes curiously. "Will I be able to come visit him?"

"Yes. We have weekly visiting hours."

The Goodstein's regarded each other as passengers on a journey, who must temporarily part ways, but with the resounding promise to return to each other as soon as possible.

As tears welled up in Mr. Goodstein's eyes, he said to his wife, "I don't know. It's a lot of money. It seems crazy, no offense doc."

This objection felt very familiar to Priya, too familiar in fact. Emboldened by the events of recent days she protested, " It's not crazy. Believe me. The science is practically there already. Your husband could be back with you before you know it. But he won't even have a chance if you put him in the ground to rot."

Mr. Goodstein held up his hand, "Whoa. Kind of a hard sell, don't you think doc?"

Priya was caught off guard by the stridency of her own reaction, she softened her voice and said, "You're right. I'm so sorry. But full disclosure, I'm not a doctor."

"Then what are you?" asked Mrs. Goodstein.

Priya answered honestly, "I'm a widow."

***

The next day, George woke up on his own in his recovery room. He sat up and stretched his arms, his body aching from lying down too long. His headache hadn't gone anywhere. No one was with him this time. He yawned and looked around curiously. *What time is it? What day is it?* No clocks and still no cell phone. He peeked under his blanket to confirm what he suspected, he had no pants or underwear on, just his crappy gown.

"Great."

He looked around the bed for some kind of button to call a nurse. Nothing. Just then, Dr. Witten whooshed into the clean room with a tray of food.

"Lunch time."

She sat the meal on his bedside tray, then went to open the curtain to let some light in. The bento box featured both steaming hot and ice cold sections, one was simply steamed yams, another was a vegetable that looked like a tomato on the outside but red cabbage on the inside, and still another was unrecognizable chunks of protein drenched in a mystery sauce. He had heard hospital food was bad, but this was next level.

"Hungry?" Dr. Witten asked, as she turned back to see him devouring the meal with his bare hands.

She offered him a much needed napkin. He saw her plainly for the first time, without the clean suit.

"Good news. The pneumonia cleared up."

"Already?" he asked with his mouth still full.

Witten responded nervously, "These drugs today. It's crazy."

"So can I go home?"

Witten looked down, she hadn't expected him to be so... inquisitive, demanding... alive. She pivoted, "I'd like to keep you a bit longer for observation, but I do think it's a good idea if you move around a little bit. Get the blood flowing. Sound good?"

"Yeah," said George, he started to get out of bed, but stopped short. "Do you think I could get some pants?"

***

Witten and George made quite the pair strolling the halls of Cryonicor. Next to the doctor, he looked like the incredible hulk in his way too small loaner scrubs. He pushed his rolling I.V. rack alongside him and wore a nasal cannula around his neck. The device vaporized pure oxygen. A far cry from the tubes-up-your nose devices of yesteryear, it distributed oxygen comfortably and effectively. He'd never seen anything like it, not even on TV. She smiled at his confusion.

"State of the art," she said with a friendly wink to ease his nerves. She continued, "Your respiratory system is still recovering. Don't want to take any chances outside the clean room."

He went with the flow, anything to get out of his little prison. Every passing person, doorway, window, object caught his attention. Witten was already getting nervous that she had made a mistake taking him out like this.

"You okay?" she asked

"I'm pretty sore."

They passed an interior office window with shades drawn closed. In the glass, he saw his reflection for the first time. He barely recognized himself. He must have been really sick before. He noticed his hair was starting to grow out as he ran his hands through it. But what was up with the color?

"Your hair is growing back fast," commented Witten.

"I can't figure out why my head was shaved for heart surgery. And why is it growing back like salt and pepper?"

Witten did a double take at his new hair growth. "Your head was shaved when you got here, I thought that was the look you were going for," it was a neat white lie, "it wasn't this color before?"

"No, my hair is dark brown." He shaved his own head? *Why?* He's never had the desire to shave his head, in fact his thick wavy hair was always kind of his thing. He was getting more intensely curious about the past sixteen months of his life.

Witten inspected his head closer, "Well, it suits you. Makes you look distinguished."

"Thanks. I like your hair too," he said earnestly, reciprocating her compliment.

Witten touched her hair self-consciously, realizing her side half-striped braid must be very unusual to him. They walked on.

"Besides the soreness, how do you feel?" asked Witten.

"I still got this gnarly headache."

"Gnarly?"

George was amused at what a sheltered square Dr. Witten must have been; surprising for someone with such progressive personal style. He educated her, "Like, terrible."

Witten stopped him immediately. "Oh no, I thought that would have cleared up with the pneumonia." She shined her light pen in each of his eyes.

While she was checking him out, he noticed behind her a room at the end of the hall labeled: TRASH INCINERATOR. Cocking his head to the side he asked, "You burn your trash?"

Trash incineration was adopted en masse before she was born, but of course George wouldn't have experience with this practice. "Yes, well that's... something new we're trying - to reduce landfill waste. Just in case one day trash consumes the planet."

"What about the ozone layer?"

"What's that?" Witten asked, simply forgetting her Life Sciences section on past atmospheres and their subsequent demise.

"What?"

"Oh yeah, no, right," nodded Witten trying to recover, "the oz layer is something to consider. Come on, this way," they moved on, but he looked back fascinated.

"Can I get my cell phone back please?"

Witten slowed down, digging her free hand in her pocket aimlessly like she wanted to disappear into it. "Right. Your cell phone. The thing is, it messes with the equipment, you know the frequencies. So it's not allowed. You'll get it back when you leave."

"Man that's messed up doc, you can't expect me to sit up in that room with no TV or anything. What do you expect me to do... read? I don't do well with boredom, social media has murdered my attention span." They passed another door that George recognized as the entrance to a clean room, but the window in the door was covered. "What's in here?" George asked, going straight to the door and trying to open it.

"That room is off limits to patients!" Witten shrieked, rushing to put her hands on his hands and looking him dead in the eyes.

"Why?" he asked, utterly confused by her objection.

"Because." She wasn't used to being questioned by anyone, except HHS.

He mimed surrender. They walked on, but she watched him like a hawk. He was twice her size and it dawned on her she had no way to control him if she had to. And she had to.

Feeling a bit constrained, he shot his eyes around uneasy, "How soon until I can go home?"

"Hard to say right now. Not long."

"What's that mean? Like a week?"

"Maybe a little longer, let's play it by ear." When confronted with sharp questions she resorted to obfuscation. This had served her well in a celebrated decades-long career in bullshitting.

She motioned for them to turn right at the next corner, but he went left without hesitation. When George walked he took long strides, and Witten scurried slightly to keep up. She had to because they were connected by the oxygen tubes. He was following the exit signs, but she didn't realize it. She tried to keep up with him. Then they rounded a corner and suddenly came to an exterior door. He looked back mischievously at her with his hands on the handle, like a toddler testing his limits.

"George," she said as a warning.

"Get some fresh air?"

"That air's not fresh."

"What do you mean?"

"Remember when you went outside before? You don't want that to happen again do you?" He looked down, remembering his burning chest and the feeling of drowning on dry land. His boyish grin fell away and he stepped back from the exit.

Witten's heart was pounding, she had never expected him to be so bold as to walk out right in front of her. What was she gonna do with this character? He was right, he could NOT stay in that weak recovery room indefinitely. And he couldn't go outside, and she couldn't keep him reigned in for long. She naively assumed they would have months to sort it all out, but that turned into days right before her eyes. This was a wild zebra in your spare bedroom kind of situation.

She finally said, "Let's get you back to your room."

He followed her, and tapped her hand pulling the cart, offering to pull it himself. He could easily handle both the I.V. rack and the Oxy cart. She appreciated it. As they rounded the corner back the way they came, George ran smack into Kelley who was power walking in the other direction, knocking his reader onto the ground, where it slid across the floor.

"Oh my god, I'm so sorry!" said George, as he scrambled to pick up the reader and get it back to its owner. When he picked it up he noticed it hadn't cracked or even scratched. Now THIS was weird he thought. He handed it back to Kelley like it was cursed with a sorcerer's magic.

Kelley regarded George with the same kind of awe.

"George, this is Kelley Baker, he's a gifted nanotech."

Kelley smiled like you do for your school pictures, "It's all in the thumbs."

George's demeanor shifted, "You're the guy from the big bus."

Witten and Kelley took a moment to wrap their minds around his ID. Finally Kelley added, "Sorry about that man, I just had to get you safe, you know?"

The sounds of distant coughing and gurgling drew their attention to the tucked away hallway to their left. Without realizing it, Witten had found herself right in front of the open door of their hospice wing. Beds full of the extreme elderly in their final days were in full view.

"It looks pretty bleak in there," added George.

Witten nodded sincerely, "Yeah, I know." She never went around the hospice wing, though working it was a cover she often used with her wife and Getty. She had managed to work her way out of interacting with the dying or recently dead since she promoted Priya to Director of Preservations. She only worked with frozen stiffs now. That's how she preferred it.

George motioned to a water fountain, and Witten nodded permission. Kelley and the doctor were alone for a moment.

"Seems like he's doing great, right?" asked Kelley brimming with his trademark optimism.

"He's a mess. Highly disruptive. He JUST tried to go outside on me. This is gonna be a lot harder than I thought—"

"Oh my god," Kelley said in a slow hushed voice looking toward the hospice entrance.

Witten turned to see what he was so interested in. George was sitting on the bed of one of the hospice patients chatting it up. He's showing off his high tech nasal cannula device. *What is he doing!?* They waved George back over to them frantically.

George rejoined them smiling, "Hey, sorry, that guy's nice. But he's pretty far gone, he told me that he's 135 years old, and that he was born in 2028."

In all her years secretly working on reanimation, Witten realized she had never thought about the consequences of success, about the aftermath of managing a full blown human being, 24/7.

Chapter 6

He's Alive

2163 B.G.

Months passed as the team worked tirelessly through the steps of Jansen's lab. Even though the work was arduous and they were racked with insecurity about their skills, they remained staunchly upbeat. They attacked everyday with the fervor and pleasure of a beginner's mind.

Even Gwen noticed a change in her wife's schedule and demeanor. She was working a lot more and could never offer a satisfactory explanation for it. She would just say she was helping out at the new hospice wing. But when she was with Gwen, she seemed lighter, more present and giving. *Did she feel guilty about something? Was she compensating?* Gwen began to suspect her wife might be having an affair. But, she tried to bury those suspicions.

Priya spoke to George when no one else was around and visited his tank in their covert reanimation chamber daily. The one way exchanges were nothing melodramatic, she treated him like a normal person: *Hey. How you doing? Do you work out? What's your favorite color? Hope you're comfortable. Do you want a coffee or maybe a tea?* One thing that bothered Priya was the expression on George's face. Firstly, it was a bit contorted. But one thing she felt fairly sure about was that he did not look at peace.

There were many conversations about contingencies among the cryonicists. Priya pushed for Witten to let her prepare a place for George to convalesce inside Cryonicor, in the event they were successful. Witten also wanted to believe this time would be different, and so she granted Priya permission - but no extra spending, she could only use what they already had. Priya worked diligently and resourcefully to make a comfortable space for her new friend.

Kelley Baker socialized with his surfer friends, but kept his mouth shut about cryonics in general. He was somewhat embarrassed that he had never become a real doctor. His friends thought he worked at a nursing home, which he did kind of. Priya was solitary outside of her friendships within Cryonicor. After John, she had taken up the, somewhat unnerving posture, of a devout conspiracy theorist thereby slowly alienating her friends. Nowadays, she had no one to tell her secrets to. But Witten slept beside her unsuspecting wife night after night, like everything was normal. Of course she wanted to share, but she couldn't get past the fear that her wife would react poorly.

As life spans increased and anti-aging treatments got better and better, people found the prime of their lives were dramatically extended. Marriage to one person began to make less and less sense as it was less and less successful. So marriage rates dropped worldwide. The wedding industrial complex was spiraling and in response it lobbied to pass a new law to make marriage appealing again. They successfully implemented a new system where marriage became a 10 year contract with an option for extension for another 10 years. If a couple did nothing on their ten year anniversary, their marriage simply expired. No muss, no fuss. Sure children and major assets had to be sorted out and they were, but the expectation that the marriage was supposed to last forever was gone. Since neither party felt like a failure or blamed one another, those divisions went much more smoothly. Most didn't have major assets to divide anyway as commitment of any kind became less and less en vogue. In 2163, 26% of all marriages still ended in divorce - couples who couldn't make it to ten years, 55% ended in expiration, leaving 19 that ended in natural causes - death. That meant one in five couples held on to the marriage is forever ideal, believing their love to be special and everlasting.

One evening in their condo, Witten was rubbing Gwen's topless back with some special cream, trying to help alleviate some chronic back pain.

"Use your elbow," requested Gwen softly. Witten obliged leaning over her wife to get at the knots in her back. "That's it. Oh my god. Thank you," said Gwen, wondering in the back of her mind why it was that Witten was being so sugary sweet these days. Maybe it was the natural rekindle that orbits around anniversaries. Gwen wanted to believe that at least. She hopped up on her elbows. "Oh I have some gossip."

"Spill it."

"Sheila and Jackie expired."

"No?"

"Yes."

"Wow, I thought they would re-up for sure."

"Shelia's going through some kind of mid-life thing and wanted to move to Italy. You know how it goes. Speaking of re-upping, I've been thinking about our trip."

"I'm so glad we're not doing the whole ceremony thing again, a long fun trip is how all re-ups should be."

"For once we're on the same page," said Gwen in her intoxicating accent, as she lay back down trying to relax into her massage. She continued, "Lower... towards my spine. That's it. I decided

I want to focus on the beaches on the southern Nicoya Peninsula."

"Not this again, we're going to go all the way to Costa Rica just to lay on the beach. We live on SANI. We can go to the beach anytime. I want to go to the Arenal Volcano, I want to try those rejuvenating thermal springs."

"Samantha, we can sit in a hot tub right here in SANI too. I want that exotic beach for our pictures. We have to outdo our first re-up. Make them crazy with jealousy. Can you get those crunchies in my traps?" Witten repositioned herself and started working Gwen's traps with her powerful hands.

"Fine, you're just gonna keep crying about it until I give in."

"Thanks babe, uh that feels so good. I needed this. They are making me crazy at work."

Witten laughed to herself at the idea that Gwen's job stress compared to her own. But she reminded herself everyone was entitled to their feelings. "What's wrong?"

Gwen got up and slipped her robe back on. "Lay down, your turn."

"Nah… ," Witten said, waving off the offer. She was so tightly wound that the slightest pressure felt like she was being stabbed with hot irons. Her back was a lost cause.

Gwen shrugged and started lotioning up her legs and hands before she tucked herself in. "I'm just getting a little bored with the out-patient ex vets I've been seeing. I miss being in the field. The stuffy office holds no excitement for me. I am trying to glean something deeper."

"Counting and timing tantrums not doing it for you these days?" said Witten, after she let the comment fly she wished she could have taken it back. It was true, she didn't think a whole lot of the soft sciences, but in her kinder moments she kept that to herself.

"Wow, you know you are the rudest person I have ever met?" said Gwen in a teasing way.

"You married the rudest person you ever met? That says more about you than it does about me." They smiled and shook off the bump in their lovely evening. Shaking off misfired barbs was a trait of all lasting couples.Witten, continued, "It's dangerous, ground war-psych. Besides Puerto Rico's dying down. Where would you go?"

"I don't know, there's always a war some-where," said Gwen.

As they laid there drifting off to sleep, Witten felt terrible about her double life. Gwen was already putting up with a huge liability being married to Witten at all, with her involvement in Cryonics. Since they first started the bizarre practice of freezing the dead in 1967, in the hopes that future medicine could thaw them, cure what killed them and give them their lives back, mainstream medicine had viewed it as a fringe pseudoscience perpetuated by delusional enthusiasts and non medical personnel. Cryonics was like the bastard son of Magnus Agrippa and L. Ron Hubbard. And over the intervening years those that supported the research, served on advisory boards, or were even publicly curious had been ostracized by the medical community.

At Cryonicor, Witten had managed to keep a low profile, she didn't make waves, she didn't draw attention to herself. The less eyes on her the better with the work she was doing. Still, if anyone looked hard enough at Gwen, they could easily find out what her wife did for a living. In fact, Samantha had urged Gwen not to take her name for this very reason, but Gwen had stubbornly insisted. They had managed to straddle this gulf between their worlds without major incident. The few people who did know what Gwen's wife did, so far had politely ignored it. Witten viewed her deception as a form of protection, a burden she chose to bear out of love. At least that was what she told herself. Deep down she feared that if Gwen found out before their anniversary, even if she could forgive her, she wouldn't have the confidence to re-up for another ten years. But if she found out after they re-upped, it would be a lot harder for Gwen to leave her.

***

The day finally arrived when they were ready

to thaw George. All his organs had been rapid-cloned, except his heart. Using scaffolding from his own DNA, they were able to 3D print a far better heart than the one god had originally given him. Medicine had also released a reimagined intestinal tract, known as the steel gut which was a tremendous help to people who suffered from diseases and cancers associated with this troublesome organ. The cryonicists had one of these too, with George's name on it. The organs all sat patiently in jars in the reanimation chamber. Of course his brain could not be replaced.Some transhumanists believed that life could be perpetually extended if bio-tech could upload a person's memories into a machine and reconstruct a person's past experiences back into something that ideally resembled their original personality. Others believed you could scan a map of a brain's neural network, essentially copying it and all the memories and personality onto a younger man-made brain.

But Witten had concerns about these ideas. For her, this was not true life extension. The original person had closed their eyes for the last time. What theoretically woke up in some machine or imprinted on some new brain was a copy. That's nice for their relatives maybe, who perhaps could not tell the difference if the science got good enough. And it's nice for the world maybe if the person was important and had an especially brilliant mind. But the actual original person was lost to oblivion. Samantha Witten was a purist as far as transhumanists went. Her only goal was to protect a person's original consciousness. She came to believe the only true life extension possible would mean using a person's original brain, and that worked best in the original body.

Of course, who knew down the line what science could do. This was the catch-all credo of cryonics from the beginning, but Witten disliked this rationale. There was an element of blind faith in this line of reasoning that was too close to religion for her. Science was not religion. It would not solve all your problems if you believed in it hard enough. She was an actual doctor and she understood to some degree the limits of medicine. She had hope for her research because of the science she witnessed herself and what its implications were as specific medical obstacles were overcome in due course. These obstacles existed in mainstream medicine, or medicine for the living as Witten thought of it. It was up to her to keep an eye out and repurpose whatever progress was made for her own aims; medicine for the dead.

Early in her career Witten had dabbled in various life extension treatments and methods. In one such experience, about fifty years ago, she had been part of a private research team that was the first to reanimate a cryonic patient's respiratory system. That was unbelievable to witness. Emboldened by that success she dedicated herself to the pursuit of cryonic reanimation, and never looked back.

Kelley, Priya, and Witten suited up. They drained George's tank, and pulled him out by his arms. There was no rigor, he was as flexible as if he had expired moments ago. They toweled him off and gently laid him on the operating table.

Witten began the transplants immediately. In 2163 organs were replaced everyday in mainstream medicine, by doctors with far less experience. Each organ was complex, but the advances in organ cloning had been astounding. They were plug and play, designed for easy installation. This part took twelve hours - It was hard work, but Witten had stamina like nobody's business. George's original organs were removed and tossed into a biowaste container. Blue and gray, organ after organ, was piled atop one another as the jars began to empty.

The giant I.V. bags of synthetic purple blood were being emptied into the corpse. Priya was applying and reapplying a cream to his skin. It was working. He was gradually turning from a ghastly grayish hue to the natural color of a living person. His preservation was quick and efficient. But his skin had slipped off the skull in places, so his face was a bit contorted and unsettling to look at. They set up the ventilator and got his heart beating. His new lungs swelled and contracted as the life support machine regulated his nervous system on behalf of his inanimate cerebral cortex. This part was always very exciting.

But they knew the heartbeat meant nothing really, it was a milestone overcome long ago. Witten had achieved a heartbeat in 15 of her last 26 attempts. So they expected this part to go well, especially considering the excellent physical condition of the patient.

Kelley wheeled out the glittering I.V. nano bag. The tiny robots entered the patient's synthetic blood stream and began to identify and repair internal damage caused by the initial preservation. When a body is preserved, its tissue must be saturated in cool-aid to keep the cells from crystallizing in the deep freeze. But the problem had always been ensuring all tissue was sufficiently saturated. Of course some tissue was not, and those cells basically exploded in the freezer. These problems were repaired by the nanobots in theory. They occurred mostly in muscle tissue, tendons, and the blood vessels themselves.

As the nanobots did their work, Kelley broke out his handheld body laser, and began rejuvenating George's appearance, focusing on his contorted face. Imagine fixing a lop-sided latex Halloween mask on a trick-or-treater. Because he was so young when he died and his preservation had gone great, Kelley did not have to do much. After George's face was corrected, a certain handsomeness returned. He looked like he was only sleeping.

And now the hard part. There was little known even in 2163 about the brain. Sure, they have made discoveries and understand more than they did a hundred years ago. But the brain largely remained shrouded in seemingly infinite mystery. Re-activating a cerebral cortex after the cessation of the heart beat, shouldn't have been that hard considering the other astounding advances in medical technology. But it had proven to be. Witten ran head first into this problem fifteen times in previous thaws. Each time, armed with more information, and the latest techniques modern mainstream medicine had unwittingly gifted her. Still she had never achieved what she believed was real success. But this time it was different. They all knew that Jansen's discovery was beyond groundbreaking. Re-animating the cerebral cortex in virtually brain dead stroke victims? People returning from years of comatose life support to be reunited with their families? Unthinkable.

Witten, Priya, and Kelley all had to work in concert to reproduce Jansen's results. Step by step they proceeded. With the help of the nano-bots, they deployed the calcium boosted neuro receptors to George's brain. The bots transmitted out a high res rotating hologram model of his cerebral cortex. The dim hologram began to light up as the receptors took hold in his neural network. Just as Jansen had observed in his stroke victims, a domino effect played out, lighting up long dormant synaptic highways. It looked like someone throwing the power grid back on after a blackout in Manhattan: Behold the lights of SoHo, then Chelsea, then Harlem, then the Upper East Side, Battery Park, and so on.

The cryonicists continued to turn back and forth from George to the hologram, like watching a tennis match. Priya saw George's face twitch. "What's that?"

Witten's eyes widened but she remained cautious. "Could be nothing. Auto-electro response?"

George's face twitched again and again. This scared the hell out of Priya. Her friend looked like he was being tortured with electric shock therapy.

Suddenly Witten shouted, "Kelley hit him with 100ccs of adrenaline."

This startled both Priya and Kelley, whose mouths were hanging open. Kelley nodded his head and quickly loaded a syringe. He swiftly administered the injection. They watched the brain activity. The twitching continued. Witten turned off the life support, and George kept breathing on his own, his brain was working at least as it was able to regulate his respiratory system. But that's not enough. That's not even a first. She tapped his knee with her reflex mallet and it didn't jump, but he was still twitching. It was getting hard to watch. She opened his eye and shined her light pen into his pupil, hoping for dilation. Nothingness.

"Hit him again!" Witten shouted, the urgency in her voice was palpable. Her eyes were bulging and desperate. This was her last chance.

"Too much. It'll kill him," warned Kelley.

"He's already dead. Just do it!"

Priya could not take her eyes off of Witten. *Is she crazy?* Kelley followed his orders. The adrenaline threw the heartbeat off, so Kelley hit him with the defibrillator paddles and shocked the heart back to its normal pace. They watched the brain hologram closely observing more activity and firing synapses. They watched the hologram so closely that they failed to notice George open his eyes, sit up, woozy, and swing his legs over the side of the gurney. Witten looked back at George.

"He's alive!"

George is panting and wild-eyed and looking around terrified. Priya gasps, clasping her hand over her mouth. She is both elated and frightened. Witten walks slowly toward George with her hands out to show she means no harm, "Whoa, take it easy big guy."

Kelley warns, "I pumped him with enough adrenaline to kill a horse, so you might want to stand back doc."

George tried to stand, but almost fell pulling his IV stand crashing to the floor. Kelley and Witten stepped back frightened. But Priya stepped forward, and said in a firm but soft voice, "Hey, you're okay. Can you hear me?"

A mute George met her gaze and held it, a moment too long, as if he knew her voice.

Kelley asked, "Maybe he doesn't understand?"

George pulled his I.V.s out of his arms roughly. He started bleeding from the wounds.... a strange purple blood like liquid. He stammered back, scanned the room then rushed for the exit grunting. Kelley stepped in front of him, but George bulldozed through him and disappeared out of the exit.

Witten helped Kelley off his ass and ordered her cryotechs to go after the patient. While Kelley grabbed a handheld tranq, Witten produced a gas mask and handed it to Priya.

Chapter 7

Blue Jay

2163 A.G.

The Iconastary was a cliff-side Michelin starred restaurant. It overlooked the Gulf of Redondo on one side and a vast empire of skyscrapers on the other. Still nowhere near the size of the Asian super cities, Santa Angeles was the biggest megalopolis in the Western Hemisphere. The Iconastary was a place for moguls. Samantha Witten sat alone at a table overlooking the water. She was wearing a nice dress and heels, but her hair was still pulled back practically and she wore no makeup, save for some crudely applied eyeliner. She looked out of place in this old money milieu. Fidgety, she pulled her trusty eye drops out of her purse and reapplied.

Martinez breezed in suited and booted, she

stood to greet him and they kissed each other on the cheeks European style. They sat, "Been here long?" he asked.

"No, just got here," she responded.

He ran his hand down the table, lighting it up with menu options. His fingers glided with ease through the screens. He made his selection and looked up at her with a knowing smile.

"How was your flight?" she asked nervously.

"You look great. I don't think I've ever seen you in a dress before," he said.

"Thanks. I'm very uncomfortable. I don't know why you wanted to have dinner here, we could have met at the facility."

"No. We're celebrating tonight."

A white-gloved attendant delivered a martini and a green smoothie to the table.

Martinez said, "Muchos Gracias" to the attendant politely.

"You remembered," she said, gesturing to her green sludge.

"I never forget a lady's drink." He raised his glass to Witten. "C'mon cheers."

"So we got it?"

"Yes," he said, clinking their glasses then taking a sip of his vodka dirty, two olives. He continued giddily, "you should have seen their faces, Sam. Man, I wish you could have been there."

They cackled together in excitement, drawing attention from the more refined clientele. Martinez couldn't care less. Let them look and wonder, he thought. Witten sampled her drink and leaned in for the juicy details. She asked, "What did your father say?"

Martinez replied, "He said, 'I knew she could do it.' He's always had faith in you."

Witten rolled her eyes at the blatant mischaracterization of her relationship with Javier Martinez, which had always been contentious. Cryonicor was Christian's pet project, one Javier had never approved of. In fact, it felt like Javier wanted Cryonicor to fail just to put Christian in his place. Competitive father-son bullshit. The patriarchy and their pissing contests. Why was Martinez trying to butter her up, she wondered.

"So, 25 billion dollars?" she asked to confirm.

"That was the deal right? We fund twenty years of research at 100 million per year, with a 25 billion dollar kicker if you reanimate. Look at what humans can do when properly motivated. God I love venture philanthropy." She nodded her head, but inwardly couldn't help but wonder where his brimming commitment was only weeks ago, when he was stonewalling her pleas for an extension. Still, she couldn't refute that his strategy had worked, she performed only once her back was to the wall.

They clinked glasses again and she started to relax. It was rare for her to really allow herself a moment of relief. Her work was still illegal, the threat of discovery lurked behind every corner, her breakthroughs unknown to mainstream medicine, even to her own wife, and to top it off she had a wildly unpredictable reanimated corpse living in a retrofitted work room inside her facility. But just for tonight, she wanted to let her guard down and enjoy herself.

Witten sat back in her chair and said, "This is great. We've got so much work to do. God, I need, I don't even know, I never thought this far ahead. Didn't make sense to."

Martinez followed closely, "I'm way ahead of you."

"What do you mean?"

He said matter-of-factly, "We're bringing someone in to help you." He took another sip.

Witten slowly set her glass down and placed her elbows on the table. "Help me what?"

He smiled, putting his drink down too, "Don't be so stubborn. This is a good thing." Of course she needed help but this was not what she had in mind. Her phone was vibrating. She silenced it without looking, focusing all of her attention on the billionaire before her. She considered him for a moment, then it hit her like a mack truck. She scanned the room, then looked back at him.

She said, with progressive but restrained anger, "Is that why you brought me here? So I won't make a scene? You're just gonna take this thing away from me after I gave twenty years to this? And give it to *who*?"

Then a man stepped forward, appearing almost out of thin air, wearing a suit, the same quality and caliber as Martinez's. He read like he was in his early 40's, but who knew how old anyone really was in 2163. His hair was neatly trimmed suggesting he might be generation iota like Gwen. His eye color and shape gave him a vaguely exotic edge, suggesting some Pacific Islander or possibly Native American ancestry.

He addressed the table, feigning awkwardness, "Excuse me, didn't mean to eavesdrop but - you're just so loud."

Martinez stood to introduce them, "Dr. Samantha Witten, meet Dr. Elijah Owens."

**

George was furiously pacing around his room like a killer whale doing laps in its tank at sea world. He had ripped out his I.V., and was yanking on the door, locked from the outside.

"Hey! Hello! Excuse me?! Open the door!" he called out, rattling it with a vengeance. No one came. He turned over his bedside tray in anger. *What the hell? Are they stealing my kidneys?* He checked his abdomen for scars. No scars....yet. Good.

He went over to the one small window, it was high up, like a basement window. He recruited the stool to help him get a leg up. He peaked out and saw some side walks connecting a few buildings, a little landscaping, but nothing that interesting. He checked all four sides thoroughly looking to open it or pop it out, though he wasn't sure he could get through it as big as he was. It didn't open. He climbed down and noticed the camera tracking his movements.

Priya was on watch duty, she was texting Dr. Witten their code word for a George related emergency: BLUE JAY. But she was getting no response from the MIA top doc.

George pointed straight to the camera and shouted, "What the hell is this? Why's the door locked? Open it right now, I'm not joking. If you don't open it right now, I'm going to rip it apart."

Priya believed him. She had to make some quick decisions. She pushed the red button and took off for the elevator. When George went back to the door he found it unlocked. Before he stepped out he remembered his breathing problem. The nasal cannula and oxygen tank were there next to his bed. He set himself up as best as he could remember and took off down the hallway.

***

Witten's eyes widened with outrage as the interloper, Owens, sat down at their table. What had he done for the cause to earn a seat, she bitterly asked herself as she braced for a fight.

"I can't believe this."

Owens said to Martinez, "I thought you said she wasn't going to make a scene."

Martinez tried to level with Witten, saying, "Come on Sam. You really think we're gonna give you 25 billion dollars carte blanche? You said so yourself, you need help."

"With 25 billion dollars I can hire my own damn help."

"You can't have sole discretionary spending. You need a second. Checks and balances."

Witten nodded her head, that kind of nod you give yourself for taking back a cheating lover only to get cheated on again. She needed autonomy, it's all she'd known for the past forty years for good reason. Bureaucracy and decision by committee were a death sentence to real progress and truly daring innovation. After all, she needed to perfect the process in her own lifetime, and the clock was ticking. The dark river waits for no one. "Checks and balances," she repeated.

Martinez continued, "With the backing of our foundation, Dr. Owens has founded and sold two very profitable biotech startups—"

Owens interjected, "Nanotechron, the nano repair program you modified, to get patient zero back online. That was mine. And we also brought Regenadrips to market. Those preservatives keeping that skin of yours so supple? That's me, I did that." Owens grinned from ear to ear. Modest, he was not.

Martinez added, "He's got an MD/PHD and an MBA from Harvard. He can help us."

Witten asked Owens, "Why would you want to leave all of that to come down here and slum it with me in the underworld? Ain't no glory in what nobody knows about."

"The truth is I've been following cryonics for a long time, if you check your records I've been signed up for preservation at Cryonicor for years. I know who you are. This is what all my work in regenerative medicine has been leading up to. And that was great. But what you are doing here? This is it. This is the final frontier."

Witten leaned in and asked, "Then where were you for the last twenty years?"

Owens responded coldly, "Touché. I guess I just cared too much about what people think."

Ouch. Witten knew she was persona non-grata with the mainstream medical community. It was a fact she tried to accept. But it wasn't easy. There was part of her that yearned for the recognition someone like Owens enjoyed, for far more trivial accomplishments. She aspired to be above it, but she was only human. She reminded herself what her mission was, and not to let ego or this pre-madonna get in the way. "My priority right now is George Gilroy."

Owens adjusted his jacket and began playing the part immediately, "What do you need?"

"I need a hyperbaric chamber," said Witten.

"Whoa, that's a big ask. Those things cost a lot of money. Are you sure about your course of treatment?" Owens asked.

Witten said, without breaking eye contact, "Nope. Welcome to the final frontier."

***

George was on the loose and he was headed straight for the door to the other clean room. The elevator opened and Priya ran out at top speed, her nurse shoes squeaking on the linoleum floors as she hit corners making her way to George's room. He wasn't there, but at least the door hadn't been ripped apart. *Where is he?*

George got to the other clean room and started yanking the door handle but naturally found it locked. Tell him he can't do something, he wants to do it all the more. It was a quality he honestly loathed about himself, but so far had been unable to tame. A security device next to the door required some kind of scan. He put his eye in the scanner, then his thumb, not sure what it wanted. He leaned in to look at it closely and it scanned his entire face.

Access Denied.

"Hey George, whatcha doing? You okay?" said Priya, who was now standing behind him trying to act casual.

He turned back, "No. I'm not okay. I'm starving and—" he stopped mid sentence at the sight of her. He didn't know her. But he did somehow, it took him a moment or two to place her. "You were on the bus too, with the mask."

She hadn't expected him to recognize her. She hoped he had forgotten all about that incident, if it were her, she would have a lot of questions about that bus. Luckily he didn't seem to recall all that much. But the thing about George was that he never forgot a face.

"That's right. That was me. Guilty." She said, raising her hand awkwardly. This time she wasn't in a hazmat suit, his first thought was that she was pretty and she felt familiar to him, but he wasn't sure why.

"Do we know each other? I mean before all this? Have we met?"

"Before the bus? No. I would remember you, trust me. I'm sorry you said you were hungry, but you just ate like three hours ago, so we didn't have another round of meals scheduled until—"

"Well I eat a lot, what can I say?"

She was looking at him. It was her first time being this close to him, in clothes, standing up especially. He made an impression for sure. She said, "I will get you something to eat right away. Let's go back to your room."

"Why's the door locked?" he asked, remembering his anger.

She blabbered out, "Well, it's a clean room, and we have to follow protocols to go in and out... to keep the bad stuff out... it's standard to lock the clean room."

She swatted away a wayward fly.

"Well how am I supposed to know that? And where is the call button for the nurse or whatever, you can't just leave me in there unattended. There's no TV or anything in there. Really uncool," he said, feeling slightly embarrassed.

She touched his arm gently and pushed him toward his room. He took a deep breath, and allowed her to walk him back. "I don't want that door locked anymore. It makes me feel like I'm a prisoner, like I'm trapped. I don't consent to that."

"Ok, I'll talk to the doctor about leaving it unlocked so you can come and go as you please. Does that sound okay?"

"OK, yeah. Good. And I know um... I can't have my cell, but I want to make some calls, I need to talk to my Mom already. She's probably worried sick. I gotta call my job and check in, and like," he cut his eyes over to her curiously before this next part, "... and my girlfriend."

His girlfriend? Priya felt terrible lying to the poor guy. He wasn't ever going to talk to any of those people again.

***

The next morning, Dr. Witten and Jack were wogging together, a walk/jog hybrid, along the waterfront near the old Hollywood Bowl. Witten didn't break a sweat, but Jack was as red as a tomato. She invited him to run with her because she wanted to talk to him outside of Cryonicor, a place she feared was becoming compromised. Witten never wanted to get a coffee or a drink like a normal person. She had to be ever active, dragging people on long hikes, mountain bike excursions and humiliating attempts at tennis. She shared with him the previous night's events.

"Director of Innovation Management or some bullshit," said Witten, looking over her shoulder.

"What does that mean?"

"Fuck if I know. He's going to observe our operation, evaluate our procedures, and assets, then make formal recommendations to the foundation on how to move forward."

Jack's eyebrows betrayed his worry. "Then tell them to get lost. We won't take their money. We'll find another way!"

"I thought about that too, but this is too big for me to do by myself - George had another incident last night, he's a time bomb. Without the foundation's funding we won't have the resources to help him. Priya's right about that. Hell, I won't even be able to make payroll next month. Plus, if I go shopping for new funding, more people find out, we risk being exposed. I don't think we have a play here."

"You think he's going to bring in a bunch of new people?"

"Yep." Her no nonsense answer stopped Jack in his tracks. Hearing your biggest fear validated felt like getting punched in the guts. Witten stopped too, taking note of a jogger running past wearing an oxygen-pac face mask. "I need to make a stop real quick."

Chapter 8

George Finds Out

It was Dr. Elijah Owens first day at Cryonicor. He came in dressed down, wearing casual pants and a classic white doctor's lab coat. He was already at work recreating their image as a hip biotech start-up. He had seen George in the video that Martinez had presented to the foundation. But reanimation, resurrection, coming back from the dead - sure this was science, it wasn't a miracle or magic, but still it required seeing for believing. He made a beeline for George.

The room was double doored naturally. Through the small window in the hallway door he could see the bottom of George's dirty feet. That would not do at all. He leaned into the facial scanner.

ACCESS DENIED

He would have to wait for Witten to arrive and start activating his security clearances. It was frustrating being so close to the six billion dollar man and not being able to see him. But Owens was a pro, he shook it off and got to his next order of business, evaluating the staff.

He had a certain prejudice against the 'self-taught' that seemed to dominate this industry. Yes, they had done something amazing here, but Owens wasn't just a doctor, he was also a businessman. The whole amateur-hour stuff was bad for business. He looked at his primary task as one of rebranding cryonics. He needed the support and buy-in of mainstream medicine, in order to get the public's acceptance. He needed the public in order to get the government. None of that would happen overnight. But now that Witten had demonstrated proof of concept - Owens felt confident he could attract more mainstream medical talent like himself.

He spotted a disused office and set up shop. The first appointment in his calendar was with the Director of Preservations, CR. Priya Cayhill. She knocked, and he signaled her to come on in. She cleared a box off the only guest chair in the office and took a seat. Priya was reluctant about the whole thing. Her first impression of him was that he seemed arrogant and entitled.

"So, you are our Director of Preservations."
"And you are?"

"Dr. Elijah Owens. I'm just trying to get my bearings. I hope you don't mind helping me out."

"I report to Dr. Witten." His nice guy routine made her sick. His office was stuffy so she took off her cardigan.

"Right. I'm here to help take some of the load off her shoulders, but I need to know our team."

"What do you want to know?" she asked him coldly. His presence clearly undermined Dr. Witten's authority. Priya was her name and open hostility was her game.

"Okay, I notice that you use the prefix CR in front of your name, can you tell me about that?"

"I earned a certificate as a cryonicist, so it means I can use the CR prefix."

"A certificate? From where?"

"Cryonicor has a program."

"Oh from here? And what governing body oversees that program?"

"You can ask Dr. Witten, it's her program."

"I'm asking you. You are the one with the CR in front of your name - you should know what it means."

"It means cryonicist. I don't believe there is a governing body that oversees the credential."

"Not much of a credential then."

"Can I go now?" *What-a-dick.*

"In a minute. I want to get your opinion on spearheading our outpatient program."

Now he had her attention. Witten never wanted to talk about the after care of the reanimated, she was more of a let's-cross-that-bridge-when-we-come-to-it kind of doctor. But maybe Priya had underestimated Owens' value. After a lengthy discussion about half-way housing, job training, and financial stipends, Priya started to get comfortable in Owen's stuffy office.

"I know you started some biotech companies in the area of regenerative medicine—" she said.

"Regenadrops, that's right."

"Why did you decide to come here and work in ....?" She was eternally curious about how people found their way into the bizarre world of cryonics.

"I've always been interested in Dr. Ettinger's theories. Never brave enough to pursue it outright though, because of the obvious stigma, no offense."

"What changed?"

"My son was about five years old, maybe 5 years ago now and he fell. He fell off our balcony. Died... instantly."

"Oh my god, I'm so sorry." Priya felt terrible about doubting his character, as if anyone who had ever lost a child was ipso facto a saint.

"Thank you." He pulled his cell out and showed a picture of himself and a little brunette boy with big blue eyes.

"Did you preserve him?"

"I wanted to, but the damage to his head was so severe, it was something my ex wife couldn't imagine any medicine from any time being able to treat. She thought it was madness frankly, she was probably right. So we agreed to have him cremated like she wanted. Anyway... as I dug into the research, I started noticing that so many of the classic roadblocks to reanimation had actually already been cleared by medical advancements and," Priya was smiling and emphatically nodding her head. He continued, "Plus, Christian Martinez is a hard man to say no to."

She left Owen's office on cloud nine. But she forgot her cardigan and went back. As she reached the door she overheard Witten in Owen's office. She stopped and heard Witten insist, "We have to tell him the truth."

"You said he might spin out. Plus, think about who he might tell, what is he gonna demand?"

"I get it, but we can't hold him here like a hostage. He has rights."

"Does he though?" asked Owens coldly. "I mean... he's legally dead, there's a death certificate somewhere. As of now there are no laws to protect someone like him."

Priya stepped back from the room. She didn't want to hear anymore. *Wow, whatta two-faced son-of-a-bitch.* At that moment she spun on her heel and headed for the clean room.

George sat on his bed, with his head in his hands. There were stacked up empty bento boxes on his bedside table. Priya whooshed in and he was instantly relieved to see her.

"You again."

She tossed him one of Kelley's hoodies. "Put this on, where we're going it gets cold."

She knew Kelley was on George watch upstairs and he wouldn't think twice about her taking George for a walk. But if Witten were to check the cameras from her cell, it would be curtains. There was no time to waste.

Moments later, Priya had led George into the freight elevator, they were going down to the foxhole. Priya had to lean in for a facial scan before the elevator opened to the high security floor. George had seen that in movies, but that was top secret CIA spy stuff - not for nurses at a small hospital.

He pulled his own oxy tank behind him and wore the nasal cannula device around his neck. She led him into part of the foxhole filled with miniature versions of the cryostats. He was intrigued by them and their mysterious steaming chimneys.

Priya hoisted herself up onto a countertop, her feet dangled above the ground. She watched him inspect the steel vats.

"What's in these things?" he asked.

"Pets."

"What do you mean?"

"People freeze their newly deceased pets here, hoping one day when science gets good enough, they can thaw them out, cure what killed them, and give them their lives back."

"Nooooooo. Are you serious? What kind of

hospital is this?"

"What do you think about that?"

"About freezing your dead pets?" he asked looking back at her, she nodded. "I don't know. I just don't think it's ever going to work. When you're dead, you're dead. I guess it makes the owners feel better but—"

"—Okay fair enough, but let's say hypothetically it did work for some of them, eventually."

"It won't. But, even if it did - their owners would be long gone by then. They would be strays, why work so hard to save a bunch of animals to put them back in a shelter. Seems like a waste of resources to me. Anything for a buck I guess." He smiled at the novelty of the concept.

George got to the end of the stacks of miniature tubes and saw beyond it into another cavernous warehouse, filled with giant tubes, 9feet tall at least. He paused.

"What's in those? Horses?" he asked, his smile fading away.

Priya slipped back down to the ground and approached him. "No."

"Then what?"

"What would you say, if I told you that people were inside those?"

He turned around and looked back at her, suddenly feeling uneasy with the slightest touch of vertigo. He asked, "Is that true?" with a lump in his throat.

"Would that upset you?"

"I thought that was just in movies like Demolition Man and Austin Powers."

"And Captain America" she said, referencing her own inside joke with Kelley about George. She continued, "those movies are fiction, you can't cryogenically suspend a living person and then just thaw them out whenever you want, their cells would explode. But, they have been freezing the newly deceased since 1967."

"Creepy."

"What if you just thought about it like, they're just waiting. Waiting for science to find the cures to what they died from, so maybe if they're lucky they might get a little more time?"

A mysterious nausea crept over him. "But they're not waiting. They're dead," he said, with his eyebrow raised.

"Only legally."

"What's that mean?"

"Legal death is defined by the cessation of the heartbeat."

"Oh is that all?"

"You got sick. A heart transplant saved your life, right?"

"That's what they tell me."

"But what if there wasn't a heart available in time? Wouldn't you want more time, even if it was far off in the future?"

"I don't know. It would never even cross my mind honestly. I'm just not that kind of person."

She nodded empathetically, unsure what to do

next. Maybe Witten was right. Maybe this would be a bigger obstacle than she had realized. When she didn't respond, he lingered for a moment then looked back toward the full sized cryostats. There was something about them that attracted his curiosity. Something wasn't right about this. Why hadn't anyone come to see him? Where was Alison? Where was his Mom? And what was the self-driving mega-bus about? What do these tubes have to do with it?

He tried to resist these thoughts, but bubbling up inside him was a nameless suspicion. It was more of a feeling than a thought. His heart rate was rising and the nausea was getting stronger. He gripped his oxy cart harder to steady himself. Try as he might to resist, he still wanted to see the tubes up close. He began drifting over to the border of the two bays.

Priya warned him, "Are you sure you want to go down that road? You might not like what you find."

He stopped and looked back at her, considering her warning. He decided it was worse not knowing, whatever was down there he needed to see it for himself. He nodded his head, and took his first steps into the foxhole.

Outside in the Cryonicor parking bay, Getty sat in his pod, nervously bouncing his knee. He needed the bug to make the case, and why not make the case? He was doing the world a favor by shuttering a sicko place like Cryonicor. He finally sacked up and went inside. He was surprised by the changes he saw. There were more personnel and bustling construction crews. He approached the receptobot behind the new sleek desk and asked to see Ms. Samantha Witten. It politely told him to wait in the lobby. He looked around annoyed and took a seat. Now he was more anxious than ever to get his hands on that footage.

Dr. Owens appeared from the back offices to greet him with finger guns. "Hi, are you Inspector Getty?"

"Yes," said Getty, standing slowly, surprised by this new face. "I'm waiting for Samantha Witten."

"Oh yeah, she's unavailable at the moment. But I can help you out."

"Okay… and you are?"

"Sorry about that." He taps his cell phone to Getty's glass reader, giving him his e-card. The words appeared on the reader.

Dr. Elijah Owens MD/PHD/MBA

Cryonicor/Director of Innovation Management

"Impressive. When did this happen?"

"Recently. So what brings you by today? I noticed you just logged a surprise inspection not that long ago. We do something wrong?" Owens flashed a cheeky smile. He had that affable way about him, he could turn his charm on and off.

Getty was stoic by nature and found people like Owens, highly social high achievers, to be... overwhelming.

Getty swallowed, and said, "Well it's the damnedest thing. See when I was here last time I forgot to check on your trash incineration set up. I made a note here, see?" he said pointing at his reader, "A few months ago I noticed driving by that the smokestacks wcrc putting out white smoke. Supposed to be black. And I forgot to check that out when I was here last."

"So you came back to check this last item off the list?"

"I'm nothing if not thorough."

"It takes a special breed. I'm not good with paperwork, ask my assistant. C'mon let's check it out together." Owens put his hand on Getty's shoulder as if they were old war buddies, and ushered him into the back. The inspector forced a polite smile. He needed to recall the bug, manually upload the footage, recharge it and re-release it. But in order to do that he had to lose this creep.

Meanwhile Witten was in her office recovering from her own encounter with Dr. Owens. Some people had a stiff drink when they needed to shake off something upsetting, but Witten never touched the stuff. Instead, she coped with her negative emotions by taking it out on the speedbag in her office. She had another one at home too. She wiped the beads of sweat from her brow with her wrapped fists and finished dribbling the bag.

She was unwrapping her hands with her teeth when she commanded her cell, "Show me George." The device accessed the app linked to his closed circuit monitoring system. His room was empty. Witten's eyes widened. As she started for the door, something about her last walk with George gave her pause. She needed a way to control him, so she grabbed a device from her bottom desk drawer and bolted up to HQ.

As Getty and Owens walked to the trash incineration room, Getty was tracking the FlyGuy on his app, he had initiated the recall, and the glowing red dot on the screen was moving toward him.

Once they reached the trash incineration room, the ultra smooth talking Owens had given him a dazzling plethora of facts, figures and charming anecdotes. The bug arrived as Getty was looking inside the trash chute. Owens eyed it and waved it off, making a mental note about facility hygiene.

Getty re-emerged and motioned to the chute, "take a look, the incinerator is caked with white dust and all kinds of stray matter." Owens agreeably peaked his head inside the hatch and illuminated the dark with his cell. Getty continued, "you need to get this thing serviced. I'll give you a warning this time."

Owens took his head out and dusted off his hair, he turned back, "Thanks a million–" to find he was suddenly alone.

Witten arrived at HQ, where Kelley was sitting in front of the monitors. He was working on something else while the monitors showed an empty room.

"Where is George?" she asked desperately.

"On one of those walks, keep his blood moving." Kelley smiled like an idiot.

"With who?" asked Witten, sure that Owens was behind this.

"Priya."

Priya? What the hell is she doing?

"Get up, we gotta find 'em. Let's go." Witten and Kelley went from room to room, break room, reanimation chamber, trash room, the offices, the supplies bay. Witten checked the restroom and saw a pair of feet in the stall. She threw the stall door open, and much to both their surprise, found Getty sitting on the toilet fiddling with some wires and his reader.

"Oh my God, I'm sorry." She turns around embarrassed, thinking she may have caught him literally with his pants down. He stashed the recovered autonomous surveillance drone into his bag as his reader showed the ominous message:

Manual Upload Complete

"Do you mind?"

"Getty? What are you doing here?"

"What do you think I'm doing? What are you doing in the men's room?"

"Nothing, I'm sorry. It's gender neutral. I'll leave you to it," said Witten, leaving confused and mortified. They had no time to worry about what the other was doing. Kelley and Witten had checked everywhere for George but the foxhole.

Kelley stated the obvious, "He couldn't have gone outside."

"No, he's gotta be in here. Shit." Witten was realizing the problem with George being in the foxhole as they got into the freight elevator and descended. As soon as the door opened they rushed down the rows of tubes searching for him. Witten called out, "George!"

Priya and George were walking down a row, when they heard Witten's call. George froze looking at Priya for direction.

She said, "They are coming. You don't have much time, so get a good look."

He nodded and noticed an alphanumeric code imprinted on each tube. It was familiar. The code on his hospital wristband had the same configuration. That mysterious uneasy fear began to creep back over him.

Witten knew they were in there somewhere, she could hear the rattling of George's rolling oxy cart. George had noticed the codes were in a sequence. He was following the sequence to something, like the Dewey decimal system leads a bookwork through library stacks. If he understood the patterns, in theory the sequence should lead him to the tube matching the number on his wristband. His breathing was growing labored. He was almost there.

Witten and Kelley rounded a corner and ran right into Priya! They knocked her down in fact. Kelley stopped to help her up. But Witten just looked at her betrayed and asked sharply, "Where is he?"

"I don't know, he was just with me, then he must have wandered off," lied Priya - buying George another moment.

Witten and Kelley pushed past her. George was halfway down the row. They got to him and could see he was in physical distress. Witten asked, "George, are you okay?"

He looked at her, then back to the gap in the row. There was no tube where the tube should be that matched his wristband. "Where is it?"

Witten reached into her pocket, covertly grabbing the small device. She tried to answer him calmly, "Settle down George. Everything's okay."

The tubes were all stamped: Property of Cryonicor. "What is Cryonicor? You asked me before, if I had, had, had ever heard of cryonics. Is that the freezing shit?" No one answered him. "That's what this place is isn't it? It's not a hospital at all." Suddenly he snapped and screamed at them, "That's why you got no TV in the goddamn room!!"

Witten pulled her device from her pocket, it was a tranq. Priya had rejoined them, she was worried about George, it was too much for him.

But there was no backing out now.

George screamed, "ANSWER ME!"

They didn't know what to say. George lost control, trembling with rage. "Why does my ID bracelet look like these labels?! What do I have to do with these tanks?!" Then his breath caught in his throat, his voice cracked. "Oh my god." A sickening understanding hit him like a Louisville slugger. He started feeling woozy and unsteady on his feet, tears began rolling out of his blood shot eyes. He looked to Priya, who had a tear or two rolling down her own cheek. She didn't know how to console him.

The patient spoke, so quietly it was barely audible, "I was in one of these?" He looked at them for confirmation, their silence spoke volumes. He thought about the strange super bus, the mysterious glass devices that didn't break or scratch, the hi-tech breathing apparatus he wore around his neck, and what that weird old man told him. "For how long?"

At last, Witten answered him honestly, "142 years."

George doubled over and started getting sick. He threw up. Sweating and convulsing, he called out desperately to himself for help, "George wake up! George wake up!" He threw up again.

Witten hit him in the neck with her tranq and he slumped down into Kelley's waiting arms.

Chapter 9

Favors

Getty sat at his desk in his corner cube, he was riding low in his chair slurping the last of an ice coffee while he covertly scrubbed through the FlyGuy footage. It had been filming for months, and he wasn't sure what he was looking for. He was hoping he could get them on an infraction when it came to mishandling biowaste. He kept coming back to Elijah Owen's card on his reader. He looked him up. The guy's resume was stacked. What was a real doctor like that doing at a dump like Cryonicor? And where was the influx of cash for capital investments coming from? He saw that Owen's background had nothing to do with cryogenics. His work was all anti and reverse aging. Where did that come in? He leaned back rocking slightly in his chair and linked his fingers. Then he went to Cryonicor's website and he watched a commercial for their preservation services. In it, an elderly woman talked about not being ready to die and leave her grandkids, about loving to travel and loving her garden, then a picture of her as a young beautiful woman appeared. A text overlaid the photo, reading:

> If you could be restored to your younger self and do it all again, would you?

He tapped the screen pausing the video and shook his head at the shameless treachery. He found it physically revolting. How did anyone fall for this? Then it dawned on him, most people don't want to come back to life looking like they did going into the grave... they didn't just promise you would come back, they promised you would be restored. If they did manage to bring back an old geezer, with their modern medical technologies he had to admit, they could probably fulfill this secondary promise, partly at least. But even in his wildest fantasies he hadn't truly believed that they would try reanimation on human subjects, and even if they were stupid enough to try that, they would never succeed for obvious reasons. But if they hadn't succeeded, why would they need someone like Owens?

And that's when he started to suspect that roping in Owens and refreshing the look of the business were part of an elaborate ruse to entice a new crop of gullible godless customers. It was either that or they were actually experimenting with human reanimation. Either way, he felt he should double his efforts - he sat up straight and rubbed his eyes awake then leaned in refocusing on his task. He had learned grit at West Point, when things get hard, escalate commitment.

Not long after that, he came across some footage between Witten and some olive skinned adonis in a suit. He turned up the volume and heard them clearly talking about someone else, someone important, someone named George, who was going to change everything. He didn't understand the context but he felt the hairs on the back of his hands stand up.

He accessed the Flyguy app AI toolbar. He asked the app to search the footage for anytime anyone in earshot said the name 'George.' 254 Hits. He cocked his head unsure of what to make of it. He did the search again, this time for the name 'Dr. Owens.' 29 Hits. Whoever George was, he seemed much more top of mind.

***

Witten sat at George's bedside, she wasn't looking over his vitals. She wasn't worrying over her glass reader. She was just sitting, el-bows on her knees, hands clasped, watching him. George's tranq had worn off 24 hours ago. But he hadn't regained consciousness. His eyes had opened, but it seemed no one was at the wheel. He was totally non-responsive. They were get-ting close to having to put a feeding tube down

110

his throat. She contemplated his future as an eggplant. He seemed okay physically. Maybe he was in some kind of shock or had some kind of severe PTSD? She wondered about his inner life.

"I know you can hear me. I'm a brain surgeon, kind of. "

He stared blankly ahead.

She glanced up at the monitors. She was on duty right now so no one should be watching. She continued, "Can I ask you a question? And this stays between us…"

He remained unresponsive, which she took as an undying vow of discretion. "What happened to you after you died? Where did you go? Is it really a devouring blackness?"

Priya gently stepped into the recovery room. Witten composed herself, wiping the worry off of her face. The cryotech was braced for a confrontation, she wanted to get it over with.

Priya spoke first, "How is he doing?"

"Do you want to put the feeding tube down his throat or should I?"

***

Back at HHS, Getty searched the personnel files for anyone named George working for Cryonicor, 0 hits. His first instinct was that this George character was another regenerative scientist like Owens, only bigger and better. But now it didn't seem that way. He leaned back in his chair thoughtfully. His afternoon coffee had long gone cold. He tapped his finger, just one, on the table top rapidly and then it started to slow down as a new idea came to him, unbidden, but there it was. He sat up slowly and tried to access Cryonicor's human storage database.

ACCESS DENIED

"This is bullshit." He got up so fast he left his chair spinning lonely in his cube.

Moments later, he was in front of his superior. Bruno Phillips was a mountain of a man, pacing around his office bouncing the newborn baby strapped to his chest. Getty was unnerved around kids but was trying to push through.

"What do you need that kind of clearance for Jimmy?"

"Too early to say, it might be a deadend, but I have a hunch."

"A hunch?" Bruno mocked him just as his baby spit up on him. "Oh hell." He shook his head at Getty, then said, "this isn't the CIA, you're a health inspector, asbestos, wash your hands after you go to the bathroom, that's it, no hero shit, ok?"

Getty's shoulder's dropped in defeat.

"Now when are you and my baby sister getting one of these?" He motioned to the infant below his chin.

"We're working on it." He said it with the polite restraint of a driver who has to say thank you to the cop who just gave him a ticket.

"If you're going to sit there and mope then fine you can have your clearance." The rookie inspector gently pumped his fist in celebration. Just as Getty turned to leave, Bruno added, "but if you want to go back in their records more than 100 years, you're gonna need a warrant." Getty closed his eyes slowly. "You could just ask for them, you know? Flash your credentials. Most companies are dumb enough to hand that stuff over."

"Hey, guys, sorry to interrupt. Family meeting?" said CJ, as he poked his head in the door.

"Not at all, I'll be right with you CJ, let me just get cleaned up, wait here."

After Bruno dipped into his executive bathroom, Getty and CJ rocked on their heels and stared each other down.

CJ finally broke in, "Did you get what you asked for for Christmas?"

"I need a higher security clearance to investigate wrong doings within my sector. I'm trying to protect the public."

"And we have to right wrong doings with our regular basic clearance, without any special favors. Could you even imagine having to slum it like us?" He narrowed his eyes.

"Sorry you feel that way, you should have whatever clearance you need to protect the public."

"Protect the public from who?" said the senior inspector. After a moment he continued in a hushed voice, "We have these things called regulations, due process, you know... the law, we operate within it as best we can. It's a thankless job, not for glory hounds. I doubt you could handle the paperwork involved in shutting down a lemonade stand, West Point."

Getty seethed with an unstable, but all too familiar rage. Escalate commitment.

**

Witten's suggestion of intubating George hit Priya like a punch to the gut. Did she mess up? It's not like she told him, she just gave him a choice and he made it himself. But still, she couldn't help feeling responsible.

Priya said, "I'll do it."

"I'll take you up on that. But not yet. So what was the idea... taking him down there?" she asked bluntly.

"I just wanted to formally introduce myself. I thought if I asked you, you would say no."

"Better to ask for forgiveness, than ask for permission?"

Exactly. She stood silent. But Priya couldn't stand the idea of her mentor being truly angry with her. She had to try to make peace. She said, "And I know Owens is gonna be looking to change things. I wasn't sure I could trust him so I —"

"—You can't trust him," said Witten abruptly. She didn't care if he was watching them from the monitors, which of course he was. "Look, I don't like seeing George like this, and I don't agree with your tactics, but part of me is glad he knows the truth. So let's just forget about it."

Owens was at his desk, loosening his tie while watching the live feed of George's room on his cell. He was none too impressed with how Witten ran her team, letting them off the hook for willful and flagrant disobedience.

Priya was relieved that Witten had not grasped the true extent of her sabotage.

"One more thing," said Witten, as she proceeded to retrieve a gift bag from hiding and presented it sheepishly to Priya.

"You remembered," said Priya, surprised. Witten wasn't much for gift wrapping, the item was simply folded in the bag, no card or bow or colorful tissue paper. Priya pulled it out, a lab coat. It had CR Cayhill embroidered on it. Priya pulled it close to her, moved by the gesture. "I love it." In fact, she found herself a bit self conscious about the CR part after her talk with Owens.

"Now you can stop wearing that raggedy cardigan everywhere you go."

"Thanks."

"Look, normally only doctors get to wear these, and I know you didn't go to medical school, though you could, you're smart enough, but around here, to my mind, you've certainly earned it." She motioned over to George.

Owens' jaw was on the floor. He promptly dug

his office whiskey out of his box of yet unpacked personal belongings and poured himself a stiff one. How was he supposed to get mainstream medicine to give them their blessing when they were letting kindergarten teachers wear lab coats?

"Thanks." said Priya, determined not to cry. It felt good to be seen. But the feeling was bittersweet, knowing that George was lying there catatonic because of her. She hardly felt she deserved the white coat. "What are we gonna do about him?"

"There is only one other thing I can think of."

***

Gwen was almost twenty five years younger than Witten, though they looked much closer in age. Wide gaps in age for romantic partners were common since there was so much overlap in prime of life nowadays. At one time there was a fear about getting involved with an older person because, though it might be fun and sexy now, what would it be like in twenty years? But with longer primes and shorter marriage contracts those fears had dissipated and the dating pool got a lot bigger. People didn't even identify with the decade of their physical age, thirties, forties etc... now they classed themselves by their generation and its quirks. Dating someone from two generations ahead of you was like dating someone from another country who had a different style of dress and manner of speaking. But these differences were usually quite superficial and every person was totally different than the next. Still, everyone told Gwen, who was genIota, that dating a zeta gen like Witten was going to be tricky. It was true they were different, their values, their music, their vocabulary, and their relationship to work to name a few.

That night, Samantha and Gwen were out for a walk together. They had a routine of walking in the evenings. It was a way they could spend time together and Witten could still get in some activity. Gwen, knowing Witten tended toward feelings of guilt if she wasn't working or exercising, had figured out this little loophole. But nothing was ever easy, while Gwen was on a romantic walk with her wife, Witten was trying to increase her pace to get her heartrate up. Their evening strolls were peppered with stopping and waiting and getting irritated and snappy with each other. But there were good times too, like today when they actually held hands.

"Oh! I cleared my schedule for the trip. And I overpaid for a bikini."

"Trip?"

"Yeah, Costa Rica? Hello, we leave in two weeks. But I'm sure you won't have a problem getting away. It's not like your patients need your undivided attention. No offense," said Gwen, trying to keep it light in spite of this feeling in her gut that something was wrong.

Witten knew now was not the time to tell her wife, there was no way she could go on that trip. Gwen's vest pocket started ringing. She checked it and said, "It's Private Anwar. I told him, I don't take work calls on Saturdays. Boundaries people." She ignored the call and put the cell away.

Gwen was raised in the church of work-life-balance like her fellow genIotas. But Witten had no concept of her own identity outside of work. It was her purpose with a capital P. She couldn't imagine ignoring a call like that, it actually got on her nerves.

"Maybe it's important. What's wrong with him?" asked Witten.

"You know I can't discuss it. Combat vets are tough though, he's dealing with an ongoing internal crisis."

"Who isn't?" Samantha asked no one in particular. Gwen laughed agreeably. But she noticed Witten wasn't laughing, in fact she was even more aloof than usual, and that was saying something.

"What's with you?"

Witten stopped and took a deep breath. It was moment of truth time. There was a bench along their walking path, she sat down and said, "I need to tell you something."

"What?" Gwen joined her wife on the bench, her heart pounding out of her chest as she futilely attempted to brace herself. Gwen expected to hear Witten confess to cheating on her, to maybe being in love with someone else, maybe even to be leaving her. "Look if you're having second thoughts about re-upping again we can talk about it. I had just assumed—"

"—No, that's not it, I'm not having second thoughts about us." Witten knew telling Gwen her secret would have irreversible ramifications, the extent of which she could only speculate. Needless to say she feared the worst of them and would have preferred to do this after they had re-upped. But in her mind, the circumstances at present left her no choice. She swallowed hard and began, "I'm gonna tell you this because I need your help with a patient."

Gwen smiled incredulously, "with one of *your* patients?"

She nodded and continued, "And I need your total discretion. Promise me." Gwen nodded seriously, beyond relieved no one was cheating on anyone. Witten went on, "I have been experimenting with reanimation."

Gwen was taken aback. "What? You could go to prison for that. For how long?"

"Twenty years." Gwen reared her head back stunned, her concern turning into a scowl. She contemplated for a moment the length of Witten's deception over the majority of their marriage. It felt like finding out that your partner had a secret second family on the other side of town, and their oldest kid was graduating high school today.

"I couldn't tell you."

Gwen's far away stare, slowly returned to meet Witten's. "But you can tell me now?"

"Just, please, let me explain. There was a breakthrough in Amsterdam, they recovered cerebral cortex activity in a brain dead stroke victim. We were able to reproduce the experiment in our work and - we did it."

"You did it?" said Gwen, not even sure exactly what *it* was.

"Well yeah. Kind of, but we've run into a little problem in the rehab and I need your help."

"A problem in the rehab," Gwen repeated to herself.

Gwen sat back wondering about the timing of this confession and the motives behind it. Who was she married to? For the first time, she began to realize there was a gulf between them, a mist filled expanse, whose distant shore was too far gone. In that moment, she began resigning herself to the fact she had resisted for so long, that Witten was only pretending at marriage, and was incapable of real partnership.

"And if you didn't need my help, would you have told me?"

That night Gwen packed up a small overnight case and didn't say where she was going or when she would be back, just that she needed time to think.

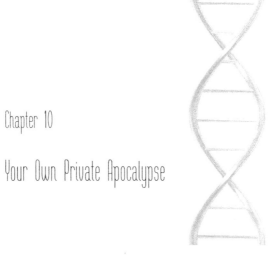

Chapter 10

Your Own Private Apocalypse

Three days later, Dr. Gwen Kim Witten entered George's clean room. She was dressed in over-sized loaner scrubs. She was clearly someplace she was not supposed to be. Her eyes were fixed on the catatonic man lying in the bed. She approached slowly as if he was a dead body she had come across in the woods.

She said softly, "Hello George, I'm Dr. Gwen Kim, I'm a psychologist." She sat on a stool and sized up the shabby make-shift recovery room. *Yuck.* She continued, "I saw your brain scans, and it's very evident to me that your present condition is not physical, but psychosomatic." She leaned over George, with a devouring curiosity.

"I wonder if this encounter might send me into a similar state," she said a bit tongue in cheek. Her eyes wandered to the cameras in the

121

ceiling.

Upstairs in HQ, Witten watched with Owens. He shook his head, and said, "I can't believe you told her."

Witten shrugged and watched intensely. "Did you have a better idea?"

Inside the recovery room, Gwen was in fact, spinning out a little. She couldn't resist the urge to touch him, to see if he was real. She rested her hand on his hand. Her heart broke for him, but she could not get over the strangeness of it all.

"You don't look that much different than us. I know this is unprofessional but... you know Freud once described a feeling. The feeling of being confronted with something that is strange yet familiar. He called it uncanny. Like that uncomfortable feeling you get seeing a life-like android, or even a cadaver. I'm experiencing that feeling now. You look like us, you feel like us. But you are not like us. You are something else entirely."

George's empty eyes at last began to wander over to her. She recognized his surfacing awareness. She nodded, signaling it was okay to come out.

Upstairs in HQ, Owens was alarmed by Gwen's unorthodox approach. "What the hell is she talking about?"

Witten raised her finger to shoosh him. "Look, he's responding."

George was looking in Gwen's direction, but

not really looking at her. He was following her voice so she kept talking. "This uncomfortable strangeness is terrifying for all of us I think. But none more terrified than you. I didn't expect such a young man. You are grieving everyone you've ever known all at once. What did they expect? Can I tell you a secret?" Now George was looking directly at her. He nodded his approval. She admitted, "I never thought this would work."

Her honesty cut Witten. Even Owens caught the dig and for a moment felt sympathy for his hostile coworker. It must be painful to know even your closest and most trusted companion thought you were nuts this whole time.

George spoke at last, "What happens next?"

"I don't know, but I sure do want to find out. Don't you?" she asked, and nodded up to the cameras.

***

Moments later the staff had gathered in George's room, wanting to witness his recovery in person. They were all relieved that he was out of his catatonic state. They were also dying of curiosity to see his reaction to the reality of 2163. It was a historic moment, one that changed the direction of mankind for better or worse. If enough people lived to tell about it anyway.

Jack, Priya, Owens, and Kelley all stood behind Dr. Witten who was speaking with George.

He was lucid and drinking water. He listened to her with a wincing caution, like every word she spoke was his foot slowly stepping on broken glass.

"Once I realized you'd lost all memory of the end of your life, I knew this wouldn't make sense to you - and in your condition—"

"—end of my life?"

Witten nodded regretfully, "Okay. From our records, looks like you got sick. Congenital heart problem, like I told you. And sadly you didn't get a transplant in time and you passed away in 2021."

George and Priya locked eyes. Her hypothetical mortality question from the foxhole wasn't so hypothetical. She had been trying to prepare him for this. She was a truth-teller. He was certain about her but no one else. He tried to do the math, "I died two hundred years ago?"

"142 years ago, yes, but your remains were cryonically frozen."

"Chronically?"

"Cry-on-ically, cryonics is an offshoot of cryogenics, it's what we call the freezing of cadavers for future—" Hearing himself called a cadaver was like taking a bullet. Witten saw his eyes cast downward and his heart rate on the monitor skip a beat. She course corrected, "Cryonics - that's what we call this whole thing, this place is a private company called Cryonicor we specialize in human preservation but really until you, the reanimation part of the equation had been theoretical."

"So you are telling me that I am the first?" he asked.

"Not technically, no. But this is as close as we've ever gotten to a... desirable result."

George sat up eager to learn more, "Wait. Why can't I breathe outside?"

Witten waded into this one carefully, "Our air quality is not like it was 150 years ago. We've got super pollution, crazy CO_2 levels and a slew of airborne super flus - But we've adapted in different ways, we have maxvaxes to inoculate us from the viruses. Our genomes have been edited generations back to help us survive. I can't change your genome at this point, we will eventually give you a boost, once you're ready. As far as the carcinogens in the air - our lungs are a bit tougher than yours because we've grown up in this atmosphere - but we still rely heavily on these when our capillaries start to contract from exposure." She holds up an inhaler. The rest of the staff hold up their haleys in solidarity. They are all personalized with patterns and stickers. "Of course your lungs are not even your lungs. Those are regrown from your DNA, so they have no interior callusing from thirty years of breathing. They're showroom new."

George snapped,"So that's it. I have lungs like a baby's ass so I can't ever go outside? Does that mean I'm trapped inside this place like some kind of bubble boy invalid? This is your idea of a desirable result?" He looked at Priya there at the end. She held his gaze straight on. This was not what she meant by giving someone more time. All she could do was shake her head, no. The staff's triumphant mood had downshifted. Their hi-minded dreams of extending the sacred lives of our noble species, thereby allowing them to miraculously travel forward through time had given way to a dreadful *Monkey's Paw* reality.

Witten ordered everyone to clear the room. Owens elected to stay much to her chagrin. George watched Priya go, she looked back at him regretfully.

Witten sat on the stool and tried to reassure her patient. She explained, "We are working on this. Nothing is permanent right now. Your recovery is going to be long and ongoing, of that much I'm sure. We're figuring this out as we go but... there is something else you have to understand George. You cannot ever tell anyone about this, about who you really are. What we are doing here isn't government sanctioned, in the strictest sense, and if it were to get out, they would shut us down and well... I don't know what they would do to you."

The reality of George's situation began to sink in. He was alone. Even if he could escape, he couldn't breathe outside, and if he told anyone about this, he could be what - turned into a circus attraction at best and dissected by the military at worst? This was a hellscape there was no waking up from. Death would have been a gift compared to this.

Then he asked the question foremost on his mind, "Why me? Who gave you the right to do this to me?"

Witten and Owens looked at each other puzzled a moment before Owens answered him honestly, "You did."

***

Back at her condo, Witten found all of her things had been moved from the bedroom to her study. Not a great sign, but at least Gwen was back in the house. Maybe Gwen held out hope, or maybe she was just waiting for her new residence to become available. At any rate, Witten only had a couple of weeks until they expired. She didn't know how to begin to make things right with Gwen. But she knew she had to do something. She went to the study and made her bed up on the little sofa. When Gwen eventually got home from work, Witten waited nervously for her partner to come to the study to talk, but she didn't. She just went to bed...

2020

George sat at his kitchen table. He had a full head of wavy hair. He was tan and muscular, a stark contrast to the broken down George of

2163. The second floor one bedroom apartment was large with a good deal of natural light. He worked on a laptop at the table. He was bare-foot, wearing a t-shirt and jeans. Whatever he was doing on his computer, he was very proud of himself.

He took a swig of his afternoon canned energy drink. The landline rang and the caller ID read a number he recognized, but had no compunction to answer. The phone stopped ringing and his beautiful live-in girlfriend, Alison, sauntered into the kitchen … on the phone.

"Babe, it's your Mom." Alison held the phone out to him, the mouthpiece covered,

George shook his head. And said barely above a whisper, "Just tell her I'm not here."

"She just wants to talk to you."

"I know, but she goes on and on. Please? I'll call her later I promise."

"Hey Julie, you just missed him. Did you try his cell? … You did. Maybe he's in a bad area. As soon as I see him I will tell him to call you… Sorry… While I have you - I wanted to ask you a question…" George straightened up nervously. "Do you remember what time George was born, like down to the minute by chance?" she asked.

Alison smiled and nodded, jotting down the answer on the back of a piece of mail while George slumped back over his laptop.

"Thank you so much Julie. A mother never forgets, so true. Talk to you soon, bu-bye."

Alison sat down at the table, unable to make eye contact because she was furiously searching the internet on her phone.

"You little liar," she said.

"I never lied."

"You said you asked her and she didn't remember."

He sat back defeated, "Ok maybe I lied. But, this is so stupid Ali, it's nonsense—"

"I know, I know astrology is unscientific blah blah blah, but let's see how nonsense it is - are you ready?"

"No. Because I'm a rationalist. There is nothing you could read to me that would convince me, and it's embarrassing that you buy into it at all."

"Shut up," she says abruptly. "According to this you are very analytical and strategic, you do not like to take a chance if you aren't prepared to deal with the worst case consequences..." she looked up at him knowingly. He shrugged his shoulders, guilty as charged.

"So what?"

"You are generous, curious, you are fair, but you don't want to work harder than you have to, you put a great deal of thought and stock into your rigid convictions, but will betray them if sufficiently motivated, and you always think you're right."

"That's unfair!"

"See, that is one of your hang ups, everything

has to be fair."

"Everyone wants things to be fair, no one is out there totally fine with unfairness, especially at their expense. But I mean, I always think I'm right? C'mon. That's like you are kicking my legs out from under me there, if I try to defend myself against this character assassination I am automatically proving your point because I am defensive and I think I'm always right, right?"

"I just think it's funny, because you are so anti-astrology but never in my whole woo woo life, among all my new age hippie friends have I ever, ever, ever met someone so much a textbook case of their sign as YOU."

She got up from the table victorious and he grabbed her quickly and playfully pulled her into his lap and kissed her. "I bet you say that to all your boyfriends. What are we doing this weekend?" He was giddy with Alison's new full-time presence in his apartment. No more sleepovers, messy overnight bags, or goodbyes. They were in their domesticated bubble, and for him nothing existed outside of it.

She said, getting up from his lap, "Well I've been wanting to hike up to Mount Baldy, if we leave soon we could make it to the summit before dark. Supposed to be really beautiful at the top. We could build a fire, spend the night under the stars."

His expression soured, "Why can't you ever just suggest a happy hour down the street?"

While half of him meant this, the other half was secretly stowing this suggestion away in a file called - proposal scenarios. This would be scenario #4 so far.

She rolled her green eyes and grabbed a turmeric and pineapple juice out of the fridge.

"Besides, mountaineering is dangerous babe. You could plummet to your death."

She said with a smirk, "Maybe you could. I'm gonna live forever."

2163 A.G.

It was a quarter past midnight when George emerged from his sweet memory into the chilling loneliness of the present. Alone, emaciated, and slightly soiled, he sunk into his sheets and pulled his covers up to his chin. He wondered what happened to Alison after he died. Was she sad? Did she ever get married or have kids? How did she look when she got older? How long did she live? What did she die from? Did she leave him when he got sick, or stay by his side until the end? He wanted to remember to give her credit for that, but part of him was grateful to be spared the memory of their final goodbye.

He had this false sensation that he had time traveled forward. But this wasn't like the movies. This was a dark one way highway. Now he was a traveller forever stranded. The comfort, the warm embrace of those intimate connections he had lived on and built his identity around, were irrevocably lost to him forever. It was like everyone he ever knew died in the same plane crash. Every waking moment he was fighting back the overwhelming grief. But that's what death was he reckoned. Every relationship you have is taken from you in a moment. It's the end of the world - your own private apocalypse.

He let a deep guttural scream out into the night.

Back at Owen's cliffside estate he found himself unable to sleep. He had to get started recording George for future marketing and limited docuseries projects. And if he was going to lure big name medical and entertainment talent to a cryonics facility, he would need tantalizing sneak peaks. But he couldn't work with George the way he was. A bitter angry homebound invalid - look at what we've accomplished! He racked his brain thinking of strategies to get George camera ready.

He turned on his side and pulled out his cell. "Show me George." That's when he saw his six billion dollar man tearing his room apart like an animal.

Chapter 11

Thin Ice

Twenty minutes later Owens found Witten and Priya had beaten him to Cryonicor. They were watching George break everything in his room like it was made of balsa wood.

Owens couldn't believe what he was seeing, "You're both just standing by doing nothing? Sedate him!"

Witten shook her head in refusal, "No. We can't drug him forever, he has to process it."

"Where are you on this, huh, you're his primary right?" he yelled, getting in Witten's face. His nice guy routine sure had faded fast. "How could you miss the signs!"

Witten had been waiting for an excuse to scream in his face, and he had just given her one. "There is no playbook for this man! There's no best practices. There are no signs to miss! We are all in the dark here, it's not like I'm a shrink!"

"This is unacceptable, doctor. You're not out here with no one watching you anymore. When you mess up, I'm gonna be all over you, you know why, because when we don't have accountability is when people get sloppy. And THIS is a pig pen," he said motioning to hurricane George on the monitors.

"I don't need this. I got a lot on my mind. Why don't you do something about it, hero?" Witten grabbed her jacket and left.

Priya had never seen anyone speak to Dr. Witten that way. She didn't know how to feel about it, but she knew George deserved better.

***

The next morning, Witten was still MIA, and Dr. Owens examined George in what was left of his room. Priya and Kelley were at his side observing, like residents watching the attending physician at a teaching hospital. Kelley watched Dr. Owens, intensely curious about his methods and techniques. But Priya was focused only on the patient himself.

"Sorry about the room," said George, he was sincere, but he was also partly numb.

"It's okay, I'll get you a better room," said Owens forgivingly. "You can sit down. Your skin's looking a little sallow." He retrieved a mysterious vial of clear fluid from his lab coat pocket and plugged it into George's IV drip. "This ought to help you out."

"What's that?"

Owens answered with a trademark aire of self-satisfaction, "this is a little cocktail I call Tiger Blood - steroids, regenerative stimulants, preservatives. It's gonna help return you to your prime, and keep you there for a very long time. Do you have any questions?"

"I have a headache all the time. I don't want to take any painkillers, I know what happens to people who get hooked on that crap. I just want my head fixed, what's going on with that?"

The others were a little out of touch with George's fear of painkillers, because the infamous opiate epidemic of the twenty teens was overshadowed in the annals of medical history, by the ensuing pandemics. George had missed those entirely. Since then painkillers had been made safe and non-habit forming.

Owens really wanted to fix George's headaches rather than manage them. He shined his pen light into George's pupil, who recoiled.

Owens said, "Sorry about that. You have any nausea, light sensitivity?" George shook his head. Owens made a note on his reader. "I'll look into it right away and come up with a game plan for this. I am sorry you are going through it. Anything else?"

"When do I get to go home?" He asked it, as if it was the most natural question in the world.

Owens, slightly stunned, stared back at him

with even parts compassion and morbid curiosity. At last, he asked him earnestly, "Where do you think home is?"

**

HQ was the nerve center of their operation, which was mostly automated and required a minimum staff. Floor to ceiling windows lined the rear wall overlooking the Santa Angeles skyline in the distance. Name brand drones and birds of prey casually zipped past the windows.

At the presentation center Kelley and Priya illuminated a holographic projection of George's brain; they could move it around with their hands. Owens was right behind them, he was pleased by the fast work of these medical enthusiasts. He sat down close to the hologram and eyed it with great interest. If Witten wasn't going to do anything meaningful about George's headaches then he would.

Priya began, "George suffered two major cleaves during his initial vitrification that we had to repair before even starting his heart transplant, one in the medium temporal lobe cutting from the hippocampus through the thalamus"

Kelley continued, "And another here, in his medulla. That's probably why he can't remember some stuff."

Owens liked Kelley, even though he didn't sound especially educated when he spoke, he was actually right about this. "Wow. I can't believe you were able to modify my code to do this level of repair."

Kelley shrugged his *no-big-deal* shrug, but inside he was on cloud nine over a compliment like that coming from *the* Elijah Owens. The doctor, in a rare moment of self awareness, had to check his privilege and ask himself why it was that he liked Kelley, but not Priya or Witten. Was he a misogynist? He made a mental note to work on that.

The doctor circled the hologram, "But I'm not sold on using an HBC. What do you think?"

Priya said, "Dr. Witten knows what she's doing. I trust her instincts."

Owens noted Priya's loyalty to Dr. Witten. This wasn't the military, loyalty had no place in medicine as far as he was concerned. He left it alone for the moment, rationalizing that they had no opinion, because maybe they didn't really know what was happening from a medical standpoint.

Owens sat back down, straddling a chair backwards and said, "Earlier you said, George was a stage 1. Can you tell me more about that?"

Priya reluctantly walked over to the wall and with the stroke of her hand illuminated it, the entire wall was a giant glass reader. The display was segmented into four scrolling columns; each containing entries with photos of different preserved patients. The database was Priya's baby. She spent years creating a centralized platform to store and sort their patients.

She explained, "Every patient is cataloged thoroughly. We compile cause of death, conditions of preservation, life history information. Anything we can get our hands on that's relevant. Then we use that information to rank them."

"OK. In stages?" Owens followed.

Priya nodded and continued, "In four stages. A patient categorized as stage 1 has the best chance for a successful thaw, because we can now cure or replace what killed them. And their preservation was immaculate."

Owens' eyes lit up as he viewed the scrolling lives of thousands before him. He asked, "you made this?"

"Uh...yea," she answered, distracted by his shift in tone.

He raised his eyebrows and pursed his lips, starting to see the kindergarten teacher's value. "And what variables go into the preservation?"

Priya answered, "The first is the quality of the cool-aid. These chemicals have improved a lot over time. Also, not all patients' tissue absorb it to the same degree, some fare better than others. If large areas of tissue don't absorb the cool-aid, then they are destroyed by the ice crystals and the nanobots can't do much for them... at this point."

Kelley interjected, "And some preservations happened like that" he snapped his fingers dramatically, "but sometimes they don't get into the ice fast enough. So their cells become necrotic or decayed."

"Got it."

Emboldened, young Kelley went on, "These are stage 2s. Their preservation was immaculate, but science still hasn't found a cure for what killed them in the first place. Once medicine has found that reversal, they can slide... to a one.

"In theory," said Priya.

Kelley echoed, "In theory. Stage 3s already have a reversible cause of death, but their preservation was spotty. If we can find a work around for freezer burn, they can leap frog over a 2 to a stage 1. But that's even harder than reversing cause of death most times."

"What about stage 4s?"

Priya said, "Their preservation was so-so."

"And we can't fix what killed them yet," added Kelley.

Owens bobbed his head with understanding, "So they're screwed."

Kelley and Priya mumbled in unison, "Basically... Essentially...."

Suddenly, the lights flashed and a synthetic female voice announced, "Dr. Elijah Owens, you have a visitor in the lobby."

"Who is it?"

"US Department of Health and Human Services."

Owens shrugged his shoulders, unsure what

this could be about. "Again? This isn't good," he said, cutting his eyes between the two cryotechs, "He knows something or he thinks he knows something."

***

Getty shifted his weight in Owen's guest chair. He looked around the minimal but chic office. He noticed the whiskey on the credenza, and made a mental note. He also noticed a bizarre object next to it. It was a soda bottle cut in half, the bottom was filled with a sticky brown substance and the top half flipped upside down like a funnel, sitting in the bottom half. He looked at it with a raised eyebrow.

"DIY honey trap. We gotta fly around here."

"Oh yeah? Good luck with that." His body temperature rose three degrees though you could never tell it by looking at him.

Owens nodded his head and continued their discussion, "Yeah, so like I was saying, without a warrant, I don't see any reason why we would release our human storage database."

Getty knew he might get stonewalled, but he wasn't expecting Owens, a relative newcomer to the cryonics game, to be so well versed on the fine print. "Fine, but if I have to get a warrant and I find anything untoward—"

"I don't understand what you think you are going to find," said Owens, squinting and cocking his head.

Getty's countenance was unchanged. He had to think on his feet. "I'd like to see your books, those you are required to provide." He knew he was showing his hand, but he needed more than a name to make a case and he couldn't watch hundreds of hours of footage by himself. Where was the money coming from?

"Our accounting records? Purchases orders, invoices... ?"

"Ledgers and bank statements."

Owens stood up and extended his hand, "I'll have them sent over ASAP."

"You will?" They shook hands.

"Yeah. But next time you show up, do me a favor and make an appointment, I'm pretty busy."

After Getty left, Owens phoned Martinez, who appeared as a projected half hologram head. He was rattling slightly because he was riding in a car on his way to BKK in Bangkok.

"Talk to me," answered Martinez enthusiastically.

"HHS is sniffing around here hard. Did you know about this?"

"No, I had no idea.... Do you think they know about our man?"

"I don't think he knows exactly, but he's got it out for us for sure, and if he keeps pushing, with the way things are around here, he's going to find something... or someone."

"We might need to speed up our path to legalization."

***

Samantha Witten was hiking alone through the snowbank alongside a frozen lake. She was enjoying the stillness of nature as she clomped along her path. But her peace was short lived when her cell started ringing. She struggled to pull it out of her coat pocket with her gloves on. It slipped from her hand, ricocheted off a rock and flew out onto the icy lake. It lit up ringing. Her wife's name, GWEN, flashed on the screen.

Witten stepped cautiously onto the ice to retrieve it. A few feet from shore, the ice cracked and she plunged into the freezing water. She struggled to surface, but the lake froze over again, trapping her under. She beat her fists violently against the ice from underneath. Her eyes were flooded with desperation and terror as she struggled futilely to break through the ice.

She sat bolt upright gasping and distraught. She was on the sofa in her study made up like a bed. Gwen was seated at Witten's desk, she was wearing her silk robe drinking coffee, watching her wife suspiciously.

"Bad dreams?"

"Yeah."

"Same one?"

"This time the lake froze over me, and I couldn't break through it."

"That's a new twist."

It had been a couple days since Gwen had returned to the condo. But they moved about like strangers, barely speaking. Was Gwen's presence in the study an olive branch?

Witten wiped the trauma off her face and started right in, "Look, I'm sorry—"

Gwen stopped her with a raised hand. "I'm not ready to have this conversation with you yet, I get doctor-patient confidentiality but—"

This half statement alerted Witten to another danger, "Well you know you can't tell your therapist about this." Gwen was disappointed by her wife's preoccupation with the logistics of deception. "Or your mother," she added, for good measure.

Witten's emotional obliviousness was exhausting to Gwen. "I can't do this with you right now. Just tell me how George's doing?"

Well, it might not have been an olive branch, but at least they were talking about something. She thought that was good. It was actually a sweet relief to talk to her wife about her work. "His vitals are getting stronger everyday, but he's got these terrible headaches and the whole breathing outside problem is—"

"No, not physically, how is he *doing*? Mentally and emotionally."

Witten took her point and leaned back. "He's been pretty quiet."

"And what are you doing about *that*?"

"I'm trying to fix his damn headaches, what

am I supposed to do?"

Gwen flared her eyes wide at her wife, who promptly went into listening mode. After a silence settled between them, she began, "In combat when a soldier loses a piece of themselves, like their legs, or their sight, or their hearing, they can experience a retreat inward. It can get very dark in there. The further away they get, the harder it is to pull them back to us. It's critical to George's recovery to do whatever you can to build up his connections to new people and new places."

Witten considered her wife's words, and got an exciting idea. She had a surprise in store for George Gilroy.

Chapter 12

No Atheists in Foxholes

George explored his new quarters. It reminded him of getting upgraded to the high-roller suite in Vegas. There was a bed, a lounge area, a desk and an ensuite bathroom with a jacuzzi tub. The room was done in pastel metallics. The far out interior design wasn't exactly his taste. It was sort of a blush neon desert starship aesthetic.

"You do you 2163."

One of his windows spanned the entire rear wall, he was on the top floor of the building and saw skyscrapers as far as the eye could see in either direction. There was even a peek-a-boo view of the ocean in the distance. On a shelf next to the bed there were some vintage puzzles and a few tattered books including *A Brave New World* and a Shakespeare Anthology. He picked them up and shook his head baffled by their clumsy effort.

Who did they think he was? And there was still no television. He scratched his head, wondering if this was for his benefit or if people in the future really had done away with it all together. He rolled his eyes either way.

As he turned back he caught a glimpse of his reflection in a mirror. He almost didn't recognize himself. Owen's cocktail had transformed his face. What was sallow, sunken and lined was now glowing, tight, bright, and just the right amount of supple. "Wow" he said, turning his head from side to side.

He looked up for the camera, there they were, two of them, tracking his motion. *Great*. He turned back to the view, looking for familiar landmarks to ground him. Hollywood Sign? The Capitol Records Building? The Staples Center? It was unrecognizable. It was closer to what he imagined Tokyo looked like, though he had never been.

He wondered first and foremost if the Lakers were still playing, and how they were doing this season. Then he thought of his best friend Mac, who loved the Clippers. They used to text each other non-stop trash talk during the season. Those memories brought a smile to his face. He didn't want to let himself think about Mac being dead. Still he couldn't help but feel his stomach sink at the reality that he would never talk to his friend again. He became overwhelmed with sadness, panic and dread when he imagined the lifetime of lonely struggle stretched out before him. He had taken up a one-day-at-a-time coping strategy. He pushed those thoughts out of his mind, closed his eyes and focused on his breathing. In and out. In and out. Just be here.

A bell rang. He opened his eyes, unsure of where it had come from. He looked around. On the desk? Next to the bed? It rang again. He noticed a light going off over the door. He went over to examine it. Then he heard a clear voice from the other side of the door ask, "Can I come in?"

"Come in?" he asked, cocking his head back. Was there a button he needed to push?

The door whooshed open and Witten walked in carrying a black oxygen assisted performance workout suit and a pair of running moccasins. This was her first time seeing the quarters Owens had renovated for George. On one hand she was upset that he had gone around her, and on the other impressed with the fast results. Maybe he wasn't worthless after all.

When she refocused on George himself, she was struck by his appearance. "Wow." She stepped up to him closely, her brows pushed together trying to figure out which chemical combination had produced these results.

"Not bad huh?" George said, smiling and turning his head for her.

"How did...where did...?"

"That doctor guy gave me something yesterday."

"Dr. Owens?" she said, forcing nonchalance over her white hot rage.

"Yeah, I think that's what he said his name was."

"Well, how do you feel?"

"I'm kinda numb mostly, except for my headaches."

"I have an idea for how to treat your headaches. I am just waiting for some materials to arrive, I expect them today or tomorrow."

"Good, because I don't know how much more of this I can take," said George, running his hand over the side of his aching skull.

"And what about your... accommodations? Is it satisfactory?"

"Good view. Thanks for the books, but I'm more of a video game guy. Now that could be cool, I would actually love to see what your video games are like in twenty one whatever it is... "

"Hmmm..." said Witten, "not really my wheelhouse, but I'll see what I can do." She held up the suit and shoes, "I was thinking it would be good for you to take a walk outside, get some earth under your feet?"

He took the gear from her, but not without some trepidation.

It was an especially smoggy day in Southern California. The overcast sky was a septic blend of white, brown and lavender. Witten and George rounded a corner on the grounds of the Cryon-icor compound. The landscaping was minimal and mostly dried out, filled in here and there with plants native to the arid climate. George was wearing the oxy suit, which fit his athletic frame quite well, a little tight in the shoulders maybe. He was not used to the sustainable fabrics of 2163. The suit was a blend of bio-elastic, bamboo and soy fibers - so it itched a little. But it was black and flattering. The head piece fit a little bit like a ski mask, except over the mouth and jowls there was a vented plastic oxy-pak with a small green light indicating it was full and ready for use.

"What do you think?" asked Witten.

"I feel like a freak."

"Believe it or not, this is what people wear when they workout. The oxy-pak supplements our poor oxygen level which improves our physical performance."

"So if I wore this out in the world, no one would look at me crazy?"

Witten winced at his uncouth vocabulary. "Well, I wouldn't wear it in a grocery store. But outdoors, yes, you'll blend in. People would assume you are between sprints. Also... we don't really use the word, 'crazy' anymore. It's problematic."

A whiff of white hot shame hit George smack in the face. "Oh. Okay, sorry... Um this mask... how long does it last?"

"Couple hours."

They rounded another corner and came to a cleared lot of land on the far right edge of the property. It was dotted with steel markers in neat little rows. There was a bench all by itself where Witten stopped and took a seat.

George could see this was their destination. "What's this?"

"Cryonicor Cemetery." He didn't get it. Witten squinted in that brooding way she had, as she looked out over her markers and into the late afternoon sun. She continued, "I started it around 18 years ago. Each of these mark a thaw that failed. These are my real angel investors right here. None of this would be possible without their sacrifice."

"They're just dead bodies that are still dead," he said, keeping a rationalist's distance.

Witten shrugged it off, "You were a dead body, and now you're not. You're alive again. They went through a lot of trouble... a lot of trouble to have a second life. That is what they sacrificed. What you have now."

"I doubt any of them would want what I have."

"You sure?"

George joined Witten on the bench. After a moment he said, "Look, I get that I should be grateful to be alive but... I just can't understand why anyone would do something like this, much less my own self."

His point of view flew in the face of Witten's

entire life's purpose, and she naturally felt attacked. With a little more bass in her voice she asked, "What's the alternative?"

"I don't know, rest in peace? Ever heard of it? It's like if I were ever faced with life in prison or be put to death, put me to death every time."

"Apparently not kiddo. Or you wouldn't be here. Big talk, but when you're facing down a meeting with your maker, you might find you aren't so sure as all that. Why do you think we call the cryostat storage the *foxhole?*"

George knew he couldn't refute this point logically, but emotionally he still couldn't accept it. It was like waking up from a coma to find out you had been in a gunfight, and had used your baby brother as a shield to save yourself. Your entire essence, all your beliefs and convictions that you thought defined your character had been betrayed by instincts you seemingly couldn't control, remember or deny. He looked down at his weird moccasins ashamed, "Well I was a damn fool, anyone can see that."

This only further angered Witten, who was already raw from her troubles at home, "How can you believe that? We're not allowed to fight for our own lives now? Let natural causes take us all down?"

George repeated his programming, "I mean we live and we die and however much time we get, that's how much time we got. Doesn't mean anything if it just goes on and on."

Witten shook her head appalled and stood up as Priya approached with caution, seeing they were in an argument.

Witten fired back, "That's it then? Long life isn't worth having? When does it shift over to meaninglessness exactly? Where is that threshold? Thirty years old, like you?... No, that's clearly a tragedy right? So much good life to live. OK, how about fifty years old, a heart attack?... Still pretty sad. Let's speed up to sixty-five. That's "old" for sure, right?... But wait. What about those grandkids and a brand new retirement to enjoy? Tough one.... OK, let's factor in quality of life. Are we talking about eighty years old wasting away in full blown senility? Put them out of their misery right? But what if that same eighty year old was strong, vibrant, contributing and looking forward to the future everyday?... How's that threshold feeling now? Priya can you take him back to his room? I gotta lot of work to do." Witten stormed off fuming over the ungratefulness of it all. If he knew what she had sacrificed....

George nodded his head, trying to hold onto some dignity by pretending he was above it, while inwardly feeling bothered that she had gotten the last word.

Priya sat down next to him, after a moment she said, "You know she is seventy-five."

George was gobsmacked. "Her? How?"

Priya shrugged, "The miracles of modern

medicine, we don't age at the velocity you guys did back in the 2020's. They have developed all kinds of ways to slow down mother nature."

It was a little clearer to George now why Witten was so passionate about life extension. If you look and feel forty-five at seventy-five, maybe you would want more years. But still, his feelings struggled to keep pace with the intellectual understanding. Witten's aggression only inflamed his defensiveness. He was reeling in that adrenaline soaked rip tide that sucks you away after a confrontation. Priya could sense it. She sat quietly allowing him to process things. Her energy was a welcome change of pace, but could he trust it?

"Are you here to play good cop?"

She smirked, "Oh, I'm not the good cop... I'm the hot cop." She lifted his oxy-pak mask up and saw his amused smile. "I want to try something." She lifted the mask all the way up, and it rested over his head, his mouth and nose were fully exposed to the untreated air of 2163. He moved to snatch it back down over his face, but she stopped him. "Trust me for a second. Try to relax."

George obeyed. He started to wheeze, harder, then harder - he looked at her with growing desperation but did not reach for his mask. Then she pulled her inhaler from her pocket and gave it to him. He took a hit. His breathing relaxed as he gratefully examined the haley.

"Can I ask you something?" George asked.

"Okay."

"What's the plan, for me I mean? It's been what, a couple weeks? I can't stay here forever."

"I know. I wish I could tell you something more definite. I probably shouldn't be telling you this, but truly you are the first and there is a certain amount of 'making it up as we go' happening. I *want* to build a robust outpatient program. I *want* to have a good answer for your questions. But I don't yet..."

"Not right now, but soon more answers, I know. But what about like at the end of the day when it's all said and done and I get my walking papers... What am I supposed to do... out there?" he asked, motioning to the city in the distance. "I'm not supposed to be here."

"You have just as much of a right to be here as anyone else." He had no words for her, just a far off look in his eyes. Priya was no psychology student but she knew that people didn't do what they were supposed to do, or what they were expected to do, they tended to do whatever the hell they *wanted* to do, which begged the question: "What do you want to do?"

He looked down at the inhaler, then back at the setting sun. "I have no fucking idea."

Her comm device suddenly went off. "It's a code blue. Dead already, huh? That was quick. I gotta go." She stood to leave then turned back to George. "Hey, you wanna see something cool?"

Chapter 13

The Worst Kind of Magic

Priya was wearing her white hazmat-like uniform. She was in the Preservation Chamber. This was the mysterious inner sanctum where they thrust their recently deceased clients into the deep freeze. The cryonics industry had been perfecting these procedures for almost two hundred years. While the reanimation work they did was totally experimental, they had the preservation side down to best practices. Priya was in charge of a small team of on-call part-time assistants and directed them with confidence.

George watched with intense curiosity from an observation deck above. He had changed out of his oxy suit back into his scrubs and was wearing his nasal cannula. The thrill of this spectacle had almost eclipsed his upset feelings after his row with Witten. Almost.

A couple of assistants rushed in the body bag on a gurney. Upon unzipping it, it appeared to be full of ice! Pushing the ice away they revealed the lifeless face of Mr. Goodstein. Priya had spoken to him only days ago, he was funny, expressive, gesticulating, a muck with conflicting emotions like fear, gratitude, hope... an entire world unto himself. And now... he was transformed... meat in a bag. Presto change-o. It was the worst kind of magic.

Maybe for now, but not forever. Not on her watch. Priya took her duties as director of Preservation very seriously. For her, she knew that any chance her patients would have at a successful return to life came down to this thirty minute window. Their preservation was everything, she knew this all too well from the database. A delay or mistake could mean the difference between stage 1 and stage 3. She was skilled at pushing away her emotions, thinking clearly and efficiently, not unlike an army general in battle.

At Priya's direction they began the process of drilling holes into the skull, and inserting various tubing. In mere minutes devices were switched on and George could see red fluid going out through the tubes, and neon green fluid going in. An assistant quickly shaved his head. George raised his eyebrow at this, and ran his hands over his own missing mane. *Oh*. At least one of his questions had been answered. After this the patient was lifted off the gurney and placed in a glass box. He was naked except for a neck brace. The box was sealed and began to fill with a cloud of white vapor. George's heart sank. He felt the back of his own head for a scar from the tube holes, it was faint, but it was there.

Once the patient was frosty and the internal temperature readings met Priya's satisfaction, the glass box receded into the floor and the patient was transferred to a mylar sleeping bag. The cryostat on standby, was opened and the client was loaded into it, head down, the fourth and final client added to this specific tube.

Priya was all too pleased with herself, and when she walked George back to his room, she failed to notice that he was as white as a sheet and awfully quiet. She mistook his pale color and introverted manner as a sign of simple overexertion.

***

The next day, Witten waited outside of George's quarters with a pair of googles and a small box. She felt terrible about how she had snapped at him in the cemetery. It was unprofessional. The fact was, she wasn't used to patients who were... alive. Her bedside manner was sorely out of practice. She took a deep breath and hoped her gift would help to smooth things over.

On his say-so, she entered. He was shirtless doing side crunches on the floor, his feet tucked under the platform bed, his arms crossed and his hands locked together. She noticed two trays of uneaten food on his desk.

"Hey, I brought you some video games."

He finished, "98, 99, 100" - and slowly stood up. He pulled a hoodie on and took the strange items from her without offering her a greeting.

"What is it?" he asked while slyly eyeing her closely for signs of her true age. He looked at her hands, her neck, her earlobes and found a bit of thinning skin tissue here and a couple sun spots there. Still, if someone hadn't told him, taking into account the total package, he would never have suspected.

"Those are the games," she pointed to the dice-sized black box, "and that is the interface, the Googles."

"Goggles," he corrected her, inspecting them closely.

"Goooooooogles, like Google, the huge multi-national corporation, or at least what's left of it. Doesn't matter...I'll send Kelley by to set this up and show you how it works, because honestly, I never touch the damn things."

"Ok, thanks." He sat them down and tightened his face into a macho lipless non-smile, the kind guys make when they are trying to take expressionless selfies.

"Nice form on your oblique crunches. I do 100 of those a day myself."

"Well it shows," he said, complementing her impressive physique.

She smiled slightly, "Got to get it in where you can."

"Got to." He smiled slightly too. They did have something in common. "What do you do for your triceps?" He pointed to the defined underside of her upper arms peeking out from her short sleeve scrubs.

"Speedbag."

"Nice."

"You don't like the food?" she motioned to the uneaten trays on the desk.

"It's okay, I'm just not hungry."

"Okay, well, I'll leave you to it. Have a good one."

"Thanks. You too."

Witten headed out, feeling good about their exchange. It was the best she could do as far as apologies went.

***

Her victory was short lived as she found herself moments later getting chewed out in Owen's office. "Did you know that Priya let George observe a preservation?" asked Owens with a manic energy.

"No."

"No. Of course you didn't. You have no idea what your people are doing! This guy is a basketcase and she's just making it worse."

"C'mon man, don't say basketcase."

"Fine. Highly unstable then.... You know he hasn't eaten anything in twenty four hours? He's

159

just up there doing prison work outs. This is not what I need."

"I get it. I'll talk to her, I'm sure her heart was in the right place."

"Good. Martinez is breathing down my neck about getting legalization going, but that's a ways off still. I have no delusions about that, but we do need to position George as our... "

"Poster boy."

He snapped his fingers and pointed at her with excitement, "Yes! I'm going to start filming him, we need early footage of his... re-entry... to make this whole thing look good, feel sexy, you get me? You have to give the people what they want. We're not talking about releasing it now, but we need to start collecting it for later packaging. All we have is this terrible surveillance footage, no one wants to see this."

"None of this is my problem, I'm a doctor."

"Not your problem? You're his primary right? His well-being is your priority. What are you doing for him, for his mindset?"

"Gwen... Dr. Kim Witten said we need to strengthen his connections to the outside world. So I took him outside yesterday, just around the campus, in an oxy work out suit to.. I don't know... give him a better sense of mobility and independence."

"Clever. And I like that people can't see his face." Owens was pacing. "How did that go?"

She sank down into the guest chair trying to

disappear. Her expression indicated, it had not gone well.

Owens finally settled on standing in front of his desk and leaning back on it slightly, his hands clasped at his waste. "Now what?"

"I gave him a video game."

"That's it?!" he guffawed.

"Okay, I'll schedule him for a mental health check up with Jack."

"Who?"

"Jack Wagner, he's my in-house guy."

"That guy? He's a two bit grief counselor. He belongs in a church basement."

"I trust him, he can handle it. But honestly I think his mindset will improve on its own once we get his headaches and breathing outside under control. When am I getting the HBC?"

"I saw the specs you sent me on that, but in my medical opinion that is unlikely to generate the results we want, and we're not going to flush money down the toilet because you have a feeling... what would you try if you had gotten the hyperbaric chamber and it hadn't worked?

"You want me to start with my back up plan?"

"Yes. Work on that, but even if we do get that all sorted out, there is no guarantee it's going to right his mindset, so let's play this from both ends for now." She nods and starts to rise, he pointed at her again, warning her, "your boy Jack better do this right - or I don't see a need to keep him around."

Witten stood up and leveled his gaze. She did not like him threatening the livelihood of her loyal staff. But she knew she didn't have much recourse here. Jack would have to earn his keep on his own.

"One more thing," said Owens before she left. "We're going to have to duplicate these results. So clear your schedule." She knew they would have to duplicate. They needed to pull out more George's to prove this wasn't a freak accident. More subjects would bring more varied results and it would offset any specific problems of any particular patient. She knew Owens was counting on that, but what he wasn't counting on was the unique horrors the next crop of lucky subjects would face. After George, she was a little gun shy to find out.

Once she left, Owens went back over to his credenza to pour himself a scotch neat. Was he getting too old for this shit? Was it worth it? He noticed the pesky fly had returned. His home-made honey fly trap seemed to have generated no interest. What kind of fly was this? Perhaps they were evolving a distaste for sweets? It ceased buzzing and casually landed on his credenza. He had the empty tumbler in his hand, as yet unspoiled by the alcohol. Seeing an opportunity, he slowly turned the glass upside down in his hand, moved ever so slightly above his prey and - BOOM- he swiftly brought the glass down... trapping it. He lit up with sweet satisfaction. Then he noticed, magnified under the glass, this wasn't an ordinary house fly. He leaned down, angling his head for a closer look.

"What do we have here?"

Chapter 14

The Monte-Carlo Theory

The next morning Priya was feeling so good she was bordering on manic. She and Kelley were palling around in a disused examination room in the hospice wing. He was administering a cosmetic treatment to her face with a hand-held laser.

"What's the special occaishe?" he asked.

She tried to answer without moving too much, like one does with a dentist's hands in their mouth. "No occasion, I just want to freshen up my look."

He was totally focused as he carefully worked his mini-laser. They noticed George walking past the window wearing his NC, pulling his Oxy cart like a lonely little boy pulls his red wagon. He didn't see them.

Priya lamented, "I'm worried about him."

Kelley nodded, "Me too. Uncharted territory."

"Poor guy. Imagine what he's going through."

Kelley echoed the age-ole credo of the cry-onicist, "Beats the alternative though, right?"

"I think so, but it depends, I guess. What do you think happens after we die?"

"Well to be honest with you, I have been working on a theory for a while."

Priya started to crack up. "Hold still dude!" he ordered.

"Spill it."

Feigning reluctance, he spoke slowly and deliberately "Ok, after you die, you go into a casino. Like a nice one, like in Monte-Carlo, wearing a tux, like James Bond."

"Okay... " said Priya, trying very hard not to smile.

"You step up to the roulette wheel and every wedge is a day of the life that you lived."

"Okay..."

"You spin the wheel and you land on some random day of your life, and you have to live that day over and over again for eternity. But you don't know you are repeating the day."

"And it's totally random?"

"Totally."

He finished her treatment and stood back to admire his work. It was subtle but effective. She was radiant. He shrugged unimpressed with himself, and handed her a mirror.

"I did my best, but you can't fix ugly," he

teased. She slapped his arm while admiring his work.

"But wait, that sucks. If it's random... what are you supposed to do?"

"The only thing you can do, stack the odds in your favor. Live as many great days as you can."

She leaned back smiling, and said with her hands on her hips, "You should, like, start your own religion. But how do you know that you aren't already dead and today is the day you are reliving over and over?"

"You don't," he said straight faced. "So I hope you'll understand why I need to leave early today to go surfing."

***

George arrived at Jack Wagner's office for his mental health check up. Jack was somewhat excited by the opportunity to counsel someone about something other than their impending death. But he was also very nervous because of his lack of experience. His office was inviting and smelled of eucalyptus, a sharp contrast to Witten's sterile office which reeked of self-discipline.When George arrived, Jack stood up wearing a huge fake smile and awkwardly pulled out the guest chair for George like they were on some kind of date. Cringe.

"Thank you for coming, George. Can I get you anything, water or tea maybe?"

"I'm good. It's just nice to be outta my room."

"Okay, well today I just wanted to check in with you. See how you're holding up and what not." George began to cough slightly. Jack looked around, and noticed his office window was cracked open. He was a sucker for a nice breeze. He shut the window, and George nodded appreciatively. Jack continued, "Sorry about that... I know this is a very difficult, confusing time for you. It's important that you can talk about what is bothering you."

"So you're some kinda shrink?"

"I am some kind of mental health professional, yes. So, tell me... how do you feel?" said Jack as he straightened objects on his desk.

George rubbed his temples, exhausted by the unoriginal question, he felt like he got asked that a million times a day. "Well I guess I feel pretty shitty."

"Why is that?"

"Uhhhhhhh, everyone I care about is dead and I can't even go outside by myself."

"That's fair. No, that's totally.. yeah. I get that. What else?"

"Does there need to be more?"

"Only if there is more..."

"You know there are cameras in my room watching me all the time? All the time."

"It's for your own protection George."

George put his elbows to his knees and shook his head, "that's what they keep telling me. But how would you feel?"

"That's hard."

"Man…" said George in frustration, scratching his head, "I just want to get the hell out of here." He was sullen but at least he was talking.

"What else?"

"Honestly, I am pretty pissed off at myself for signing up for this. I can't really believe it. I keep thinking someone else went behind my back and did this to me."

"I assure you, they did not."

"Well I am struggling with that… I guess…."

"You thought you knew how you would react to the news that you were about to die, that you only had a couple months to live- at thirty one, you thought you knew how you would react to that?"

"I'm sure. I was sure. I have strongly held personal convictions."

Jack really had no idea what he was supposed to say here. His online Christian therapy certificate had not exactly prepared him for this situation. So he improvised.

"I don't know if this will help but… have you ever heard of Thomas à Kempis?"

"No."

"Alright, well he was this man in the 13th century who wrote this really famous devotional book called *The Imitation of Christ*."

George rolled his eyes hard at the mention of the C word.

"—I know, believe me, I'm not even…. it

doesn't matter. Anyway listen, that book was super popular, he was famous in his own lifetime and even after he died that book was reprinted for like ever. So when he died he was buried on holy ground which was the tradition, right?"

"Okay," said George, repositioning his slouchy posture.

"But later, they moved his body to an ossuary. When they opened his coffin they found these crazy claw marks on the inside lid. And his fingers were broken to bloody bits," said Jack, pushing his red glasses back up his nose.

"He was buried alive?"

"Yeah. And he of all people shouldn't have been afraid of death. I mean this guy was gonna get a ticker tape parade when he went through those pearly gates, right? ...But he *was* afraid." When Jack really got going he would talk with his hands a lot. "And the Catholic Church decided they couldn't make him a saint because of this. They took it as proof that he had lost his faith. Can you believe that?"

"Brutal."

"Yeah."

"And what's this got to do with me?"

"You're only human, George. Death will do *this* to the best of us. The church was messed up, what they did to him, what they held against him. Have a little grace with yourself. Don't be your own Catholic Church."

George considered the words of the chatty

counselor as he stood on the elevator that lifted him up to his penthouse. From here he had an escalating view of the world of 2163 in all its madness and glory. He couldn't live like this. Something had to give.

***

That night, inside Priya's compact home, she had laid some clothes out on her bed. She held her wedding dress up to herself in the mirror listening to music on the container's all-room sound system. Her reader leaned against the bathroom mirror, displaying a photo of herself from her wedding day. She stretched her jaw away from her face trying to match her former tautness. Honestly, it looked like no time had gone by. She tossed the dress on her bed and took her reader to the kitchen with her. She propped it up against the backsplash and began to open a bottle of wine. She realized with some self satisfaction that she hadn't logged into Facebook Legacy in weeks, not since George joined them. Maybe she was finally past that unseemly compulsion...

"Play John Surprise" she commanded the reader while her hands were occupied with the corkscrew. The reader played a short cell phone video file from her personal cloud. It was a video of John surprising her when he came home from his last deployment. Soldiers routinely recorded these in secret, it was tradition. The short clip played on a loop. It was after midnight when he returned so the video was all night vision. He placed the phone on a shelf facing her as she slept, dutifully to one side of the bed, as was still her habit. He climbed in gently, wearing his uniform sans boots. He laid his head on his pillow next to her. Seconds later, she screamed and recoiled up into the corner - as he bursted out laughing uncontrollably. Then realizing it was her husband in her bed, and not a rapey intruder, she kicked him resentfully, "John!" Then they kissed and embraced.

Pop. The cork was out. She smiled at her reaction in the video file. This moment was the last truly happy memory she had, but boy was it short lived. She remembered the conversation that night. He was home unexpectedly because he had abruptly left his deployment in San Juan. At first she was thrilled by the prospect of having him home full time and saying sayonara to the angst of being an army wife. Then she realized something serious must have happened for him to be discharged in the middle of war time deployment. And it had, he was medically discharged.

As she sipped her imitation Burgundy pinot noir, her eyes fell on her new white lab coat, thrown over a bar stool. That symbol of her life in cryonics took her back to her introduction to Dr. Samantha Witten and to her last night with her beloved husband…

It was ten years ago now when Captain John Cayhill sat up in his hospital bed at Kaiser Sinai. He was emaciated and pale from disease. Death hung in the air. The soldier had lost this battle, that much was clear. His wife Priya was by his side along with Dr. Witten, at the time a stranger to both of them. The doctor watched the monitors closely. Two of her assistants hauled in a man-sized tub of ice.

John asked, "What's the ice for?"

"I think they're gonna put your body in there, after.... you know," said Priya.

"Is my Mom still here?"

"She went home."

"Good, She doesn't need to see this. You don't either, should go too."

Priya said, "Oh no, I'm not going anywhere."

He insisted, "Priya I can't stand the idea of you having to carry this memory around with you for the rest of your life, when you think of me I don't want you to think about this—"

"This isn't about me John, you're the one in this bed, I'm not going to let you be alone when you... " she clearly couldn't bring herself to say the word, so she wiped yet another tear from her face with her elbow and continued, "—So don't say it again."

John looked at her, beyond exhausted, her eyes swollen from crying and she still took his breath away. He smiled his dimpled smile, and said "Can't believe I survived three tours disabling bombs in Puerto Rico and I'm going out like this. If I was gonna die young I always thought it would be so much cooler. At least I still got my good looks right?" He didn't. He chuckled himself into a violent coughing fit, blood came out of the sides of his mouth and he winced in great pain.

The doctor approached the couple, she said "Everything is ready."

"Tell me again how it works. What happens... to my body?"

The doctor sat on a stool next to him and began to explain it again. She said with a cold detached confidence, "We'll begin the preservation here. First, to prevent ischemic injury we need to lower your body temperature as much as we can, as fast as we can—"

"You're gonna stuff me in the tub?"

The doctor nodded, "The most important organ is your brain. We'll have only a few moments to get this right."

Priya asked, "Wouldn't we have a better shot on the back end if we do it now? Before his organs you know..."

The doctor shook her head, "If we do it now, it's murder. Legally we have to wait until his heart stops on its own."

A subject change was in order so he asked, "Where do you keep me?"

Witten and Priya cut eyes at each other. "Don't

look at her!" John shouted. "Look at me, I'm calling the shots!"

"A steel cryostat, a special air-tight container that remains super cooled at negative 196 degrees Celsius at all times."

"So there's no coffin, no burial?"

"Many people still choose to have funerals - for closure, others believe their deanimation so temporary a funeral is misleading. It's up to you."

John finally asked, "Okay. But just to be clear, no one has actually ever been brought out, right?"

The doctor sighed, she'd never claimed otherwise, the entire prospect was a gamble. "That's correct. But we are doing serious research. Testing on human remains is not yet permitted but we are making a lot of progress."

Priya interjected, "—We don't have to tell anybody you're not in the coffin John, if that's what you're worried about."

John slammed his fist down onto the medical tray next to him and shouted, "That's not what I'm worried about! Everybody out! Everybody out! I wanna talk to my wife."

The doctor handed Priya her reader as she gave them the room. Priya was destroyed by John's outburst and struggled to compose herself.

John's chest was heaving, he was silently staring at the tub of ice. This 'opportunity' was interfering with his 'acceptance stage.' Priya looked at the reader, it was a form: **CRYONICOR: Cryonic Preservation - RELEASE OF REMAINS**.

She timidly handed him the reader and a stylus. "You need to sign this."

He grabbed her forearms roughly and she dropped the stylus. He pleaded with her, "They are taking advantage of you. Why can't you see that?"

"I don't believe that. All I know is I can't live without you. And now I don't have to. They could find a cure in six months and—"

"—This is crazy! I don't believe them." He swallowed, getting ahold of himself and lowered his voice. "And you need that life insurance money."

Priya shook her head, tears streaming down her round cheeks, "I need you."

John was going now, but as his pulse headed toward the flatlined ever after, he held on to say, "You don't need to waste your life pining after some piece of meat in the freezer. You have to let me go. It's okay." His eyes closed and he went limp as the monitor let out its monstrous uninterrupted beep.

The only man she'd ever loved, who she built her entire life and future around, was gone, blinked out of existence. She stepped back in shock - her body shielding her for a moment, flooding her nerves with a numbness that allowed her to think. She looked back at the tub of ice and then to the reader in her hand. In a split second, she picked up the stylus and forged

John's name on the form.

The doorbell rang unexpectedly, snapping Priya out of her lucid but conflicted memory. She frowned with unpleasant suspicion. Literally, no one ever came to her place in The Keys, especially unannounced.

She peeped through the doorhole but could only see a woman's face and long hair in shadow. She grabbed a tire iron out from under the couch next to the door. A woman living alone couldn't be too careful. John used to drill that into her when he left on long deployments.

"Who is it?" she asked in the upbeat and welcoming tone of a person you do not expect to be holding a tire iron.

A mature but demure voice from the other side answered, "This is Madeline Goodstein. I was looking for Ms. Cayhill? Do I have the right unit?"

The widow of her latest icy interment? This was a surprise indeed. Priya quickly unlocked the door to welcome her guest.

"Mrs. Goodstein! Hey! What are you doing here? Come in, come in!" She ushered her visitor inside. Mrs. Goodstein was truly touched by the warm welcome. She had been nervous to approach Priya at home like this.

"Downsizing. I just moved in."

"Here?" Priya said with a touch of concern for her new friend.

"It's quaint. I saw you earlier in the tunnel, so I thought I would say hello. And please, call me Maddie," she said. 'The tunnel' was what they called the underground commuter train that shuttled residents back and forth to the mainland. In truth, it was a terrifying cesspool.

"Small world. Well, sit down. Wanna glass of wine? I just opened a bottle of red," asked Priya.

Maddie instantly felt a connection with this young widow. Priya abandoned her evening plans of self-amusement/deception and gave all of her attention to Maddie. They went through a bottle of wine discussing their husbands, their lives, and how they ended up on The Keys.

Priya asked, "So how you doing?" as she opened a second bottle.

Maddie nodded solemnly and admitted, "It's hard."

"It'll get easier." Priya rejoined her guest on the sofa and handed her a refill. Maddie caught a glimpse of her wedding ring.

"That's a beautiful ring. I didn't see it before at Cryonicor."

"Oh no, I can't wear it to work, no jewelry on our hands allowed. But I always wear it at home."

"Did you get remarried?"

"No." Priya chuckled, surprised by the premise of the question. She continued, "'Same ring. Remarried? Can you imagine, John comes out of the cooler and I'm like, 'let me introduce you to my new husband."

Maddie smiled politely while she tried to reconcile this statement with the intelligent and thoughtful woman she had been bonding with for the last hour. Maddie took a slow sip and said politically, "I hadn't thought of that. How long ago since he...?"

"Ten years last March."

Maddie took another sip and began to survey the compact home again. This time she noticed the wedding photo that hung next to the entryway. She also noticed the clothes on the bed in the back, including what looked like a wedding gown laid on top. On one of the bedside tables, she clocked a man's watch, out of date phone and two rings. The objects were a still life from the past, lovingly preserved in a Havisham-like denial of the present, complete with cobwebs.

The beginnings of a sorrowful and cautionary understanding crept over her.

Maddie was admittedly loose after 2.5 glasses of wine and feeling a bit more emboldened than usual, she asked, "So does that," pointing to Priya's ring, "mean you haven't had sex in ten years?"

"That is correct," a buzzed Priya quickly answered.

Maddie delighted in Priya's openness. Girl talk was her favorite kind of talk and she was happy to find such a curious case study in this new friend.

"What about children? Don't you want kids?"

Priya nodded, "Sure we do. Let me show you something, come on." Priya stood up and led Maddie to the door of her second bedroom. She unlocked it with a key. Maddie noticed the bottom of the door was covered in the cat's scratch marks.

Priya opened the door and turned on the lights, revealing a half-painted nursery, with a crib filled with boxes. There was also a bicycle, weights and other random guy stuff crammed in. Everything was covered in dust.

"I was actually expecting when we got John's diagnosis. Didn't take. Stress."

Maddie nodded sympathetically before asking, "What if he doesn't.. come back out in your lifetime?"

Priya answered confidently, "He will."

Maddie saw the far away look in her friend's eyes. She was confused by Priya's sense of certainty. She was more than confused, she was disturbed. But why? After all, she herself had signed up for the same fantasy. Their contrasting attitudes threw their shared faith in cryonics into sharp relief. For Maddie, she could carry her hope around with her like a locket, close to the heart, but compartmentalized. She was still a grieving widow, prone to sudden bursts of emotion. But Priya didn't appear to be grieving anything. Maddie wondered which approach was better. She couldn't help but feel sorry for Priya, sensing her attempt to preserve her old life was putting off the business of living itself.

But she didn't know what Priya knew. She didn't know about George.

Chapter 15

Mistakes were Made

George darted his eyes back and forth nervously at the ceiling. The diodes on either side of his temples were cold. It wasn't without hesitation that he agreed to this experimental treatment. But at this point, he was ready to try whatever the doctors wanted to stop the ever present throbbing in his skull. Witten and Kelley checked his vitals and adjusted accordingly. She had concluded that George's headaches were a secondary symptom to an underlying primary issue - but she had competing theories as to what that primary issue could be. One theory was related to his elevated blood pressure. She hypothesized that this might be because he had no blood in his veins.

Cryonicor had designed its own synthetic

blood replacement called PURP, named after its deep purple hue. The viscosity was thicker than natural human blood, but it had proved to be an adequate delivery system for oxygen and nutrients in their animal research. However, they had never used PURP in a human subject, except for one, but he didn't count. Witten felt terrible about the dozens of dogs she had reanimated using PURP. Who knows what they had suffered.

If the blood vessels were being stressed, due to the PURP maybe she could use a frequency to relax them and allow the nerve endings in his skull to decompress. She had read a study from Myanmar regarding this breakthrough technique which had some success in a limited test group. George felt like he was about to have wide awake lasik eye surgery at a shady storefront in Koreatown. They were using his original recovery room for this treatment. Owens and Priya were watching on the monitors from HQ.

After another night on the sofa bed, and Gwen giving her the cold shoulder, Witten was somewhat depleted that morning. But she had gathered herself and focused as best she could on the task at hand. Afterall, she had to try something. She took a deep breath. "Okay George, I'm going to count down from three, brace yourself. You may feel some slight discomfort. It should only last about ten seconds." George nodded. "Three, two, one." She pointed to Kelley like a conductor, and he ran two fingers up a touch screen console simultaneously to initiate the frequency.

Immediately George's eyes shot open, as blood shot as could be, he let out a howling scream that betrayed an unspeakable agony. His hands were restrained. but his entire body was seizing.

"What the fuck happened?!" shouted Owens in HQ.

"Abort!! Abort Kelley!!" ordered Witten. The whirring of the machine wound itself down as Witten removed George's restraints and caressed his face. "George, are you okay?" He jerked his head from her touch and brought his hands to his temples. He was unable to respond, tears streamed down his face.

In HQ, Priya's palms were at her cheeks and her mouth was agape with shock and worry. *What happened?!*

"I'm not sure what went wrong doc, everything was set just like you wanted," said Kelley as he removed the diodes from George's head revealing bright red imprints where they had been. "Jesus."

"Give him a sedative right now, and let me see," said the doctor as she went over to the console herself. She put her hand to her mouth in disbelief. "You have the frequency set wrong, this says 2.0, it's supposed to be .02. Could have given him a stroke!"

"You told me to set it at 2.0," refuted Kelley sternly, hurt by Witten's outright accusation of carelessness on his part.

"The hell I did," she pointed up to the camera, "run back the video!"

Priya quickly pulled up the playback file on another screen and scrubbed backwards. They did not have to bicker over who said what when they had instant replay. As she watched, wearing headphones, the answer was clear as day. Priya shot a quick look to Owens then leaned into the microphone, "you gave him the input 2.0."

Witten's shoulders fell, as the news echoed down from the loud speaker. She looked back and forth between George and Kelley. "I'm sorry... I don't know how I..." she had no words. Frustrated with herself, she kicked over the bedside tray of instruments and stormed out.

***

After making sure George was comfortably sleeping off a sedative in his quarters, Priya went looking for her mentor. Witten was on her speedbag. She was stripped down to her sports bra, her hands taped, really giving it her all. If she could punch a hole in time and go back to that moment when she gave the wrong direction to Kelley, she would. But she couldn't.

Priya knocked lightly, indicating that she came in peace. Witten didn't acknowledge her presence, she just kept dribbling the bag, crossing from right to left like a pro, sweat dripping down her face. Priya could see Witten was going through it and probably did not wish to be disturbed. But if she truly didn't want her there, she would have told her to go away. Her silence told the cryotech that she in fact did need a shoulder to lean on. So Priya went in, closed the door behind her and took a seat in the guest chair.

"I thought you would want to know, he's resting comfortably. No permanent damage." Witten didn't respond. Priya continued, "You're allowed to make a mistake, you're only human."

"I'm a doctor. It's not okay, can't be that careless…"

"That was bad. I know. But what are we gonna do? We have to learn what we can from a situation and move on." Witten stopped dribbling and cut her a glance, recognizing her own words. She started unwrapping her hands with her teeth and sat down in her desk chair. She was spent. Priya continued, "You're fatigued. Anyone can see that. What's going on with Gwen?"

"Exponentially higher frequency than prescribed…" ruminated Witten, shaking her head and deflecting Priya's direct questions. "Too risky to try it again, plus we've lost trust with him."

"So you think it's too late to fix it?"

"No… if I had an HBC, I would have a real shot —"

"I meant with your wife," said Priya. Once again she heard that familiar buzzing and spotted that damned fly, she waved it off.

Witten put her elbows on her desk and tried

to rub the worry from her brow. "I don't know." She inhaled a long breath and then leveled Priya's gaze in an unusual but desperate moment of personal disclosure. "She's at home, which is good, but she won't even talk to me. Our anniversary is a week away. She's so angry with me, I think she actually might let us expire."

"You said she won't talk to you. Have you really sat her down and tried?" Priya knew Witten well by now, and felt it was unlikely she would go looking for an opportunity to talk about her feelings.

Witten cracked her sore neck. "She's told me she's not ready to talk about it yet and I don't want to push."

"You expire in a week doc. You don't have time to let the dust settle."

"What am I supposed to say?" asked the doctor, genuinely at a loss for words.

"Tell her you love her, tell her you want to spend nine more lives together, to re-up forty five more times and that you will do whatever it takes—"

***

"—to win your trust back. I can't imagine how betrayed you must feel, but you must know I didn't do any of this to hurt you," said Witten looking into her wife's big brown perfectly lashed eyes. She barely got it all out and thought she might cringe to death. But Priya was right. It was now or never.

They were seated on the sofa in the study. Witten had lit an aromatherapy candle looking for any advantage, no matter how small. Gwen took her wife's stiff and rehearsed words into consideration. She took another sip of hot lemon water, which she drank habitually.

"I just can't stop thinking about the hundreds of conversations we've had over the past twenty years about our day at work, and to know that you were doing this dance of omitting, minimizing, outright lying all that time…"

"I have no excuse. But I do have an explanation, you might not like it but it's the truth." Gwen wanted to forgive Witten and had already reasoned out why her wife had kept her in the dark, but emotionally she really struggled to get past her wife's capacity for deception. But she gave Witten a chance to explain, because she wanted to be convinced. Witten summoned her bravery to continue, "When I started in cryonics, working for Dr. Hester's lab reanimation research was legal. I went into this field because of the success we had in that lab. Then as soon as I got my own R&D facility—"

"— they reclassified all cryonics facilities inadvertently handicapping all reanimation research, I know. I was there, remember? By your side. Supporting you through that terrible time."

"I know. But you had a career of your own.

Your first book had just come out, remember? They wanted you on all the talk shows, then you left to go to a war zone for months."

"You told me to go, if that was where I was needed."

"And while you were gone, I made the decision to go where I felt I was needed. But where that was... you couldn't follow. If I had been... even now if I am found out... What's gonna happen to you, if they find out you know? It's plausible deniability."

"Bullshit. That's a copout. Let me decide if I want to stay and take that risk or walk away. You do not lie to me for twenty years."

Witten dropped her head. "I didn't want to lose you." She lifted her head back up, "I still don't."

"Look, do you think I want to blow up my life? Of course I don't. But it's a trust thing. If I can't trust you... I know our re-up is around the corner, but—"

"What if we think of our renewal as a fresh start? We both want this to work... "

"Honestly, it's difficult for me to visualize that at this point. I am just trying to get through my day, as you are I am sure."

"But—"

"Stop Sam. I need time to process it all. I'm tired, I'm going to bed. Tell George hello for me."

Gwen went to their room, her room, whatever. Witten keeled over, sick to her stomach. But then, she sat up and steeled herself. She went to her desk rooted out her trusty regenadrips and applied it to both eyes. After a few blinks for good measure, she grabbed the tape from her drawer and began wrapping her hands...

***

Owens was on his second Credo Sour, a lactic acid-based whey cordial that's shaken with vodka, aquavit and an aperitif wine. He was seated at his favorite table on the upper terrace of the Iconastarey. Christian Martinez was twenty minutes late. Owen stewed over it, but he knew he couldn't really lecture a billionaire about not valuing the time of others.

Finally, the debonnaire businessman cruised into the restaurant and spotted his acquaintance from the bar. He was dressed in all white. Monochromatic outfits were very on-trend. In all honesty, it was a beautiful combination with his olive complexion.

"Sorry man, I got hung up with this girl, you would not BELIEVE," said Christian as he raised his eyebrows up and down in that way that invoked an unspoken international gentleman's agreement allowing for tardiness where a beautiful woman was involved. "You started without me I see, can't blame you. Let me catch up - order me whatever you're drinking."

Owens bristled under the inconsideration, as

he did not subscribe to those same guy-codes of conduct. Nevertheless, he remained composed and professional. He wasn't there for a casual chit chat, this was a progress report with a big price tag. Owens ran his hands across the table lighting up the menu and ordered Christian a drink.

"Did you hire the film crew yet?" Martinez liked to be late and he liked to start out pushing. He found it put him in control of a negotiation off top.

"I haven't hired them yet," said Owens, flattening his shirt and tie with the palm of his hand.

"He's not ready yet?" said Martinez understandingly. "What's the problem, I know his situation is not the.. But I mean, come on... would he rather be dead or something?"

"Look," said Owens, as he pulled his reader out of his satchel and showed footage of George tearing his room apart like a maniac. Martinez covered his open mouth with his hand. Owens continued in hushed tones, "He still hasn't regained his memory and I don't think he will. Also he has no independence because he still can't breathe outside - that's taking longer than we wanted to get sorted out, if it ever gets sorted out...we may have better luck with another subject."

"No way. I'm not giving up on this guy, he's perfect. He looks like a quarterback had a baby with a … another quarterback.. You know what I mean. We legit won the lotto with him. He died young, tragic, through no fault of his own… cryonics gave him back something owed to him. You can't write it any better than that. I hired you because of your skill in bringing controversial biotech products to market, right? And with HHS up your butt, we have to stay ten steps ahead. You have to get him camera ready, like now. No excuses. Do whatever you have to." Martinez knocked back his Credo Sour.

Owens decided not to tell Martinez about the bug he found that he was sure belonged to Getty, it was a truly amazing piece of technology, one that perhaps he could use to his own advantage inside Cryonicor. "I'm having some difficulties with Dr. Witten."

"No shit. Is she a ball buster or what?" said the billionaire playboy, flashing his movie star smile and darting his eyes around the room.

"Frankly, I think her involvement might be counterproductive at this point. We'll have better luck if we cut her loose altogether."

"What's happened?"

"She doesn't follow directions, she's not collaborative, she's unstable, she yelled at George about him feeling sorry for himself. And she wants to try these highly experimental, highly expensive treatments. She's exhausted and making careless mistakes, she almost gave him a stroke yesterday because she mixed up a decimal point. I don't know how she even got this far..."

The waiter dropped off Owens' third and Martinez's second cocktails respectively. They waited until he was out of earshot before they resumed their conversation.

Martinez bit his lower lip a moment, trying to think before he spoke. "Sam's not perfect, but she's not going anywhere. Because first and foremost, you cannot do what she does in the reanimation chamber, can you?"

"Not yet..."

"So you need her," he said, opening his hands and shrugging his shoulders. "Besides, she knows too much. Now if you were actually good at your job, you would figure out how to bring the best out of your people. Why is she exhausted? What is distracting her?" Martinez was leaning in, tapping his index finger to his temple. Then he finished his drink and got up to leave, "Look I'm gonna head out, I have a chopper waiting to take me to an oil rig my father just bought.... You're there to support Dr. Witten, don't forget that."

That had not gone as Owen's had hoped. He was an overachiever among overachievers, and was a grade grubbing teacher pleaser when it came down to it. He hated having his competency questioned. If he was actually good at his job...??? *How dare you!* Now he had two problems to solve, get Dr. Witten back online, and work with her to get patient zero back online.

Priya was waiting for a delivery, but it didn't look like it was arriving today, so she decided to go home. She could see from the monitors that George had roused from his sedation. On her way out she stopped by his quarters to check on him.

She entered on his say-so. At the sight of her, he stood up straight. She approached him like a friend.

"I'm so sorry George. The doctor made a mistake, it shouldn't have happened." She could see he was still red where the diodes had been. She went to touch the side of his face, and he didn't pull away. "Does it hurt?"

"A little tender." They sat down in his lounge area on the sofa. His hair was a mess and he had a desperate look in his eyes. He looked up at the cameras resentfully. He had some hope that they would be able to cure his headaches and restore his respiratory system, so he could have some semblance of a normal life. But after this morning, he had tremendous doubts about his chance at a 'normal' life. He was grateful for the sedative, because being awake was demoralizing. He went on, "I just wish I could understand why I did this to myself, like what *was* I thinking? *Did* I do this to myself? I keep thinking someone else must have signed me up for this, like without me knowing about it..."

Priya felt a hot flash when he said this. God,

she would never want John to feel betrayed like George did. But that didn't happen to George. "Hold on," she removed her glass reader from her backpack and accessed the Cryonicor human storage database, she pulled up George's original signed contract and showed it to him, "Is this your signature?"

George took it from her, fascinated, a clue from those missing sixteen months of his life! He saw the date, August 6th 2021 and there was in fact his messy stupid signature. He nodded his head and handed it back to her. He got another idea, "What about social media?"

"Oh all social media was outlawed about eight years ago now because of these really violent worldwide riots that kept happening. Why do you want to see that?"

"Well I was a heavy poster, I thought maybe there could be some clues there as to where my head was at…but guess it's all gone."

She hesitated for a moment, wondering if it was a good idea to open Pandora's app. She cautiously pulled out her cell. "About a hundred years ago the social media corps removed the profiles for all its users who were… dead….and consolidated them into one pay per view platform."

"Wow."

"I know such sleaze… And whenever a user died after that, their profiles immediately disappeared across all social media platforms and reappeared a moment later on the consolidated ppv," she pointed to an open app, it was the familiar Facebook F, but in black instead of blue. "This is Facebook Legacy."

He took the phone from her. It was the first time he held one since he'd come back, weirdly it made him feel human again. She went on, "try it, search your name." He typed in his name and quickly found his master profile.

"Oh shit. That's me."

She nodded and got up to leave, slipping her backpack on. "You pay for everything you click and it adds up, but knock yourself out, it's on me. I'll pick it up from you tomorrow morning. I hope you find some clarity."

He looked up at her sincerely, "thank you Priya." And just like that, he would finally be able to see how his story had ended, and those of all he loved.

Chapter 16

FOMO

It was 3 AM and George's face was illuminated by the comforting blue glow of a cell phone. But he didn't look comforted, he looked... devastated. He had started with his own feed of course, then moved to Alison's feed, then to his Mom's. Images of aging faces, new borns, weddings, cancer treatments, vacations, Christmases, and more than a few gone-too-soon posts dedicated to his truly flitted across the alumina silicate composite screen. What struck him the most was what happened after he'd ceased updating his accounts. Life went on without him. It made him feel... insignificant. For the most part people looked happy. Happy without him? But were they really happy? Of course not... Social media doesn't represent the truth of a person's experience, he knew that, still he couldn't balance his feelings of gratitude with those of resentment. Deep down on Alison's timeline he found a video she had posted when she was gray haired and less confident than he remembered her. Even at that age she still posted regularly, though mainly about her kids as they were getting married and having children of their own. So the subject of this video caught him off guard.

She was seated at the kitchen table in her home, with a tablet in front of her, speaking directly to the camera. She said, "My George would have turned sixty years old today if he had lived. So in honor of George I wanted to read you all his horoscope, because he would have hated this, but I love it." George watched agasp, smiling through a bittersweet cascade of emotion. "Darling Libra, Another trip around the sun. We're coming out of back to back eclipses and Neptune was in retrograde and you were pushed to your breaking point. As reality begins to resume some semblance of normalcy—you have the perspective to look at your circumstances from a birds' eye view. What do you need to release to ensure that you're truly living a truly aligned life? On September 23, the Full Moon in Aquarius will illuminate everything with its powerful nocturnal radiance. Under this sky, you'll be inspired to take a good, hard look at your current realities. What's working? What isn't? Take the best and leave the rest." She put the reader down and looked into the camera again, speaking through time with a cool elegant wisdom, "Happy birthday my love."

He laid his whole body down supine on the floor, with the phone face down on his chest. Not only had she stayed with him until the end, she never stopped loving him. And there was nothing he could do to get back to her. He couldn't profess his love or buy her flowers, or show up to her job. The finality of it all killed him. He tried to catch his breath and stared out of the big windows up at the black sky, the room seemed to spin him around counterclockwise. He went back to what she had taught him. *Breathe. In. Out. In. Out. Just be here.*

After his heartbeat had returned to normal, he found himself alone again, in the middle of the night, and no closer to sleep. He had often used social media as a way to escape from himself... typical. And when he got too uncomfortable, he fell into his old patterns predictably. He played with the app hunting for something to take his mind off himself for a moment, just to take a breather, and he discovered the search history function.

Priya's search history seemed to be dominated by a single user. Who was John Cayhill? George had seen her wearing a labcoat that said CR Cayhill, so it was likely a relation of hers. He looked at the man's profile. He was white, she was Bengali American, so probably not a blood relation. As soon as he opened the guy's photo album, he saw their wedding pictures. She looked so beautiful then. She was married? No, this guy wouldn't have a page on the platform if he was alive. She was a widow. She was single. He watched a candid video John had posted, of a time when they were on a plane on their way to some vacation. She was ugly laughing, and when she saw John filming her she suddenly stopped and tried to shield her face from him, shouting at him to quit. George smiled at this and replayed it...a few times.

***

Owens showed up late to work the next morning. He knocked on Dr. Witten's office door with an extra cup of $45 single serve coffee that justified its high price tag because it was brewed using reverse atmospheric infusion.

"They gave me an extra cup of RAI, do you want it?"

Witten signed with annoyance and looked up from her docked reader, "No thanks, I don't drink coffee."

"Oh." The single syllable word contained all the surprise and mild humiliation you could imagine. "Tea drinker?"

Witten took another belabored sigh over the fact that Owens was still trying to ingratiate himself to her. Pathetic. She stood up and slipped her lab coat over her muscled arms. "I drink date coffee, made from dates. They've been using it in Jordan for a thousand years, it's part of standard prenatal care there. It wakes the body up with potassium. Caffeine use is linked to dementia, if you knew anything about life extension you wouldn't touch the stuff. Excuse me." She pushed past him on her way to HQ. From the hall, she paused and turned back to him, angling her head. "I'm sorry, did you need anything else?"

"No, um, how are you? Is there anything you want to talk about?"

"Like what?"

"Just like... anything..?"

"Yea, I want a hyperbaric chamber for George. Can we talk about that?"

"I'm still thinking about it."

"Pshhhh...," she exhaled as she rolled her eyes and defiantly walked away.

Back in his own office, Owen's knee bounced wildly as he drained his second cup of RAI. How could he get Witten to open up to him, when she hated his guts? He was only trying to help her. Of course, he understood that this was only after he had tried to have her removed, but still she didn't know that. It seemed unfair. He started looking up the hyperbaric chambers against his better judgment, until he got a better idea.

He opened the FlyGuy app on his reader, which he had managed to identify, install and pair thanks to the bug's tiny serial number. He had already downloaded the files it had on it, which was how he got a front row seat to Witten's cemetery-side tantrum with George. But he held out hope that the more recent footage might give him the insight he needed to help his tight lipped subordinate. And she was his subordinate no matter what Martinez thought.

Being in such close proximity to the bug, the download completed easily for him. He began to scrub backwards through the footage and after about an hour and a half of diligent and systematic scrubbing - paydirt. Elijah Owens could systemize a task and stay focused on it until it was completed. This was one of his super powers. It was like his body produced its own adderall. He turned up his earpods to listen to the conversation between Priya and Witten.

He heard Witten say clearly, "I don't know... She's at home which is good, but she won't even talk to me. Our anniversary is a couple weeks away. She's so angry with me, I think she actually might let us expire."

Owen's steel gray eyes lit up. He replayed this part again. Even he felt a little guilty for prying into something so personal. If anyone took that type of liberty with him... it would certainly piss him off. Still, now that he had the information, he asked himself how he could leverage it to get Dr. Witten to perform better? He was no love doctor, and he had an expiration and two divorces to prove it. For him an expiration was a godsend, a blessed light at the end of a dark tunnel. That was clearly not the case here. He knew

Witten's wife, knew of her, had seen her talking to George through the monitors. He leaned into his reader and pecked out with two fingers his search words: DR. GWEN KIM-WITTEN.

***

Witten was in the supply freezer examining a curious vial of chemicals when Jack stuck his head in. She waved him in and said, "We're missing some liquid nitrogen. Kelley said he did his inventory three times and he's still coming up short. I don't see it either."

"That's weird. But it's not like the Martinez foundation can't afford all they want. Whatcha got there?" he pointed to the vial in her hand.

"Owen's rejuvenation cocktail. He gave this to George without even running it by me.'"

"Can he do that?" said Jack, taken aback.

"I don't even know. But you know what really pisses me off?"

"What?"

"Kid looks great, this shit works."

"How are things going with Gwen? Are you talking again yet?"

Witten bristled at the personal question, it seemed everyone wanted to know about her marital problems. "No, and honestly, it's not looking so good. I think she's really going to let us expire" said Witten matter-of-factly, as if she was reporting the weather.

Jack was stunned, as long as he had known Samantha Witten, she had been with Gwen the mighty. It was such a defining part of her persona to him for so long. All of his other friends were single or crossing between single/expired/married/engaged and back, but not the Wittens. They were goals. And he was always a bit starstruck when Gwen was around, not only was she gorgeous, she was also famous.

Witten was touched by Jack's nonplussed reaction, she put her hand on his shoulder, "you'll be alright." He smiled at her little joke. "By the way, nice job with the kid the other day."

"Yeah? Dr. Owens didn't seem impressed when I debriefed him, in fact he—"

"Don't worry about that jerk, I'll protect you." Jack sure hoped so. Witten continued, "So what's your take on George's—" suddenly, a truck driver got their attention on the other side of the supplies bay.

"Excuse me! I gotta delivery. Can somebody sign for it? We're backing the truck up..

Jack and Witten looked at each other surprised. They weren't expecting any deliveries for weeks. As they headed over to attend to it, Witten covertly pocketed the vial.

***

Upstairs in George's penthouse, he gladly handed the cell back to Priya. "I was on it all night until it died," he confessed sheepishly. "My girlfriend told me I was addicted to Tik Tok.. please take it away from me or I will never stop looking at it. She was right, I have a problem."

With a slight smile she tucked the dead cell phone into her lab coat, and noticed he didn't eat his breakfast that morning either. He wasn't looking so hot. With her eyebrow raised, she asked him, "What did you find out?"

He sat down on his bed prepared to spill his guts, she looked for a more appropriate place to sit, and pulled over the desk chair. He began, "my social media got pretty quiet about a month or so after ... the last thing I remember, which was going to a Laker Game with Mac. I figure that was when I must have... you know.. Found out about the... heart thing." He couldn't even bring himself to say it.

"Then what?"

"I saw my Mom post one of those cryptic thank you for all your thoughts and prayers for our family type posts, but didn't say what she was actually talking about."

"Probably you."

"I assume so." He was clearly a little emotionally numb after last night. He continued, "Then I saw some pictures of myself with some of my really old childhood friends, guys I hadn't seen in a million years you know.. We were um... camping out in New Mexico looking for Finn's Treasure, we were obsessed when I was younger. Bucket list type stuff I guess...?" His eyes were wide as if he wanted her to somehow confirm the suspicion. She shrugged a noncommittal confirmation. "And I had wondered if my girlfriend, Alison, had stayed with me or if she might have bailed, but she was there til the end, so that … I don't know... made me feel a little better I guess."

"That's so nice, she must have loved you a lot."

"She did." He was surprised how easy it was for him to open up about Alison with Priya. "And there toward the end of...the feed, Alison was even posting stuff, like about me, from her account, like how we, us, you know were planning to get married and stuff."

"Wow. That's big."

"I don't think I thought I was really going to die, if I was going around proposing to people."

"I bet it caught you off guard. It's crazy, one day you're there, the next day you're not."

George's eyes fell to the floor and he nodded with understanding. "So I spent the rest of the night cyber stalking everybody I knew." He laughed a little, trying to deflect his own emotions. "It was pretty bleak watching them all get older, get married, have kids. It was so hard to see all that, I was worried I might actually die again, from FOMO."

"Oh my god," she said, concerned. "Wait, what is that?"

"FOMO… you know, fear of missing out." She tilted her head, then gave him a knowing nod. But in truth, she had no idea what he was talking about. George continued, "It was also strange looking at it with foreknowledge, you see them and you know that they are all marching happily toward their own well documented deaths." Priya didn't encourage his morbid tangent, and he digressed thankfully. "And some of the political views of my friends took a sharp turn in their old age... that was nuts. Then one after another their timelines stopped. Just cut off. Mom lived to be 92, Alison lived to be 109, can you believe that? She looked just like pictures she showed me of her great grandmother." He shook his head in quiet disbelief.

"Are you glad you got to see that?"

"Yeah."

"Right?" Priya leaned in smiling and touched his knee, but then removed her hand quickly. She continued, "Look I know that you feel like you would never sign up for this type of thing but, the truth is this was probably your backup plan. Like you didn't think you were gonna die, you probably thought... you were in amazing shape," he blushed, "and you would get a transplant, marry your sweetheart, and live out your days like everyone else. This was just something you had in your back pocket, something you probably didn't even take all that seriously, right?"

"Right," he said, wanting to be convinced. And in light of the bigger picture he scrolled through all night long - life, death, age, kids, love - his rationalists agenda didn't feel all that significant.

She nodded her head, feeling like they had made a real breakthrough. "I gotta get back." Once she stood up, she noticed his googles and game dice on the desk. "I'll remind Kelley to stop by today to set that up for you. I'm gonna take this old food and send you something fresh, you hungry?"

He looked at the food on the trays she was gathering, he hadn't thought about food in days, he said nonchalantly, "I could eat." She nodded and took off. "Hey one more thing. I saw your search history." Priya's slight smile fell away. "Next time you visit me, tell me about this John character, will ya?"

***

The delivery truck rolled up the back door revealing a huge wooden crate. Witten said, "What in the world? - The HBC?! He got it?" She looked to Jack for confirmation, but he clearly knew nothing about it.

They watched a forklift pull out a two-ton steaming crate, as it spun around they saw it stamped: CRYONICOR N. DAKOTA.

"What the hell?" asked Jack.

A dreaded realization dawned on Witten. "Oh no."

"What?"

Jack could see it was a cryostat from their North Dakota facility, but only Witten understood the meaning of it's arrival. She flagged down the truck driver while Jack collapsed the new age crate, revealing the frosted over tube, spewing a steady trail of evaporating liquid nitrogen.

"Can I see that?" Witten asked the driver gruffly, gesturing to his reader. She scanned the QRP code with her cell and reviewed the transfer request form, signed by: CR. P. Cayhill.

Jack located the nameplate and wiped the frost away, there were four names, one was Cptn. John Cayhill 2153.

"Shit," said Witten.

"What are we gonna do?"

Chapter 17

Silence and Darkness Forever

Kelley was delighted to find George on the floor of his quarters. Patient zero sat cross legged, grinning like a preschooler, wearing his googles, immersed in a game he had already figured out.

"G-man! Whatcha playing?" said Kelley as he took a seat in one of George's seafoam green armchairs.

George lifted up his eyewear surprised to find the blonde bomber making himself comfortable. "Oh hey. Uh.. It's called Baby Zombies." He didn't know Kelley that well, his most memorable interactions was when he captured him on the bus and when he tranq'd him in the foxhole. Naturally he wasn't exactly relaxed around the guy.

"One or two?" Kelley for his part, acted like they were casual pleasant acquaintances, as if there had been no kidnapping of any sort.

"One?"

"Two was trash, I agree. Glad to see you got the vidja games a-werk-in. Do you have an extra pair for me? We could play together."

"No, she just brought me the one. Sorry."

"S'alright, I think I have a pair in my desk some place. I'll be right back."

A few minutes later, the two sat side by side on the floor cross legged wearing their googles, George occasionally lifted his up to peak at Kelley's native form, his hand and body motions were fluid and simple, unlike George's primitive clumsy movements.

"Are you going to get in trouble for playing games?"

"Possibly?"

"Okay," said George, grateful to have a playmate to pass the time with.

"How you like the games?"

"It feels good thinking about nothing, especially when you have a headache all day. Whoa! Did you see that?"

Kelley made a dipping motion with his head. "Look alive G-Man c'mon. If you like this two bit two player stuff you're gonna lose your mind when you see our online multiplayer games."

"I never really got into those, I don't like how you can't pause the game."

"What are you talking about G.I. George? You can totally pause online multiplayer."

George shook his head and kept flailing his hands around crudely, while Kelley looked like he was guest conducting for Dudamel. He insisted, "No you can't. How are you going to pause while other players keep playing in real time?"

"I'm not a video game designer, and I don't know how they did it where you come from, but not being able to pause the game is savagery."

George took off his googles too, disgusted. "You're kidding me! That's so unfair, you know how good I could have been if I could've paused the game?"

"I'm sure you would have been one of the greats, now are we playing or what?" George snapped out of his daze and reset his googles. "You think video games are unfair... wait til you see what modern medicine can do." George's dancing hand suddenly stopped and his arms fell limp to his side.

"Can I ask you something?" asked George.

"Yes you can."

"That girl, Priya, is she... what's her deal?"

"No comment."

"Oh you like her?"

"No, we're just friends. If you wanna know about her, ask her yourself." Kelley starts coughing and takes a hit off his own inhaler, then hops back into the gameplay.

For his part, George was a little stung by Kelley's stonewalling. So far he hadn't been rewarded for his vulnerability. He had to remind himself where he was, this wasn't a resort, this was basically a medical prison and he had a life sentence it seemed. His mind turned back to his desire, no matter how unrealistic, to escape. Kelley's haley reminded him of when he sampled Priya's on the bench outside. It had been very effective relieving his symptoms. George continued playing the game and casually floated the question, "do you think I could get a few of those inhaler things."

Kelley, ever trusting and aloof, shrugged and said, "I can put in a requisition for them with Dr. Witten for you." Then he dipped his head and smiled, "Nice try... Hey..Can I ask *you* a question?"

"Yes you can." George was sure Kelley wouldn't ask him the same 'how you feeling' crap as everyone else.

He slid his googles down, "Why are you so shredded?"

George guffawed wildly, and pushed his googles up on top of his head again. "Awe thanks man, That's nice of you to say. But, you're the supermodel."

"I mean, I'm pretty like an underweight pouty no name fashion model, but you - you're butch. What's the deal, are you a marine? You're tall as shit, you play basketball?"

"I love watching basketball, but I am terrible at playing it. I rowed crew in college, you gotta have long legs and arms, it's where uncoordinated guys like me get to pretend to be athletes."

"But you're 31, it's been years since you were in college."

"I keep it up, I run and I lift. I like to break a sweat every day," said George.

"Jesus, what do you bench?"

"Honestly it's mostly diet, I try to eat healthy, keto mostly--"

"Keto? What's that?"

"Just a fad diet I guess, maybe it didn't last but I'll teach you, I swear by it. It's all protein like meat and veggies and cheese and no carbs."

"You call that healthy? That's hilarious."

"Why?"

"Meat causes cancer and all types of problems. No wonder your generation only lived to be like 99."

"... is that not good?"

"Uh no... dream bigger," said Kelley giggling and shaking his head. Then he got serious, "Wait, is that why you're not eating the food here? Because there's no animal protein in it?"

"What are you talking about? There's been chicken and bacon and cheese steak already."

"Those are all synthetic meat alternatives, too processed for me, I'm sorry they are feeding you that. They probably think that's what you want."

"That stuff's not real meat?"

"Nope. But you better start eating something or your muscle will start eating itself."

George did NOT like the sound of that, but he knew it was true. He sighed and reset his googles on the bridge of his nose. "I had no idea. The whole world's gone vegan?"

Kelley followed suit, returning to their game. "Oh I wouldn't say that, you know every country is different but in North America, animal protein is available, it's just an expensive special occasion kind of thing."

"What else is different about the future?"

"It's the present my dude, and I don't know, history wasn't my best subject."

"What about money? Do you still use money or is it like Star Trek?"

"Of course we still use money! But our population has outpaced the workforce demand, because AI can do all kinds of jobs."

"So a lot of people are out of work?"

"Right."

"So are there like homeless colonies all over the place or what?"

"Oh no, I mean it's not their fault. We have universal income, so they're okay... more or less."

"Universal income?"

"Yeah you know.. or maybe you don't know... the government gives everyone like a baseline amount of money a month so they can have their bare essentials met. But if you want something nicer for yourself and you like to learn and what not then you might choose to go to work like me. "

"Sweet. What about me? Do I qualify for that, because I'm not sure what skills I could possibly have to offer, but I would need money too."

"Hadn't really thought about that. Hmmm... I don't think you can get the UI, because, technically you're dead. As far as they know."

George huffed and shook his head slightly, he felt out of control and lost. When he felt like that, one thing always made him feel better. "Is there a weight bench around here somewhere?"

"You're making the rest of us look bad, so why don't you knock it off?"

George was flattered, but it was a superficial pleasure. Deep down he felt a weight pressing heavier and heavier down on him.

***

Meanwhile, Jack and Priya were having an emotional debate in his office about the contents of the delivery.

"It's not that simple Priya!"

"What's not that simple? He's been a stage one for two years already. Why should I wait one second longer than I have to?"

"We have a queue for a reason, you know that."

"Why am I not hearing this from Dr. Witten?" asked Priya. And she was right to question Jack's authority to lecture her on this matter. He wasn't her superior. He wasn't even a 'certified' cryonicist like her.

Jack said, "Because she's too pissed off to even look at you. You abused your clearance. Besides I think this kind of drastic action speaks to some instability on your part. As a mental health professional and your friend, it concerns me."

Priya looked down, walking a line between shame and indignancy.

She clapped back, "It's not such a problem when I'm using my story to close clients for you." Jack was officially in charge of signing up people for preservations. It was an important revenue stream for them. But he had found if he let Priya give the tours, she had a higher success rate because of the whole cryo-widow angle.

As much as that seething comment hit home, Jack opted to let silence fill the room for a moment. *Calm down.* He knew from his training that common ground was the best place to start from.

"Don't you want the fairy tale?" he asked. This did knock her off her game for a moment, and she didn't quite know how to respond. He continued, "Don't you think you should let Dr. Witten get the bugs out of this process? Imagine the difference in quality of life for someone like George versus someone who comes out in fifty years."

"Fifty years? What are you talking about?"

"Or twenty-five... or ten."

"But in ten years... "

Jack tried to reassure her, "You will probably look exactly the same. And if pregnancy is what you are worried about, let's freeze your eggs right now. There are amazing options for surrogacy available in Baja and Cuba."

"I can't wait ten more years Jack."

"Is this for John or is this for you?"

She said nothing. What could she say...

Jack wanted to redirect their dialogue to a path forward. "Look, I have it from Owens directly that he's planning to recommend the foundation give us the kicker as a five year private research grant. So we don't have to make any of our findings public until we have more of this ironed out. By then, maybe we'll be ready."

Priya struggled to find a logical way out of her own spiraling emotions, but she was only human. "Next of kin can initiate a thaw on a stage 1 whenever they want. That's in the contract!"

Jack fired back, "What if George dies?"

Suddenly, instead of thinking about her reunion with John, all she had thought about for years, she imagined the reality of losing George. She was surprised by her own feelings.

Jack continued, "We have no idea what he's in for long-term. What if we thaw John and it doesn't work? Once you pull him out, that's it! You've burned enough bodies to know that. We get one chance. Be smart."

She got up to leave, and with her back turned to him he said, "Priya, can I give you some advice?"

"No," she said without looking back and left his office.

Jack sat reeling for a moment, then he activated a call. Witten's face popped up as half a holo. They spoke in hushed tones.

Witten asked, "Did she buy it?"

"If she finds out, this is on you." CLICK.

When Jack abruptly ended their call in such an insubordinate manner, Witten was a little stung, but not surprised. And after all these years she knew Jack. She knew how far she could push him. He would buck, but ultimately he would accept her decision and her rationale. After all, his pathetic credentials didn't leave him many desirable options outside the walls of Cryonicor. He was stranded on the iceberg, just like young Kelley Baker.

An alarm went off on her watch. Without hesitation, she stood up, removed her white coat, dropped to the ground and began doing push ups like a private on her first day of boot camp. As the sweat began to drop from her nose, she found herself battling back feelings of guilt. She wasn't a bad person, she thought. But she believed she truly needed Priya to get to safety. No one else seemed to understand the seriousness of the situation. This was life or death. It was true, she was trying to save herself, but in doing so she would save us all.

2097

After her mom's death Samantha Witten had become very withdrawn at Miss Arlene's. She went from a playful and curious child to a hermit, locking herself away in her room to play with the few toys she had been allowed to bring from her old apartment. At school she started eating outside by herself. In class she stopped raising her hand. It was like she was a different child altogether. Who could blame her? She also started suffering from night terrors. She used to be able to run to her mom who always let her sleep with her on a bad dream night. But Miss Arlene did not like to see displays of emotion. It was weakness and it was only hurting yourself, she would often remind young Samantha. It was then that Samantha began to bury her emotions. It wasn't easy at first, but later it became second nature. During the nights she struggled with her nightmares, she would toss and turn for hours afraid of falling back to sleep. It was then, while she was awake, alone, in the dark - that she finally felt she had the privacy to grieve and allowed herself to sob into her pillow. She cried herself back to sleep many nights. She kept coming back to the same infuriating unfairness of her mother's death. Why? So many people survived that accident, why not her mother? She saw her friends' mother around and would wonder, why does your mom get to be alive and not my mine?

One night, she was especially upset. She had really worked herself up into a fit of grief. Unable to handle it alone, she broke down and went to her grandmother's room. She was in tears and unable to catch her little breath. Even stoic Arlene was touched by the child's suffering and invited her in.

"Why did God take my momma to heaven so early?" she blurted out.

Once it was spoken aloud, Miss Arlene decided it had to be dealt with firmly, if she minced her words it would only further confuse the child. She sat up in bed and invited Samantha to sit beside her.

"Stop that crying now. Try to relax. Now, who told you that God took your momma to heaven? That's plain old nonsense."

"My momma told me that we go to heaven after we die and so do the animals."

"Your momma knew better than that, she wasn't raised to believe that mess. It was your father that got her into that way of thinking. Made it impossible to be around them all in all. Can't talk to people like that. But you listen to me now, none of that stuff is true."

Her father had been a spiritual seeker who her mother had been briefly married to during a Christian phase, but he had long since abandoned their family, off to find his next true calling. But Witten's mother had always retained the faith that he had introduced her to and had passed it down in turn to her daughter.

"So God doesn't take you to heaven?"

"There is no such thing as God. We got to look

out for each other, you see. You might as well know that now. And even though it may seem sad that there is no such thing as heaven, you don't have to worry about hell either. Isn't that a relief?"

The child poked out her bottom lip suspiciously, and asked, "Are you sure?"

"Sure as I'm sitting here."

"If there is no God and you don't go to heaven, or hell, then what happens after you die?"

Miss Arlene said matter-of-factly, "Nothing baby. Just silence and darkness. Just silence and darkness forever."

The girl's eyes widened as the first sounds of thunder rumbled from the black sky above. She imagined, with her young tender mind, one certain day in the future when she herself would draw her last breath and close her eyes for the final time, never again to behold the world. She tried to imagine it truthfully. Her chest tightened and a dreaded despair gripped her mightily. Heavy drops of rain began to splat down on the roof above.

"But don't worry about that, it won't happen to you for a long time." said Miss Arlene, as if that was some kind of consolation. But it was too late. Miss Arlene had carelessly touched the child with a naked fear her years had not prepared her for. This moment would cast a long and ghastly shadow over her inner world.

***

Gwen walked hesitantly into the sterile lobby of Cryonicor. She was summoned under suspicious pretenses. She wasn't sure she should be there at all... considering. She approached the recently installed reception-bot.

"I am here for an appointment."

"Sure thing. Who are you here to see?" said the machine in a human voice.

"Dr. Elijah Owens."

Moments later Gwen found herself seated in front of the mysterious doctorpreneur who invited her to Cryonicor to "talk about her future." He looked cool, sure of himself, and rich. Gwen had an eye for the finer things and clocked his wristwatch, which easily cost half a million.

"You are probably wondering why I asked you to come in," he said.

"Yes."

"So, let me get right to it. I am the new Director of Innovation Management here, and I answer directly to the Martinez Foundation, I'm sure you know—"

"I know who they are." Everyone in research knew the infamous Martinez Foundation.

"Your wife has done an incredible job here. I

just want to build on that by creating a reputable team to support her work."

"Reputable," she repeated, cutting to the quick of it.

"I'm sure you know where I'm going with this. These people are fantastic. But we need major leaguers if we are going to change the legislation that's holding back our work."

"And where do I fit into all of this exactly?"

"George is the first, hopefully the first of many, and we need to start thinking ahead. We need to build an outpatient program. I may be a dumb ole MD, but even I know George and people like him are going to need someone they can talk to - we can't predict the psychological impacts of reanimation and reintegration. So I am looking to bring on a board certified psychologist, full time."

"Wow. It's great you recognize the mental health needs of your patients. And you want me to do it, because I already know about it?"

"That helps, I will admit. But I read up on you after you came in to consult on George, impressive by the way. I was watching with Witten on the monitors and I had my doubts, but you showed me something. And when I looked into your background after the fact - I gotta say I was blown away by your CV. Your publishing alone... you are exactly the caliber of medical professional we need."

"I see. And forgive me, but what makes you

think I would entertain such an offer? You know as well as I do, cryonics is career suicide."

"Look who you're telling. I didn't sign up for this until they brought out George. But now we have proof of concept. We will be the first of many places reanimating people over the next hundred years. Someone is going to get to do all that juicy research. And look, the work you did with combat vets and soldiers on the ground, you might be the only psychologist crazy enough to do it."

The thought of it was exciting. And he had her pegged as an adrenaline junky. When it came to her current work, she couldn't deny she felt stagnant. She deeply yearned to explore fringe realms of existence that could teach us more about what it means to be human. "What about Jack Wagner? You already have an in-house counselor, you don't think he's competent?"

"I don't, but it doesn't matter. He doesn't have the credentials. Look, we have a huge battle on our hands with - first the mainstream media, then John Q. Public, then mainstream medicine and finally a big showdown with the U.S. Department of Health and Human Services. I think I know how to pull this off and I can tell you we don't just need competence, we need prestige. We need the best technology on earth. And we need to make it sexy."

"Excuse me?"

"I'm not talking about you. I'm talking about

marketing reanimation. And this is where I need your help right now. Let me show you something." He spun his reader dock around and replayed the footage of George tearing apart his room like a wild animal.

Gwen scooted her chair closer and leaned in angling her head. "Oh my god." On the monitors she saw a soul unravelling, a person coming apart at their seams. She'd never seen anything like it. She shot him a look of intense concern.

He opened his hands at a loss. "I can't market this. And he's barely eating. This bitter stuff is bad for business, you get me?" Gwen noted Owen's lack of empathy. He continued, "he's the poster boy for cryonic reanimation and I'm stuck with him. I need to get him interview-ready, I know Rome wasn't built in a day, but I need to fast track this and for that I need the big guns and that's you. So what do you think?"

Dr. Kim sat back a moment considering this. While she found his motivations unsavory, they both wanted George to heal and somehow become a happy, well-adjusted member of their society. Sometimes unsavory motivations got things done. She began, "We don't have the case studies or data or research yet to create a treatment plan or make a diagnosis for someone in George's condition, however we could run a standard intervention plan without any data, but..."

"—but?" Hearing words like case studies and

data were music to his ears.

"—my educated guess would be that he's going to need a lot more than psychotherapy sessions to pull himself out of this nose dive. He feels disembodied somehow. Like a floating head in a void, if you will. He needs to be grounded in our time, in his new reality, he needs contact with the outside world, he needs to care about someone, he needs people to care about him in order for him to find his way back to his own humanity."

"That's a little tricky because he's sort of top secret and... he can't breathe outside."

"You have to find a way."

"Will you help us?"

"I would be lying if I said it wasn't tempting," said Gwen. She took a deep breath and started the calculations, what it would mean for her to leave her practice, what she would be risking, what she could possibly be gaining... She looked up and asked, "I assume you talked to Samantha about this?"

"No, I figured you would do that. You guys will have to decide as a couple, obviously, if you want to take the job, but I decide who I make the offer to," he said.

"Well full disclosure, we're not exactly on the best of terms right now. And I don't know if it's going to get better. As much as this opportunity is... crazy tempting - working and living with your ex seems like a bit much even for me."

"I'm sorry to hear that you're having marital problems. Do you think you could work together, despite your personal issues, and keep it professional, respectable and productive?"

"Yes." She wasn't sure why she lied. Maybe she wanted the job more than she realized.

"Good. But I agree, you can't live and work with your ex - Something's gotta give there. But I want you on my staff, and I'll double whatever you're making at your current practice. Take a week. Think about it."

***

After Kelley's visit George was feeling restless. He took advantage of his new come and go privileges to take daily walks inside the main Cryonicor building. Today he wasn't just walking though, he was surveying the security. When no one was looking he would check each window to see if it opened and where it opened to. He still wore the nasal cannula around his neck enabling him to breathe pure oxygen, and was unsure how he could survive outside. But he reasoned if an opportunity for survival outside presented itself, a worked out escape route would come in handy.

He left conspicuous palm marks on the window he'd just tried and failed to push up. As he tried to conceal the marks by wiping them with his hoodie, he heard the sound of a woman crying from the otherside of the door across the hall. No one else was around, he looked both ways then crossed the hall towards the sound. He opened the door and saw Priya. She was in distress, sitting on the floor of this small janitor's closet next to a dirty mop-bot. George entered quickly and closed the door behind him. He sat down at her side concerned. "Hey, what's wrong? Are you okay?"

"No," she bawled, holding out her hands helplessly.

"What can I do? You want me to get someone?" he asked sweetly, forgetting his own troubles for a moment.

Priya wiped at her wet face and said, "I'm okay."

George's facial hair was starting to grow again, but it was just a little gruff stubble at the moment. It suited him. "What happened?"

"Nothing, it's just... I'm so tired of it all."

George couldn't be sure what she was referring to, though he was surprised by his own intense curiosity. He just smiled and rubbed her arm gently.

"Did your boyfriend do something wrong?"

Usually when someone asked her about her relationship status, she told them she was married. But this time, without even thinking about it, she said, "I don't have a boyfriend." She couldn't believe those words had come out of her mouth.

"You want to talk about it?"

"You should really be in bed, I'm supposed to

be taking care of you."

"I don't need to be in bed. But if you don't feel comfortable talking to me—"

She did feel comfortable talking to him. She was emotional and she was lonely, staring down the barrel of loneliness without end. George had a thing about women crying. He could not handle it. Seeing the vulnerability and emotion on her face made him want to comfort her, he wanted more than just to comfort her.

He couldn't pretend that these feelings didn't exist anymore. This was a problem because he was still in love with Alison. Even though he had seen her move on, marry someone else, get old and die on Facebook Legacy, his heart wasn't caught up with the facts. He thought about her all the time. He felt her absence. As far back as he could remember they were still together, hot and heavy even, she was the one. So he couldn't help feeling a little like a bastard when he caught himself thinking about Priya. But it was also a good sign that he could feel anything at all for anyone. He wanted a way back to the comfort of other people. Maybe these feelings were good, maybe they were what he needed, and maybe he was just rationalizing his physical desire.

He made a choice, leaned in and kissed her. She drew back from him for a moment, surprised. He didn't apologize, he just looked into her eyes, and then she let go and they kissed again, passionately. It had been ten years since anyone had kissed her. It was almost like the first time.

When they parted, she was racked with guilt almost immediately. She felt like she had betrayed John who she still viewed as her husband and she had stained her own professionalism. Her brows furled with grave concern. Whatever George might have felt during that kiss, now he could see it troubled her. They stood up awkwardly.

"Oh no," said George, suddenly startled.

"What's wrong?" She examined him carefully and saw that he had soiled himself.

"I'm sorry," he whispered, obviously mortified.

Priya said calmly, "No. Uh... it's okay—"

"No it's not. It keeps happening." *Kill myself.*

"It does?" Suddenly her own crisis was far from her mind, and part of her was grateful for the reprieve.

***

The team gathered around George's bed in his quarters. The tension between Priya, Jack and Witten had been set on the backburner for the moment. Now, George was the priority. But he was in emotional agony over the well meaning crowd gathered to witness his very public and humiliating condition.

Witten cleared her throat and began delicately,

"I think that your incontinence—"

George groaned and buried his head in his hands.

"—is due to some natural atrophy that's occurred in some of your harder to reach muscles. We thought we had sufficiently restored them but clearly we missed something." Witten cut an accusing glance to Kelley, who shrugged unbothered. Kelley had the rare gift of not feeling guilty for things, especially when he had done nothing wrong. In his mind, he knew he had done the absolute best with the information he had at the time. This was all experimental. He simply made a mental note for the next thaw. *Pay closer attention to THAT.*

George asked, "Is it permanent? And what about this headache? It's killing me."

It was upsetting for the cryonicists to hear George talk like this about his condition. And they all felt a desperate desire to resolve the poor young man's issues, for which they felt wholly responsible. George's increasingly dire quality of life only further proved Jack's earlier point to Priya. They exchanged knowing glances. But not an 'I told you so' glance, more like a 'this is fucked up, you don't want this, trust me' glance.

Witten leaned in about to answer, but before she could Owens interjected confidently. "We're going to put you on a steroid regiment and in time you should regain full - control."

Witten's blood boiled. *Who does he think he is?*

"Great," said George curtly.

Priya stepped forward adding, "But until then... " and presented a stainless steel bed pan. Kelley smiled and held up adult diapers.

George looked at both options. "No. Also no. I'm not using those. This is the future? You don't have anything better than that?"

Kelley's eyes lit up with an idea. "We can try timed eliminations."

"Yeah!" said Priya, partly thrilled with this solution and partly putting on a brave face.

Kelley explained, "Based on your age, steel gut, and BMI and tracking your fluid and food intake, we can gauge how long you have between trips to the head."

It all sounded like a lot of work to George. "This just keeps getting better and better."

Witten reassured him, "It's only temporary. We'll let you get some rest."

Priya stayed behind, after the others left. She was nervous to talk to him, but she knew they needed to clear the air. She didn't want to have to tiptoe around George, she cared about him too much for there to be weirdness between them. For George, he was praying to god she would have just walked out the door with the others. She was the last person he wanted to talk to, as embarrassed as he was.

She took a seat. "Look about before, in the closet—"

"Please, it was a mistake. I shouldn't have done

that. I have a girlfriend - had a girlfriend... Anyway, we don't need to talk about it. It won't happen again. Sorry."

Priya was relieved, she certainly didn't want to have to give him the - 'my frozen dead husband is right down the hall and I am saving myself for his return' speech. It never went over well. But she felt... a little disappointed somehow that he could dismiss their kiss so quickly. She pushed it out of her mind. "It's forgotten. Look I know this," motioning toward his midsection, "feels like the end of the world, but—"

George stopped her, "I feel like a prisoner in my own body." He couldn't even look at her.

It was heartbreaking for Priya to see George giving in to the bitterness. She knew it was toxic. She had shown him a preservation, she had given him full access to Facebook Legacy, it felt like two steps forward and one step back with him. Still, she had one more card to play... "There's someone I want you to meet. But not now. Tonight."

***

It was after hours at Cryonicor. Only a skeleton crew were on duty working security or monitoring the cryostats. The halls were all on auto-low light this time of night. The sound of George's squeaky oxygen tank carriage echoed down the halls amplifying it's antiquity. Priya and George rounded a corner, and approached the door Witten had instructed him never to open. Priya leaned into a facial scanner and the door whooshed open. She charged ahead, and George followed eagerly. Everytime he passed this door it was calling him to look inside, and try as he might he could never get it open. Finally, its secrets would be revealed.

Once inside, they followed a narrow corridor that led into a larger dimly lit room. There George saw a hospital bed, and in it lay a withered old man. Tubes connected him to various medical accouterments. It was quite a ghastly scene. His hair was salt and pepper colored like George's. A machine held a book above his face and turned the pages for him in a steampunk mechanical fashion. The man was awake, lying perfectly still, except for his eyes that were busy reading.

Priya whispered to George, "Tennyson was the first person we revived. But there was a problem with his nervous system and well... we are unable to solve it. As you can see, he's a quadriplegic."

George's eyes widened. His heart sank into his stomach as he contemplated the daily life of this pitiable creature. Now he understood why Witten had described his own condition as a *desirable result.*

"Hello Tennyson," said Priya.

The man's eyes stopped scanning the page and wandered over to meet Priya's gaze as she stepped closer to his eyeline. A nearby machine emitted a stiff electronic voice response on Tennyson's behalf, "Hello Ms. Cayhill," it said.

George looked unnerved by the electronic ventriloquist act. Priya explained, "He has a chip in his brain that's able to turn his thoughts into words which are sent to the machine. It's actually pretty old technology."

Priya approached Tennyson's side, but George wasn't as eager. "What are you reading?"

"I am reading *Swiss Family Robinson*. It's about a family, they're stranded...but they have to figure out a way to make a new life for themselves on this strange tropical island."

"Doesn't sound so bad," said Priya with a mischievous smile.

"I know right, sign me up," said the old man in the bed, who couldn't smile with his face, but managed to get across his temperament.

"Tennyson, there is someone here I want you to meet. This is George. He has just been reanimated after 140 years in the cooler."

"Great to meet you George. I always wanted a brother."

Chapter 19

New Alliances

George is gobsmacked by the synthesized voice of the living corpse before him. He leans over to speak into the machine as if it were a microphone. He says, "HELLO" loudly and awkwardly.

Priya giggled at his misstep. "No. You can talk to him directly. He has a state of the art hearing implant. His eyes are tip top too. We tried to set him up with audio books. But he insisted we build him this machine so he can read paper books. You know how hard it is to even find paper books for him? And he goes through them like water. He says the act of physically reading is the only activity he gets so... anyway... I'm going to give you two a moment alone."

George shot her a look that said, 'don't go!' to no avail. Then he approached Tennyson's bedside like a child timidly approaches the casket at their first funeral.

George spoke first, "So how long have you been um...."

"I think it has been four or five years, hard to keep track of time."

"When did you die?

"I transitioned in 2050. How about you?"

"2020"

Tennyson did some fast math in his head, "COVID?"

"I don't know what that is."

"What did you die from? You're so young, talk about the short end of the stick."

"Congenital heart failure. I didn't get a transplant in time."

"So you were born in the 1980's? Right?"

"Yeah. '89"

"Me too. '87"

George swallowed hard at this. They could have been in high school together. How could he be the same age as this bag of bones? Of course he wasn't really, but still it was surreal to look upon this man's decrepit and impotent frame. He felt as though he was staring through a portal into his own future and it chilled him to the bone. He started to feel faint, like he could pass out. He quickly took a seat.

"Can I ask why you chose to sign yourself up for cryonics?"

"Oh that? It was simple. I wanted to see the future. Growing up I loved sci-fi movies that specu-

lated about space travel, flying cars, peaceful so-
cieties, all that shit you know... and I thought
this was my chance to see some of it."

"And do you regret it now? Knowing this is
how it turned out? No offense, but if I was you, I
think I'd rather be dead."

Tennyson responded, "Wow, tell me how you
really feel. LOL. I have to say LOL, because I can't
make the computer laugh the way I am laughing
in my head. Apologies."

George raised an eyebrow and couldn't help
but be disarmed by his bedridden peer. "Sorry.
I guess that wasn't polite. I just can't remember signing up for this, or even being sick at all.
I'm not sure what I was thinking. I don't think I
thought I was actually gonna die, so it's possible I
didn't think this through."

"I see. And here you are voila. What's that
getup you got on there?"

"It blows pure oxygen in my face because the
air here doesn't agree with me. I only get to take
it off inside my quarters. I can't even go outside
at all."

"That makes two of us. It's not ideal, I agree,"
Tennyson said after what seemed an eternity.
"But I would rather be alive than be dead - always.
Sometimes I think about this passage that the
French writer Camus once wrote in *The Stranger,*
he said, 'I often thought that if I had to live in the
trunk of a dead tree, with nothing to do but look
up at the sky flowing overhead, little by little I

would have gotten used to it.' That's why I have my books. With them, I can go anywhere."

George said nothing as he tried to take in the perspicacity of Tennyson's remarks. They talked a little more before finally his escort came to get him. He promised Tennyson he would come back to visit again. Priya walked George back to his room.

"Dr. Witten told me never to go into that room? Why the big secret?" he said as they strolled the darkened halls.

"Well, you have to remember the junior staff can't know about you or Tennyson, they can't know about our true research. And if I'm being generous I would guess that maybe Witten didn't want to burden you psychologically with some kind of twisted survivor type guilt."

"And if you weren't being generous?"

Priya's chest heaved as her inward breath filled her lungs to capacity. "She wants to pretend he doesn't exist at all. She never ever goes in there. I think it's too overwhelmingly bleak for her, and in order to keep attempting on new patients she has to separate herself from a case like Tennyson's. It's a lot."

"But you do it." Priya had no response for this. George continued, "I hate that he's in there like that. Maybe there is something we can do for him? Like some future suit that acts like a skeleton or something? Is that a thing yet?"

She shook her head no and smiled, "But I like

where your head's at." They arrived at his recovery room.

"Night Priya."

"Night George."

After he retired, Priya didn't head back out to catch a people mover to the tunnel which would drop her off at The Keys, an hour long trip all told. No, she took the freight elevator down to the foxhole. After the day's events with George in the closet and all, she felt like she needed ... to see *him*.

She sat on the ground next to the freshly delivered tube which had been inserted neatly into a row. She leaned her back against it's frosty fuselage and spoke to the frozen human remains within its walls. She approached it as if she and John were sitting in an adorable city park, on a gentle sloping hillside, underneath an oak tree having a heart to heart. "It's been a minute hasn't it. It feels good being close to you again. I think I needed you near me, I was starting to... forget... to lose my way a little maybe." For it's part, the steaming cryostat said nothing. It simply sat inert, as it was wont to do. She continued undeterred, "The cat got fat. It's been lonely without you, me not the cat, well both of us... Those long deployments of yours certainly prepared me. But it is different, isn't it? I promised you I wouldn't give up on us, and I haven't. Whatever else may have happened... I won't bore you with the details... know that I am not giving up. Not after all this."

***

Owens was on an earpiece in his office rocking slightly in his chair, "I want the hydrocopter in red and that's it… well if I can only get it in black then I don't want it Frank." He was scrubbing through the footage of the team's consultation with George from the day before about his incontinence. He often rewatched interactions with George recorded in his quarters, especially if he was in the scene. He suddenly sat up straight and leaned into the reader. "Ok, if you can paint it then great. Listen I gotta go Frank, talk to you later." He turned up the volume on the part after the others left, when it was just Priya and George. He heard them discussing what happened between them in the closet. *Oh my god, what happened in the closet?* Judging from George's apologies and professing to having a girlfriend, Owens didn't have to be an MD to surmise what had happened. He rubbed his face in turmoil. He palmed both eyes with his hands, in an effort to blind himself from this infelicitous development. He paused the video. His head fell limply to one side defeated, then it righted itself in a moment of inspiration. He remembered Dr. Kim's prescription - George needed to care about someone, and someone needed to care about him. And he remembered Christian Martinez's comments about how effective managers get the best out of their people. Maybe he could make lemonade out of this mess.

He unpaused the footage. He learned about their plan to meet back up after hours? *Great.* These people do not seem to get that they are on camera.... He tracked Cayhill's badge scans, and saw that she returned to work late last night. He scrubbed to George's footage that coincided with her badge rescan and saw George leaving and later returning. "Gotcha."

Ding Ding. "Come." Priya stepped in, sheepishly holding her glass reader. Owens stood like a gentleman. *Speak of the devil.* With a graceful wave he showed her to a synthetic mahogany guest chair. She was relieved to see that he appeared to be in a cooperative mood this morning. He sat in the other guest chair, opting to forego the whole behind the desk power trip. He leaned in with his elbows on his knees and his fingers linked, very father-figure, and said, "What's up? Is this about George?"

She summoned her bravery. "No, this is about my husband, John Cayhill."

Owens was caught off guard, she's married and kissing this resurrected invalid? But at the same time, who was he to judge? "I didn't realize you were married."

"Widowed."

"Oh. Ohhhhhh." His eyes widened with a keen

new understanding. "That explains a lot."

"Some people say, 'sorry for your loss' but whatever."

"He's frozen. He's here. No wonder." This was a twist he was enjoying thoroughly.

"No wonder what?"

"No wonder you're so loyal to Dr. Witts End." She stared at him blankly. He was putting two and two together for her, "She's promised to bring your husband back from the dead? And you believed her. Reverse Messiah Complex."

"I don't think that's a thing."

"Isn't it?" No matter how hard he tried to be relatable and kind, he couldn't help but be his arrogant patronizing self. "I gotta give it to her, recruiting the widows, that's one way to pull together a loyal hardworking staff. It's almost Machiavellian."

Priya didn't want to play head games with him this morning, she was on a mission. "We don't have to like each other."

Owens reared his head back at this, "... who says we don't like each other?" She was surprised by the twinkle in his eyes. He was smooth... and actually kind of handsome in a douchey way.

"I wanted to know if you would look over John's database entry, he's a stage one and I'd like to proceed with a thaw attempt as soon as possible. But I'm getting push back from Dr. Witten and I wanted a second opinion."

"A second opinion? Sure, let's see it." She

handed him her reader, he cut his eyes back up to hers, somewhat flattered that she thought he would be able to even make a call like this. The information was rich and detailed. "Leave it with me for now?" He handed it back to her and she shared it to his reader with the touch of a finger.

"Thanks." She started to get up.

"Not so fast. Are we going to talk about last night?"

"What about last night?"

"Priya, can I call you Priya?"

"Sure," she said reluctantly, as he had just agreed to do her a favor.

"Please don't be dishonest with me. I don't like it. Last night I saw your badge swipes, I can also see George's room so I know you took him out in the middle of the night. Where did you take him?"

It was true that she hadn't been very careful, if she lied, and he pressed hard enough he would find her facial scans for Tennyson's room. "Fine. I took him to see Tennyson."

"Why would you do that?"

"Because he needed to see his glass as half full. He needed perspective and I think he got it."

"Priya, you're not a mental health professional."

"No I'm not, I'm his friend. I did what was in his best interests and I'd do it again. If you don't like it, fire me.

"Careful Cayhill. Do you want this favor from

245

me or don't you?" He motioned toward the reader with John's information.

"I don't want a favor chief, I just want the truth."

***

Witten marched back into her office, smoldering about half a dozen things. She found Owens in her office making a fool of himself on the speed bag.

"That's not how you do it." She said laying her reader down on her desk and closing the door.

"No? I thought I was doing pretty good. I'm a lacrosse guy."

"Really? Still?"

The corner of his mouth popped up, "Nah, I do spin class like a total girl. It's fun."

"What do you want?" She sat in her guest chair.

He leaned back on her desk and spun the docked reader around to show her John Cayhill's patient profile. She was visibly affected at the sight of it. His smiling face took her back in time to that day at Kaiser Sinai when she performed his preservation ten years ago.

"A couple days ago this guy's wife, Priya Cayhill, maybe you've seen her around here before, she came to see me. Wanted a second opinion. You and Jack are telling her it's too soon, not yet... but he's a stage 1 right? So what gives?" Witten eyed him hard and shifted her weight. He went on, "took me awhile to check it out thoroughly, I learned a lot. But um, I have to agree with you that these human remains are not a viable candidate for reanimation right now."

"Okay...," she said, anxiously waiting for the other shoe to drop.

"Not with all this damage to his brain stem and major arteries. Looks like his cool aid saturation is around 77%. When you actually look at the scans that is. Not when you look at the stats on the profile which you entered... right? Those say 94%, just squeaking by to a stage 1. So what does that mean?

"You tell me, smart guy."

"I like to think so." He stood up flattening his shirt and tie with his open palm as he went to the window. "I think you falsified his stats so, to the layman, which in this place is everyone but you, John Cayhill would appear to be a stage 1 when you knew all the time his preservation had gone poorly and he was a stage 3 at best. But you also knew the only layman bothering to look at his status would be Priya. So your intention was to... trick her."

She shot out of her chair. "That's a hell of an accusation, you pathetic excuse for a scientist. You have no idea what you're talking about. This is basically your first day in cryonics." *Deny. Deny everything.*

Now they were standing eye to eye, or eye to chin in their case on account of Owen's height advantage. "Don't pull that shit with me, I know crystallized cells on a scan when I see them. When you compare George's pre-thaw scans to John's - it's apples and oranges."

"It's possible we could thaw John, we are making progress everyday in our nanobot repair programs, this isn't a pipe dream."

"No, it's not a pipe dream, that's why he's not a stage 4. But he's not a stage 1 and you've lied about it since day one. Why?... Because he ain't comin' back in her lifetime. And you have to keep feeding her that hope... dangling that carrot... or else she's not gonna serve you, especially at what you're paying her. Ouch. I didn't think you had it in you."

"A little hope never killed anybody."

And there it was. Her great justification. "Didn't it? Even I can see that this is wrong, and I have almost no moral compass at all. She's suffering."

Witten was sick to her stomach. The fact is she knew it was true. She'd known all along what this had done to Priya, how it had held her down in a relentless limbo, slowly suffocating her prospects for a healthy life. But hearing it out of the mouth of someone else, made it real. Jack had warned her about this for years, but she had shut him out. She buried her head in her hands. "Are you gonna tell her?"

"If I tell her she's gonna leave. Trust me, I'd prefer an MD/PHD from Oxford to a kindergarten teacher with a certificate she printed off the internet but you know what they say…"

"What?"

"Hell hath no fury like a woman scorned. No NDA in the world is gonna hold her tongue after this. We can't have that."

"So what are you saying?"

"It's cheaper to keep her."

"Stop talking like that!"

"Shut up!" He hushed her with a finger to his lips. "Someone's gonna hear you shouting. Look, we need her to move off this John idea without telling her the truth. I have some ideas. Just trust me."

She realized her seething distrust for him was a case of the pot calling the kettle black.

***

On her way home, Witten stopped to buy some flowers for Gwen. They had never been at odds like this before, and she was really getting worried. She had even brought up going to a couple's counselor and had suggested Jack, since he already knew about George and they could be totally honest with him. Gwen felt using Witten's best friend and co-worker as their personal couple's therapist would not be in her best interest. She didn't want to see a therapist at all. She seemed resigned to their expiration.

Witten arrived prepared to lower herself to outright begging for forgiveness. She hated this tension between them, she missed her wife and she wasn't getting any sleep on that sofa. The place was so small it only took her a moment to realize Gwen wasn't there. Then she noticed Gwen's clothes were gone, her art was gone, all her stuff was gone. Witten walked around in a daze wondering if this was a short term thing or not. Then on the kitchen counter she found Gwen's wedding ring and the keys to the condo. She left no forwarding address.

Chapter 20

Breaking Points

"Is it too tight?" asked Priya. She was in George's quarters the next morning fitting a monitor around his ankle. It was a gray plastic bracelet that monitored his perspiration. He was strapping on a matching watch.

"It's fine. So how long do I have until… "

"Once you hear the alarm you have only five minutes, I can adjust to your preference though. But I think five is ideal. When you hear it, quickly wrap up what you are doing and then go find a toilet and wait. More time, you may get caught up in other things and forget, and less time, you may be running down the halls around here." They shared a laugh and he nodded at her logic.

"And it shows me on the watch as well?"

"See these two lights," she pointed to the ankle

bracelet, "green means number 1, and red means number 2." She smiled at the awkwardness, while his demeanor quickly turned to embarrassment. "If you are wearing long pants and you can't see these lights, that's what the watch is for. It actually does all kinds of cool stuff, measures your heart rate, your daily steps, cardio activity, your sleep patterns..."

"Like a fitbit."

"What's a fitbit?"

"A watch that does all that stuff you were talking about. Except the number 1 and number 2 stuff," he said, finally chuckling.

"Wow. You guys weren't as primitive as I thought."

"I feel that way too sometimes when I, like learn something about history, like people were using credit cards in 1959, that trips me out. I think of it as this new thing, new for me in the 2010s, but there is nothing new about it you know...?"

"Exactly!" she nodded emphatically. They giggled a bit longer. He liked her laugh. "So you're all set, no more accidents. And you're on the steroids so... you shouldn't need this at all in a couple months."

"I hope not. But does this... like... track me?"

"It doesn't. But... you should start preparing yourself, I did hear them," she pointed to the cameras, "talking about putting a chip in you soon."

"They're gonna chip me? Like a dog? Do you guys chip people in this time?"

"We can chip people with a GPS, but usually it's only used on kids during heated custody battles to combat kidnapping. It's also something that wealthy people do… to combat kidnapping. But no, normal people don't do it."

"I do NOT want to be tracked, not ever. I can't live like that."

"But it's just for your own protection."

"Ben Franklin or someone said something about how security is the enemy of liberty."

"I don't think that's the saying. But they need to be able to keep track of you in an emergency."

"No. I won't do it. I'm not a pet, I'm not property of Cryonicor."

"What's the big deal? You know your phone tracks you too."

"Yeah, I know that. But that doesn't bother me so much. I can always walk away from my phone. But if they put it inside me, I'll never feel like I'm free. Would you do it?"

She cast her eyes downward.

"Exactly," said George.

Priya didn't want to be the one to tell him, he wouldn't have a choice in the matter.

***

Back at Witten's condo, the good doctor was waking up to greet a new lonely reality. Off of the sofa, and back in her own bed, she stirred as

253

a projection of the time flashed brightly on her ceiling. She had transitioned to the light alarm at Gwen's gentle urging. And like so many things, it had been a much better fit. She wore a white mask molded to her face that flooded her skin with a special light that rejuvenated her cells as she slept. It used to bother Gwen when she wore it in bed, she said it was like sleeping next to Jason. But Gwen wasn't there to tell her what not to do anymore. She tried to eek out the sweetness from the bittersweet pill of abandonment. But the truth was, she didn't want to get out of bed at all. She thought about calling in sick. She'd never done that before, but she'd seen plenty of others do it. Then she remembered George and his headaches, which she had still found no cure for. She threw the covers off.

Witten opened the top of her hi-tech date coffee maker on her kitchen counter. She peered inside trying to determine if she put coffee or water into the compartment. She looked around for a metal reusable filter, going through multiple drawers and looking through each one thoroughly. She frowned. "Fuck it." She aborted mission and opted to simply mix the brown powder with hot water. She sipped it and spit it out in the sink. Gwen had always made the coffee. Witten didn't know where things were, she was forever putting things down wherever and relied on her wife heavily to find anything. She went to her chest of drawers to pull a fresh pair of scrubs, but found none. *Ah.* The hamper was overflowing. Gwen didn't do laundry either, she was a busy doctor too. But she managed the service that picked it up. Witten didn't even know who to call about it. She was an hour late to work washing her own scrubs. She hadn't lived alone in twenty years, and was realizing how she hadn't fully appreciated the companionship until now.

In her office she was on a holo call with Christian Martinez who was wearing a turban and tunic, which she accepted ambivalently.

"You gotta help me out here Christian. I need to order the hyperbaric chamber for George, I really believe it's going to have a galvanic effect on his physical issues. It's paramount that we—"

"We talked about this Sam, you need to talk to Dr. Owens, that's what he's there for."

"I've tried Chrstian. He won't pull the trigger. This is exactly what I was worried about, I can't treat my own patient how I see fit without—"

"—You need a second. You're both great doctors, talk it out, maybe he'll surprise you."

Witten's watch flashed: **Blue Jay**

"Now what?"

Moments later she was in George's quarters with Kelley and Priya. George was in bed, coiled into a fetal position holding his head and howling. Witten was sitting on the bed with him, rubbing his back, "Talk to me George. Is it getting worse?"

Kelley hugged himself, like he wished he could hug George. He was stressed out as his empathy overloaded. "He's been like this for an hour."

"An hour?! Why didn't you call me sooner?"

She was right, they should have called her sooner. Kelley rubbed his hands through his platinum hair in desperation, then he went back to the console in the wall, pulling up George's latest MRI scans looking for something... anything... to help him.

"I've been trying to convince him to let me give him pain meds," offered Priya, helplessly.

"No!!" shouted George from his coil. "Why don't you just shove heroin up my veins?!"

Witten looked at the others confused and unsure of her next step. "I assure you the meds are safe, it's just temporary, they can buy us time."

"No!!!"

Witten winced at his resolve. "Okay, what do you want George?"

"Put me in a coma."

The cryonicists looked at each other horrified. Witten said, "George you don't want that, we'd have to intubate you, put a feeding tube down your throat—"

"I'll be asleep, I won't even feel it, wake me up when you've figured this out," he pleaded.

Kelley could see nothing in the scans that could help them. With his head he motioned for

Witten and Priya to come to the console to consult. In a hushed voice he said, "he can't live like this. We have to force him to take the pain meds. Let's tranq him, long enough to put them in his IV. We just need twenty minutes."

Priya eyed Witten, curious about the choice she would make. Obviously, forcing him onto pain meds was an ethical downward slide, but putting him into a medically induced coma would be reducing him to Tennyson's dire state. Had Witten worked her whole life to revive someone who would prefer to be unconscious on life support than alive? They had two heartbreaking options. Witten shook her head at this shit choice. "Where is Owens?"

She located him ten minutes later in the reanimation chamber. He heard her power walking down the corridor shouting his name with extra base in her voice. He intercepted her at the chamber entry, with a big goofy smile and an open armed welcome.

"Just the person I was hoping to see! Is something wrong?" he asked, sensing her crisis but still riding high on their recent alliance. But she was not his friend, especially not today.

"You are a slimy online marketer, you know that? You run your Regenadrip ads next to sexbots ads! The truth is you're a dressed up plastic surgeon, who doesn' know the first thing about internal medicine. You think people respect you? They think you're pathetic."

"Okay..." said Owens.

"Why did you even get into this business? It sure as shit wasn't to help people or you would have ordered the HBC when I told you to instead of leaving that man up there to suffer while you try and balance a billion dollar checkbook! Company men like you make me sick. You want to press press press about getting the kid camera ready, and you know, you KNOW that the HBC could be a game changer for his painful and demoralizing condition, and you won't pull the trigger on it. Why are you hesitating? It's not like it's your money!"

"Are you through?"

Witten raised her eyebrows sizing up Owens. He stepped aside and behind him was a top of the line state of the art hyperbaric chamber. Witten walked over to it stunned. She touched its cool white surface and ran her finger along its seven foot long cylindrical body making sure it was real.

Owens was beaming. "I got two of them."

"Two?" she looked back at him.

"Why have one when you can have two for twice the price," he shrugged before adding, "I'm waiting for an apology."

In a burst of rage, she hauled off and sucker punched him dead in the face with an expert right cross. The smack of her knuckles against his skull echoed through the chamber. "What the!!!??" Owens screamed, doubled over holding his throbbing eye.

Witten shook her injured hand, she thought she might have broken it, but it was worth it. Alliance be damned. "That's for not ordering it two weeks ago!"

Owens staggered around almost losing his balance. He eyed her with fear, betrayal and revenge foremost on his mind. He took out his anger on a tray of medical instruments which he kicked over theatrically. Witten backed up and started bouncing between her feet, clenching her fists, preparing for a possible physical retaliation.

Owens stood up and shook it off. His eye was swollen and the left side of his face bright red. He swallowed his pride. He couldn't really hit a seventy five year old woman no matter how good she looked. *Get the best out of your people.* "You feel better?!"

"Yeah I do."

"Good!" he sneered back at her. Then he retrieved two cups of coffee from the ledge and offered her one. "Date coffee. Black."

She considered his gesture for a moment, looked back at the HBC, and took the damn coffee. She needed it.

Chapter 21

Everything's Going to be Different Now

"I don't like small places." George hesitated to lay all the way down in the hyperbaric chamber. It gave him coffin vibes.

Dr. Witten held up a small blue pill. "George this is a mild sedative, you are going to take this and you are going to toughen up and lay down on this little mat. This is not a discussion, do you understand?"

George was still nervous about Witten's treatments after what happened with the diode burn, so he looked to Dr. Owens who had earned at least some trust with his Tiger Blood infusion. "What happened to you?" George asked him, referring to his swollen face.

"Just lay down George," said Owens, like an exhausted father says to their kid who is asking a thousand inane questions at bed time.

He took the sedative, layed down, and pulled down the door. There was a seal release on the inside and the outside which made him feel slightly better. Once inside, it was a pleasant temperature. It was big enough for him to toss and turn. but not to sit up. He could see out through portholes on each side of his head. It was brightly lit inside and there was a console that allowed him to change the brightness. The chamber gently began to pressurize. He took a deep breath and yearned like never before, for a cell phone with wifi.

Within minutes he was asleep and Dr. Witten had returned to HQ to watch his internal monitors. She was already seeing some changes that gave her encouragement. But now that he was actually inside the HBC a quiet dread settled over her. What if it didn't work? What could she possibly try next? How could she look him or anyone else at Cryonicor in the eyes again? Priya approached to see what was happening on the monitors. Witten tensed up a little, they had not really cleared the air since the whole John debacle, and she knew that Priya had tried to go around her by taking John's scans to Owens.

Priya hated the tension between them. She knew she had abused her clearance transferring John. She knew she would get roasted for that, but she'd hoped that Witten would have been more understanding. And yes, she was angry about them stonewalling her, but she had Owens working on it. She knew she couldn't stay on the outs with her mentor forever. She needed her desperately.

"What do you think this is going to do for him exactly," Priya asked, genuinely interested.

Witten didn't make it a habit of explaining herself, but in this case, the more Priya knew, the more she might be of help. "I think underlying a lot of his symptoms is untreated decompression sickness."

"The bends?" asked Priya, fascinated.

"In a manner of speaking. When a diver comes up from the deep too quickly...it causes nitrogen bubbles to form in the tissues of the body. That's a tricky problem. Imagine the pressure his body, and brain were under in that tube for a hundred and fifty years, frozen solid? Our atmosphere is about twenty percent oxygen, give or take. What the HBC does is it forces three hundred % pure oxygen into the blood plasma, that is then infused into the cells that have been damaged or are dormant that normally the red blood cells can't get to. And that helps the body to excrete those bad bubbles and has a host of other benefits. I just hope we're not too late."

"I never thought of that."

"Yeah well, trial and error," said Witten as she finished her cold date coffee.

"I gotta save the date for tomorrow for your re-up. What's going on with you guys, did you talk to her?"

Those damn save the dates Gwen had insisted on had gone out to their friends calendars a year ago. Wishful thinking. Witten bristled over the intrusive questions, especially since she and Priya weren't on the best of terms. She had to remind herself to be nice because she had done something terrible to her young protege, whether she knew it or not.

"She moved out."

"What? So that's it? Where did she go?"

"Didn't say, didn't even say goodbye. Looks like we are expiring tomorrow at midnight."

"Did you try to call her?"

"For what? She doesn't want to talk to me. And you know what? It's fine. This is why expiration exists, people change, they grow apart. Ten years is a long time, twenty years twice as long. Think about who you were ten years ago when I met you, and who you are now? You're so different. You've grown and changed so much, you're like a little general now. We've all changed in our own ways. A lot of people think that you boil down to some immovable essence, or a soul as they used to call it, but the intrinsic self is an illusion. You're a collection of experiences and reinforcements. And how can you have a soulmate, if you don't have a soul?" Witten looked at Priya directly. She wasn't just talking about her and Gwen, she was also talking about Priya... and John. She polished off her date coffee and headed back to her office to do some crunches and be alone.

Priya sat in quiet contemplation. She pulled out her cell, "Play John Suprise." She watched the night vision video again, of a moment she insisted was her last true moment of happiness. For the first time she started thinking about how John would find her if he did come out. She had kept their home exactly the same. She had been careful to makc sure she looked as close as possible to how he would remember her. Lord knows she had been faithful. But what about the inside, her personality, who she had become? The woman in this video was a happy go lucky naive baby crazy kindergarten teacher. Priya went to wash her hands and looked at her reflection in the mirror over the sink. She saw a serious woman in a lab coat, wearing scrubs with her hair pulled back in a plain ponytail. She was now a hardcore cryonicist with a super secret all consuming career.

Even if he came back and he was one hundred percent in perfect working order, would things between them be the same? What would it feel like to need to leave at a certain time every night in order to have dinner with her husband and... watch tv together? What if things weren't the same? What if that life wasn't enough for her anymore? What if they hurt each other? What if it was awful? Then what were all these years that she had dutifully sacrificed for? That feeling, of precious time wasted, was a gut punch.

She found herself wrestling with the same paradox hanging over Witten's head. What happens if the thing you were sure would fix everything, is a total bust? What would be worse, leaving him in the freezer and letting Cryonicor make the decisions - or having him come out and he die, be horribly disabled, or be perfectly fine but end up leaving her anyway? Of course there was the possibility she could bring him out, he wouldn't die immediately, he would be fine in fact, and they would live happily ever after. The scientist in her had to recognize the hierarchy of probability was not on her side. Even though she had labored under the illusion of his impending cryonic reanimation for a decade, it wasn't the same. That had been a safe harbor for her because she had had no actual choices to make. She had spent the past decade paralyzed in fact, outside of changing her career, she had stayed in the same place she had been in every other way. But was she patiently waiting, as she liked to think of it, or was she trapped, trapped in the past by hope?

***

Almost eight hours later, Witten depressurized the HBC and released the exterior latch. Moment of truth time. She administered a nasal cortisol spray to rouse him from his light sedation. Owens anxiously observed from the back of the room, sporting a hell of a black eye. George's eyes fluttered open and he sat up grunting.

"That wasn't so bad," he said as he stretched his long arms out like a pterodactyl.

"How do you feel?"

"I feel good."

"How's the headache?"

"Gone."

"Seriously?"

He stopped for a moment to listen to his body before responding, "Yes."

"That's really good George. Your vitals are strong," said Witten, smiling from ear to ear.

"Now what?"

"We go outside and see what's good."

"Ok, just wearing the nasal cannula?" he stands and slips on his hospital slides.

"Let's try it au natural."

George pushed open the back exit of Cryonicor, with Witten close behind carrying an inhaler. He took a ten minute walk without incident. Feeling the snap of spring air on his skin was euphoria. His head began to spin with possibilities.

Moments later he was back in his quarters as Witten took his blood pressure and a blood sample for the lab. George asked her, "What now?"

"I think if you continue doing eight hours a day of therapy inside the HBC, your respiratory system should be able to handle our atmosphere unassisted for three to five hours at a time."

"Eight hours a day?"

"It's no big deal, you just sleep in it," said an extra chipper Witten, proud of her clever solution. She really needed a win, especially today.

"Sleep in that thing? Like Dracula?"

"Yes. Exactly like that."

"But I can still only go outside three to five hours at a time?"

"For now, but good news is you should not need the nasal cannula or the clean room anymore, we only have to be careful about the unfiltered outdoors. And as far as the time outside, we can push that as we go, but George, don't you see this is everything. This is real true life after death, life extension!"

"What was it before?"

Witten tilted her head and raised both eyebrows in her cheeky way and puffed. She started packing up her gear. George began to imagine his life outside of Cryonicor. That's when it dawned on him, what he and Kelley had talked about. He didn't have any money or a job or any skills and he didn't qualify for the free money everyone else got. And about what Witten had told him when he learned the truth, that he could never be honest with anyone, about who he was. His bright new day was gradually eclipsed by a dark cloud.

"Oh, one more thing, tomorrow we're going to insert a small GPS chip just under your skin, so we don't lose you."

"The hell you are!" Witten stammered back

at George's eruption. She wished she could've tagged Owens in at that moment. He was better with the living, even if he was an unscrupulous company man.

"Take it easy George, It's just for your own protection. What if you get hurt? What if you get arrested? We have to be able to get to you fast."

"It's for *your* own protection!"

Witten was nonplussed, she opted to let him cool off and went to get Owens, muttering under her breath, "I'm too old for this shit."

Alone in his room George went to put his googles on to try and relax with a game. As soon as he started it, he tore it off his face and threw it across the room. He didn't want to numb himself, that's what they wanted. They wanted him to forget that he was a captive by giving him little toys to pass the time.

Just breathe. In. Out. In. Out. Just be here now. He had to remind himself that he had no one to blame for this but himself. He knew these people weren't evil. They were doing the best they could by him. Out of the huge windows, the sun was setting over SANI.

He thought about the escape route he had mapped out in advance. But he needed the HBC, he couldn't survive without it. There was no way around that. It began to coalesce for him. He had thought that his physical problems were temporary, something that would be sorted out sooner rather than later. Like Witten, he too was waiting for the mystery box to solve everything. She seemed to think it had. But for him, a cold reality came into focus. This was what his life would be. This was it, inside this place. The difference between Tennyson's gruesome reality and his own was only one of degree. For the first time he started to wonder if a life as a chipped dependent lab rat, unable to live on his own, or make any sincere connections was worth living at all.

Chapter 22

A Promise is a Prison

When Priya returned that night to her floating domicile, she looked in on the old nursery turned storage unit. It wasn't pretty. On that night she saw it clearly for the dusty clutter it was. It represented the sheer futility of all her efforts. But, she didn't have a reason to face it yet. She had no immediate need to clear the space. So she shut the door, reasoning she could let it sit a while longer.

The first thing she liked to do after putting her things down and taking her shoes off was to slip her wedding band back on. Without thinking, she had it poised at the crown of her left hand ring finger - but she hesitated. Then she sighed and gently placed it back on the little wooden tray. After overfeeding Bear, she went to her closet to put away her nurse's shoes. The bright white mushroom leather wasn't glamorous, but it was very functional. She took in the image of John's clothes hanging next to hers. This time, she didn't overthink it. She started pulling them down one by one and tossing them into piles. Shirts. Pants. Concert Tees. Jerseys. She folded up the pants and shirts and put them in a laundry bag, the rest she deposited in the rubbish bin in a rare moment of radical honesty. All that remained from his side were his army fatigues and his dress uniform. She then started stretching her own cramped wardrobe out across the full length closet. That night she had a fitful sleep, curled up on her side of the bed.

The next morning at Cryonicor, Kelley and Priya sat side by side in HQ, watching George on the monitors. Kelley could zoom in, rack focus, pan, and even track to some extent - technically directing from two camera angles that displayed on one larger monitor giving it the effect of a movie. He had developed this cinematic technique to amuse himself while on long shifts of George watch. The duo leaned in, watching with anticipation. He sipped a childish coffee beverage while she snacked on nuts.

They watched the subject wake up on his own. His sleep patterns were remarkably predictable. Kelley had zoomed into a close up of George's face, he narrated in a fake australian accent. "And Action..." He proceeded to operate his little cinematic side-show as gracefully as he played video games. George stretched, his ankle bracelet alarm went off and he relieved himself in the ensuite bathroom. He mosied over to the windows and solemnly looked out over the bustling island metropolis. His mood seemed somber and reflective. "Another day in paradise for our hero," added Kelley. "Wait, what's that there? Looks like a bag of crap, I better investigate," said the cheeky cryonicist, as George crossed his quarters to examine a mysterious laundry bag. He'd looked inside and curiously reared his head back and cut his eyes right up to the cameras. Kelley zoomed in on his face, "What did you get me for Christmas daddy?"

"Shut up," grunted Priya, growing tired of his silly game. George lugged the bag to his bed and dumped out all of John's salvaged clothes to get a good look at the haul. He stripped off his shirt to try on a new one.

Kelley covered Priya's eyes, "you're too young to see this."

She jerked her head back, "stop!"

John's t-shirt was too tight, one after the other they either weren't long enough or the shoulders were too narrow. Each piece brought back a vivid memory for Priya. She saw John wearing them at the store, on the street, around the house. Some she had even bought for him and he'd pretended to love. It was like a tangible slideshow of his personhood. A person is partly the things that they carry with them through life. As George shrugged and moved on to the pants,

Priya's carefree mood began to darken. He started to untie the waistband of the scrubs bottoms, then stopped, turned his back to the camera and dropped them revealing his bare ass. Kelley realized no one ever thought to give George a proper wardrobe including underwear. Poor guy was wearing tight ass scrubs, one of Kelley's old hoodies, disposable hospital shoes and going commando. And he'd never even complained.

Priya was sweet to try and use John's old clothes to do George some good. Now that he could go outside, he would need something passable to wear. Like the t-shirts, the pants were too small, they were too short and skin tight. But a couple pairs of John's basketball shorts were one size fits all, even if the style of near ankle length didn't exactly suit George's taste.

She hadn't realized George was that much bigger than John had been. Whenever she thought of him, she thought of him as this larger than life army captain who had swept her off her feet. In reality, he was only 5'11. The sight of his things... being of no use to anyone, inconsequential, brought home for her that which she had denied for so long. She began to tremble with emotion, like a far off train rumbles in the distance. Sensing it, Kelley grabbed her hand, without looking at her, or saying a word. George gathered up almost all of the donations and stuffed them into his in-room incinerator.

"They're too small," said Priya, her voice

breaking.

Kelley put his arm around her shoulder and pulled her to him. "You did good... I know it's hard." She opened her crossed arms and hugged Kelley like a brother as she began to sob. A tidal wave of emotion overtook her. She couldn't say much, but she didn't have to. Kelley held her close, never shushing her, just rocking her gently. She was swallowed whole by an ocean of deferred grief. Her weeping wasn't pretty, her nose ran and she gasped for breath between pained vocalizations. Moved by her surrender, Kelley's own eyes welled, his voice cracked as he said, "It's okay Pri, It's okay to cry. He would be so proud of you."

"I promised him," she wailed, burying her face in his shoulder.

"You did all you could. You did more than anyone has ever dreamed of, but it's enough now." He broke their embrace to look her in the eyes, to make sure she heard him, "It's enough."

***

Kelley was shuffling from one task to the next after his emotional morning with Priya, when Christian Martinez cruised right past him in the hall. Behind him was a dapper suited older gentleman and the two shared more than a passing resemblance. Christian was looking at his phone and dressed for horseback riding, but he had the courtesy to give Kelley a friendly nod.

The other man ignored him completely. Martinez didn't touch down at Cryonicor unless it was really important. He ran straight to Dr. Witten with the scuttlebut.

Witten was looking over George's blood work and recalibrating the HBC in the reanimation chamber when Kelley caught up with her. Priya had told him that the doctor and her wife were expiring at midnight that night. So even though Kelley was busting to dish, he held himself back and tried to approach her with the appropriate sensitivity. "Hey doc," she acknowledged him, "so… how are you?… You, you okay?"

"I'm fine, why do you ask?" said Witten without looking up from the HBC control panel.

Well, asked and answered, Kelley felt he could proceed with the matter foremost on his mind. "Did you know Martinez is here?"

She closed her eyes at the news and brought two fingers to the bridge of her nose. "Owens called a big meeting in half an hour."

"No one told me about it."

"It's only for department heads." Kelley frowned, it wasn't often that their small staff operated by rank. It had always felt more like a family. But now that family was growing and things were changing. Witten continued, "Why would he come in for this?"

"What's the meeting about?"

"Pshhh…" huffed the doctor. "He didn't say."

"He wasn't alone. There was another guy with

him, an older guy."

"You think it's his father?" asked Witten with alarm.

Kelley put his hands in his pocket and nodded like a bobble head. "Judging by their perfect jaw-lines and matching butt chins."

Javier Martinez had never set foot inside Cry-onicor. Over the past twenty years she had only met him twice, both times she had gone to see him at their foundation's headquarters in Bar-bados. The first time, was when she initially brokered the deal with Christian almost twenty years ago. The second was after Tennyson came out, and she tried to argue for their kicker based on that reanimation. The elder Martinez had al-ways been cold and dismissive with her. In the latter incident he flatly denied the claim that Tennyson's case constituted real life after death cryonic reanimation. He said the subject didn't meet an arbitrarily imposed quality of life stand-ard. He was a reclusive figure in medical re-search, often discussed but rarely seen.

And here he was, boots on the ground, on his way to their conference room. Owens had some big thing planned no doubt. She was sure he would start by making all kinds of promises, which she would be in charge of keeping. And he hadn't ran word one by her yet. *Great.* She felt her cardiovascular tone shift as the noradren-aline coursed through her veins. This was all she needed, as if today wasn't hard enough. She had their re-up papers in her desk ready on the off chance Gwen should have a change of heart and show up at her work in some grand romantic gesture.

Kelley added wistfully, "Kill to be a fly on the wall in that room. You got nothing to worry about George is in great shape now. Thanks to your bright idea," he motioned to the HBC.

He was right, why was she nervous? Had she not done it? Had she not risen a man from the freaking dead? What in all of their careers combined could possibly compare. She tugged at her lab coat, composing herself. It occurred to her they might want to meet George, even walk him around outside a little like a thoroughbred racehorse.

"Hey, can you run out and grab some haley's for George? Get like five."

"Now?" he asked.

Kelley popped his head into Witten's darkened office. He opened her drawers looking for something. He saw the vial of Tiger Blood rattling around. But Kelley wasn't the suspicious type. He soon found what he was looking for: the petty cash fob. Reimbursement was a hassle.

Initially, he was annoyed at being sent on trivial errands like this, while the others got to pal around in top secret meetings. He may not have been a department head, and only twenty six, but he was a world class nano-technician, even if the world didn't know who he was. But Kelley was a pathological optimist, always looking for that silver lining, and he usually found it. It was one of his two super powers. Often, to regain a sense of gratitude he would question if his day, as it stood, would pass his afterlife test. If it did, then he didn't want to screw it up by harboring bitterness, anxiety, or fear. At Witten's desk he took a quick inventory: he had already gone surfing at low tide before his shift, helped a dear friend through an emotional breakdown and after work he had a hot date lined up. Depending on how the date ended, he felt satisfied that he could stand living today over and over if it came to it. He decided any excuse to leave work and enjoy the world was a gift. It was better than doing rounds in the foxhole.

Just then George walked past Witten's office, sans nasal cannula but in a pathetic ensemble; basketball shorts with scrubs on top. Probably taking one of his daily constitutionals as Priya had taken to calling his long daily walks. Seeing George forced to walk in circles for stimulation reminded him of a big dog in a small apartment with the zoomies. He had noticed how down George had seemed since he got out of the HBC. He was distant and introverted. Something was weighing on him, and Kelley had about a hundred guesses as to what that could be. He knew

George wanted more than anything to get out of the facility and get on with the business of living. Suddenly, a mischievous thought crept into his mind.

Moments later Kelley found George back in his quarters. He was sitting on the floor staring out over the city. He nodded to Kelley, "I'm not in the mood for a game today man." Kelley noted the smashed googles in the corner.

"What about roulette?"

"What....?"

"Ever been to Monte Carlo?"

A slight smile broke across George's face. "I don't get it."

Kelley tossed him a pair of his sandy flip flops from his personal pod, one of which George was able to catch. "Put these on, we need to run an errand."

George nervously looked over at the empty water glass on his bedside and checked his special watch.

Chapter 23

An Ominous Prelude

Meanwhile, Priya, Witten and Jack filed into the conference room for the big meeting. To say they were alarmed to see the Martinezes seated next to Owens, would be an understatement. Were they all getting their walking papers? Or worse? The Martinez foundation had a reputation for unsavory business tactics, and the rumors did not stop short of disappearing people, though no evidence of such iniquity existed. They didn't need the money men around to lay them all off, so that was probably off the table. Jack tried to pack away his fear of being murdered, for the far more likely scenario that this was a straightforward strategy meeting.

Owens proudly began, "Thank you for joining us, let's get right to it. You are all invaluable members of the Cryonicor system... We're about to begin a transformative period in human life extension."

Witten rolled her eyes at his theatrics. She took his use of the word *system*, instead of family or even team, as an ominous prelude of what was to come.

He had regenerated the damaged tissue around his eye and it was almost totally healed already, but nonetheless he tried to conceal it with makeup. No one said anything about it. He continued, "The foundation has been briefed on our incredible progress and they have flowed down two primary directives for Cryonicor to follow over the next five years. #1 - We bring out as many subjects as possible. And #2 - No one can find out early. Every subject has to be controlled."

"What do you mean controlled?" asked Priya.

"Not like warehousing them. I'm saying we chip 'em. Track 'em. Protect them and our investment," Owens answered.

Priya reminded the room, "Our mission is to give them their lives back."

In a stoic, gravelly voice, Javier Martinez broke in, gently but firmly, "They're going to be alive, let's start there and work our way up."

***

It was a typical cloudless afternoon in Santa Angeles. The weather was about ninety degrees. On a tree lined street of businesses, apartments, street vendors and parked pods, Kelley stood lookout.

"Nothing's happening," George called out from behind a rolling trash incinerator in the adjacent alley.

Kelley glanced at his watch and said, "Give it a minute."

George stood, legs spread, facing a brick wall, waiting for the stream. At last, he started to urinate. "Holy crap, can't believe that worked."

"'Holy Crap' … you sound like my 3G."

He rejoined Kelley on the sidewalk. "3G?"

"Great Great Grandpa."

"Oh... You guys live so much longer. Is Dr. Witten really 75 years old?" asked George. After being locked away inside the facility for weeks, he was flooded with the euphoria that can accompany blunt immersion into a foreign country. It stayed, even if only temporarily, his recent melancholy. He was almost giddy with the excitement of being out in the world of 2163, and just the ability to walk and talk to a companion like a regular person thrilled him.

"Something like that, but all gen zetas don't look as good as her, she really works at it."

Kelley came to an intersection and stopped but George kept walking unaware, because there were no pedestrian street lights. The blonde bomber put his arm out like a soccer mom to stop George from walking into traffic. A pod zoomed by, just missing him. He looked down and LEDs embedded in the street lit up a crosswalk with red dots that shifted, to flashing green arrows which led them safely across.

"Whoa cool!"

"Careful man."

Once on the other side, George kept looking backwards at the incredible crosswalk and he tripped on a crack in the sidewalk and almost biffed. Kelley grabbed him again.

"Watch where you're going Tina," said Kelley, slightly irritated.

"Tina?"

"A Tina is just a dumb person, it's a long story and its so dumb its not worth explaining."

"Cool. So it must be interesting knowing your ancestors personally," offered George.

"No it's not. How can I explain? You were born in... in what?"

"1989."

"That's nuts, just on its own. But okay, so let's say your parents were born in the 60's, grand-parents born in '30, great grandparents in 1900, and great greats in 1870? Okay? What happened in 1870?" Kelley pulled out his cell to search for an answer to his own question. "The Civil War ends," he announced in his most upbeat voice.

George scratched his head, "Whoa, that's a trip."

"A what? Where?"

"A trip? A trip, just means it's kinda crazy. Sorry not crazy, crap I mean it's wild."

Kelley cocked his eyebrow and continued,

"Yeah. Now imagine eating a holiday meal with Mr. 1870, and his ideas about the world."

As George turned this notion over in his head he spied an LED billboard of a pretty beach advertising:

GAZA STRIP'S NEWEST 5 STAR RESORT.
NOW ONLY A 3 HOUR HYPERFLIGHT AWAY.

"WHAT HΛPPENS IN GAZA, STAYS IN GAZA."

George concluded finally, "Oh.. I wouldn't want that actually..."

Kelley nods, "Cause it's torture. I mean I respect my elders and I think we can learn a lot across generations but, ideas don't die. That's why people are supposed to."

"If you feel that way, why do you work in cryo-whatever it is?

"When I was a kid, I used to steal cars - Hey hold up. Wait here."

Kelley ducked into a small shop. While George waited on the busy street, he felt eyes on him in a way that made him uncomfortable. His dress may have had a vague homeless vibe to it, he realized and found himself wondering what happened to his friend Peaches. He clocked an ad on a people mover zipping past, it was an elderly lady and her middle aged daughter, they were on a park bench together. The ad read:

SILVER ALERT - THE MOST
TRUSTED IN-ARM GEOLOCATOR TO

KEEP YOUR LOVED ONES SAFE.

Suddenly a sickening feeling returned to the pit of his stomach. He was getting chipped, today, probably as soon as he got back. He would resist of course, but what if they tranq'd him again? Kelley was taking longer in the shop than he'd expected him to. George thought, if he wanted to run, now would be the time to do it. It would be hard, he would struggle, have to sleep on the street and eat out of trash bins at first. Then eventually he would make some friends and being able bodied and hardworking he could- what was he thinking? He had no ID, no skills and he was hardly able bodied. What about the HBC? He had to be back in it in a few hours. If he didn't get back to it in time, the doctor said his symptoms would be worse than before and he could even die.

***

Back in the Cryonicor conference room, Owen's briefing continued.

"So what's next?" asked Priya.

Owens activated the reader wall, showing a dated picture of an old couple vacationing on a beach. He said, "Not what's next. Who's next? Meet Mr. and Mrs. Alpo. They were vitrified a hundred years ago, ten years apart, Mrs. Alpo went in first. We're gonna bring them out... together."

"Together? Simultaneous reanimations?" gasped Witten.

Christian chimed in, "They wake up together in the future? Awesome. We can film it, it'll make amazing ads!" Owens gave this idea a cheesy thumbs up.

Priya took one of her trademark deep breaths trying to cope with the gutting prospect of bearing witness to someone else's romantic reunion.

Witten interrupted, "—You are out of your ever loving mind. We just got George's headaches under control yesterday! We still have such a long way to go with him. No offense-" she offered meekly to the money men at the end of the table, "but shouldn't we focus on that?"

Priya said, only half believing it, "Maybe he's right. We should learn what we can from him and move on."

"If it was John would you want us moving on?" asked Witten bluntly in front of everyone.

Checkmate.

Owens continued, "We all want the same things. No one is being forgotten about. George is doing great. We can move him over to the hospice wing for now, plenty of beds over there."

Witten objected again, "No way. He is a young man, he doesn't want to rot in a nursing home. He needs independence, or else he's gonna—"

"—what can we do?" said Owens sharply. "We have to keep a close eye on him. You wanna take him home with you?" Witten cast her eyes down, remembering her own heartbreaking home life. Nurturing wasn't exactly in her wheelhouse.

There was a knock at the doorway. They all turned and saw to their surprise, the elegant silhouette of Dr. Gwen Kim Witten, sheepishly waiting to be acknowledged. Owens waved her forward.

He explained, "Perfect timing.... come, come. Some of you already know Dr. Kim Witten, some of you may know her only by reputation - but she is our new in-house psychologist. She will be treating our soon to be many, thaws." Gwen meekly waved hello and sat down near the front, trying her best to diffuse the tension by playing a student role. Witten was totally blindsided.

"I think it makes sense. We need someone and she's already part of the family. Good to see you again Gwen," said the dashing younger Martinez flashing his boy billionaire smile.

"Likewise Christian." She spoke to the higher ups like Owens and Martinez with a familiarity that made the others uneasy. Now the likes of Priya, Kelley and Jack - 'medical enthusiasts' - were beginning to be outnumbered by actual doctors. Was the writing on the wall?

Witten and Gwen locked eyes. Samantha was struggling to process what Gwen's presence meant for her, for them, for the work. Her first instinct was a strong sense of betrayal. How could Owens make such a big decision without consulting her? How could Gwen do this? How could she intrude? What does she know about it anyway? Why did she leave the condo only to turn around and work side by side with her at Cryonicor?

***

Kelley returned to the sizzling street to find George leaning against a wall, sweating through his clothes. "Hey I got the inhalers," he said. George nodded, less than ecstatic at the immediate prospect of being carted right back to chiptown USA.

"Why don't we buy you some new looks?" Kelley held up the petty cash card with a cheeky grin.

"Looks?"

"Garments, fashion, costume whatever you call it in the old days."

"Clothes," George shrugged.

"Fine. We have to get you something decent. Plus, nothing beats a little retail therapy. This way." Kelley confidently led a timid George around the corner, and down an escalator into a cavernous underground arcade of shops.

Below the surface it was cool and pleasant. The old blue line was decommissioned after the big quakes cauterized its routes. But the remaining structurally sound underground sections were redesigned for pedestrian and commercial purposes. As George descended into the depths of commerce he found himself looking forward to sampling a bit of the drone age market place. Kelley ducked into the low doorway of a distinguished but empty cedar lined shop. George followed and hit his head.

"Where are all the clothes?" asked George, rubbing his smacked head. The shop consisted of a central table and two stools and smelled of wood and leather. He couldn't begin to imagine what was sold here.

Kelley motioned to a stand alone arch, somewhat like the metal detector at the airport, but more minimal and streamlined. "So you just stand right here under this thing."

"Why?"

"You'll see."

George stood under the arch and motion sensor activated tracking lasers danced along his whole body and face. Afterward, Kelley motioned his pal to join him at the central table where a reader embedded within displayed several folders for him to choose from. Each folder was a look especially chosen by the algorithm for his corporeal dimensions. The look consisted of what appeared to be a magazine photo shoot, complete with soft lighting and flattering faux candid angles. Except the model in all the photos was George.

George double took the images, swiping through dozens of pics. "What is this?"

"These are your looks."

"But how do they make this look like me?"

"It's just 2D imaging, you just gave it all the info it needed when you stepped under the scanner. It's not that complicated really." George noticed LED poster displays of the images suddenly around the shop, life sized happy go lucky George's flitted across the screens, staring back at him. One George was relaxed on an east coast beach, one was very influenced by fashions from the far east, and another was inspired by what looked like aircraft maintenance attire. "Go on, choose one."

The fashion depicted ran the gamut from something he could see connected to his time, like athletic wear and jeans, but a lot of the cuts were far from his fashion comfort zone. He chose the safest bet: Driftwood Beach George. Then he was asked to choose a few more details, such as level of wardrobe needed, favorite colors and materials. He didn't recognize any of the materials. Once he finished two compartments hissed out from the cedar lined wall, containing a couple racks of clothes that seemed to float a few feet off the floor.

Kelley went over and waved his hand above the rack as if announcing the finale of a magic trick. "Here you are. See... you don't have to waste your time trying stuff on or going through racks of the wrong sizes. Or looking at mannequins who couldn't be further from your body type. It makes shopping for clothes as easy as picking up a six pack of beer." Kelley pulled a few pieces for George and took them to the central table.

"So I don't try it on?"

"Nope. No need. These are full proof. Let me settle up." Kelley rang a vintage service bell and a smartly dressed woman emerged to attend to him. She couldn't help but cut her eyes frequently to the unfortunate soul alongside her pretty boy customer.

As she rang up the pieces she told Kelley he had nice eyes. He flashed her a flirty smile and checked her out. Then she looked back at George, "What happened to you?"

He panicked. "I don't... really know."

"Ain't that the truth. Thanks, can I get some cash back?" The shop girl handed him a few bills which he handed to George. "Walking around money, you should always have a little dinero on you, that's what my 3G says. Don't tell Dr. Witten."

George was slightly emasculated by the sweet gesture, especially in front of the shop girl. But he tucked the money inside the pocket of his basketball shorts. He had no power in the situation. He couldn't refuse it. This, coupled with the bewildering process of purchasing clothes made him feel like a lost child, or more accurately like a useless elderly dependent.

Back top side, they were making their way through the sweltering streets of SANI to the pod that had brought them there. Finally Kelley stopped abruptly "I have to grab something for my date tonight."

"Is it cool if I wait out here?" George asked, put off after the alienating clothes shopping experience.

Kelley dipped into a shady storefront carrying the looks and inhalers. George stood there for a minute out front people watching. A young girl openly stared at him. He became aware that many people casually wore surgical masks. It was unnerving, what were they all afraid of catching he wondered.

A giant people mover hissed to a stop and let out a wave of passengers. They bumped and shoved him unapologetically. He saw many people taking hits off inhalers and some were wearing video game googles over their eyes like they were spectacles.. He stared unabashedly at one pair trying to discern their purpose and the owner pushed him back.

"What's your problem?" said googles guy.

George backed away, making sure to stay off of the street. Suddenly, the street lit up behind him signaling pedestrians to go and he got caught in a flood of people, pushing him across the intersection. He started looking for Kelley, unsure exactly which shady store he had gone into. Then a drone flew out of a restaurant and hovered at his eye-level carrying a thermal food bag. It proceeded down the street making a delicate clicking noise. He followed it instinctively around yet another corner. Mesmerized, he watched it climb in elevation and finally fly into an open window several floors above.

When George's gaze returned to street level, his delighted grin dropped to a scowl. He turned from side to side futilely trying to recognize his surroundings, searching the crowd for Kelley to no avail. He was well and truly lost.

***

After the briefing, Owens watched the father and son billionaires depart in their hydrocopters. They each used their own, and flew off in opposite directions. Didn't believe in copter-pooling, he concluded. Owens felt the meeting had gone well. He had hoped to introduce them to George, but they had to leave immediately.

Now it was time to deliver the bad news about John to Priya. He arrived at her office door reluctantly. Soon they were seated eye to eye, both knowing the reason he had come to see her. In his hands he held the reader, displaying John's scans no doubt, she thought. Witten had undermined him somewhat in front of the big wigs. So the timing of this meeting with Priya was partly payback for that. He would tell her about how Witten's science was off and that due to her incompetence, Priya had believed John was a better candidate than he was. Still, as much as he loved the idea of dividing Priya and Witten's alliance, he felt genuinely bad about hurting her with this news.

He cleared his throat, but before he could say anything she offered, "If this is about John—"

"It is."

"Well, I've been thinking about it. And, I've decided that I'm going to hold off. Leave him on ice awhile longer, so he has a better chance down the road, once we've worked out the kinks."

She was putting it in the most diplomatic of terms. Owens knew John had no shot at reanimation in his present state of vitrification. He cast his eyes downward processing her words, trying to keep up his poker face. "I think that's the kind thing to do," he said finally. "But what does that mean for you?"

"Not sure exactly. Something different."

"Change is good." He tucked his reader away in his satchel.

"Yeah, maybe it's time for a change, honestly."

Owens saw an opportunity here, where he could kill two birds with one stone. He needed George to start to even out emotionally and he wanted Priya to let go of John on what she felt like were her own terms. "There's something else I wanted to talk to you about. About George."

"What?"

"Witten's right. He can't stay here Priya. … And he can't just go out there, can he? I want the full outpatient program too. And we are going to build it. But I think… he needs the white glove treatment, you know?"

"Absolutely."

"You guys seem to get along and if anything went bad with him, I'd want you to be the first responder. You have a calming effect on him."

"What are you saying, you want me on 24/7 George call, like a buddy system?" she asked.

"Not exactly. What if George went to live with you?"

"What?"

"Not forever," he said with his palms up. "But until we are a little further along then we can relocate him to our transitional housing program. We'll pay off your mortgage of course."

Priya placed both her hands down on her desk, the blood rushing to her face. Paying off her mortgage would be life changing for her. Less stress and more freedom. He was almost making her an offer she couldn't refuse. "You know I live in The Keys right?"

He laughed, "It's not so bad. Just think about it. Maybe it would be good for the both of you."

Just then her cell blew up, it was Kelley. Owens nodded for her to take it.

"What's going on?" she asked into the silicate receiver.

"I messed up," answered Kelley.

Chapter 24

Phone Home

The Cryonicor Cargo pod came careening toward George's last known location. Priya had recruited Jack to help her and Kelley find George, quickly and quietly in hopes of saving Kelley's job. They rode in the back of the self-driving van scanning the streets.

"What if he tells somebody?" he asked.

"I pray we get to him before anyone else does. But mainly I pray we get to him before he needs to be back in the HBC. He has less than two hours, if he can last that long."

"If Kelley gave him the haleys, he should be in good shape until tonight."

The cargo pod stopped and Kelley climbed in. "I'm sorry!" he said in place of a greeting. He held up the looks and a clear bag containing five inhalers.

"Shit," said Jack.

"Let's split up."

Kelley lamented, " Guess I better reschedule my date." He got out of the pod with Priya, and looked up and down the street. "George! Where are you?!"

Priya mused, "If you woke up in a mysterious future, where would you go?"

***

George frantically wandered the streets looking for Kelley. He saw an automated trash gathering machine overflowing with garbage. It was pretty gross. He saw a sign in a restaurant window advertising Non-Vegan options. The city was much more crowded than he remembered. The sidewalks were teaming with legit throngs of people. Suddenly one of the tiny drone aircraft almost clipped him as it flew in front of him into an open shop door. He stammered back bumping into an overly cool couple behind him.

"Wake up man!" said the cool guy.

"I'm sorry, I'm so sorry. Hey, is there any way I could use your phone?"

The guy, noting George's vaguely vagrant vibe, shewed him away. He was humiliated. But he needed someone's help. There was no time for shyness. He saw a kindly looking older woman waiting for a people mover. He approached her gently, "Excuse me ma'am. I don't have my phone and I need to let someone know where I am so they can find me. Is it possible to use your phone?"

The woman shook her head in the negative and spoke to him in a foreign language. He wondered when they would invent the universal translator. Maybe they had, and the lady just leaned on her language barrier to avoid doing favors for derelicts. He walked into another mysteriously empty store and rang the bell. When the attendant arrived, he was beginning to cough slightly. He tried to explain like he had with the lady by the bus. This woman smiled graciously and produced a phone for him to use. He looked at its strange triangular configuration. It was not like the phone Priya had let him borrow. "Could you dial it for me?"

"Of course, what's the number?"

"I don't have the number, maybe you could look it up, it's a company called Cryonicor."

She nodded sweetly and searched up the number. Say what you want about the heat, you couldn't beat the customer service of 2163, he thought. She put it on speaker phone as it rang, not wanting to hand it directly to him. The automated message played, introducing the state of the art services which allow you to vitrify or freeze your recently deceased body so you can be thawed out in the future and restored. Several options were available. "Dial 1 for Full body Freeze. Dial 2 for Head only Freeze." George smiled at the attendant awkwardly as she tried her best to remain composed. Inwardly she was super weirded out. "Dial 3 for Pet Freeze. Dial 4 for Billing."

"—Representative," George blurted out.

"Sorry, I do not recognize that option. Would you like to return to the main menu?"

"Can you try pressing 0?" She did as he asked, but the menu only replayed from the beginning. "Thanks anyway." She nodded and he left. Outside he spied a city map next to a people mover stop. He jogged across the street zig zagging between gridlocked pods. A young man was studying the map as well but paid no mind to George. "You wouldn't know where Cryonicor is, would you?"

The young man responded casually, "Never heard of it. What do they do there?"

"Nevermind." George's lungs were constricting and he was struggling to get enough air. The people mover arrived and after the passengers deboarded, George thought he might ask the driver then he remembered. They were self driving. He ran his fingers anxiously over his scalp and wheezed in and out. He spied a young mother across the street with her little boy. She was rubbing sunscreen on the child's nose, reassuring him.

George flashed back to his childhood. A young George was waiting for the bus. His own mother was crouched next to him sweetly buttoning his jacket. She asked, "What do you do if we ever get separated? Remember, where do you meet me?"

Young George squealed, "Go home!"

Then they said in unison, "701 South Avenue 57 apartment 4!"

George came back to the present moment. He was caught up in his emotions. His mom was a great mom. She was always so loving and supportive. He struggled to escape the overwhelming grief that he had so far managed to keep at bay, at least in the daytime. At night, alone in his room, was another story.

That's what people did before cell phones to keep track of each other, they designated in case you get lost rendezvous points. Then he saw the street sign: Avenue 49. *Wait a minute.* He scanned the intersection, the buildings, the trees, the mountains in the distance. It morphed into a scene of this same intersection from his heyday. The streets, geography and some of the buildings were the same. But the overcrowded mob of people with sun parasols, bare shoulders and linen robes morphed into a memory of fewer people, who were wearing sweaters and hoodies. He may not have known where Cryonicor was, but suddenly he knew where he was.

He took off toward the 50's.

***

Kelley scanned the crowds while Priya focused on her reader.

He said, "If it was me. I would go home."

"Me too. My parent's house to be exact. He grew up in this neighborhood."

"Still, we need like his Mom's address. That kind of thing isn't in the database."

"That's why I logged into Facebook Legacy."

Kelley stopped on a dime and pivoted back to face Priya. "You have a Facebook Legacy login?! And you never told me?! You know what, I'm mad at you."

"Well I'm mad at you for losing George and putting his life at risk like a total Tina. Plus, I just created this account to look at John's social media. I don't really ever use it. I might have looked at George's vacation albums like once - Wait!"

"Find her?"

"Yes! Julie Gilroy, died in 2055. So let's go to her 2019 timeline, look there she posted a photo of them, caption, 'My son came to see me on Mother's day.'"

They looked at the pic on the reader; a healthy George side hugging his sun-kissed mother. They are in her home, in front of a window. Priya zoomed in on the window, to the intersection behind it.

Kelley squinted at the grainy photo, "I know where that is, you keep heading up this way, I'm gonna go down a block and head up that way. Meet you there."

***

Inspector James P. Getty entered the Cryonicor lobby unannounced with his head held high. He told the reception bot that he needed to speak with Dr. Witten or Dr. Owens immediately. Dr. Owens was the first to respond. He strolled up to Getty saying, "Inspector, I thought we talked about calling first."

"I'm here to see George."

Chapter 25

Disavow All Knowledge

On his way to the 50's George noticed something about the other people on the street. At first it was hard for him to pinpoint it, or the lack of it. There were no elderly people. The oldest person he saw seemed like a young seventy, tops. That person could have been 130 for all he knew.

Suddenly, he was stopped by the sight of a curb side memorial for a little girl. He crouched down to take in the tiny tragedy, while the unflinching world buzzed around him. These types of sights had never moved him in the past, they were just bald facts of life that he accepted. But now, he thought about this girl's story, cut short. He cleaned up the litter around the little cross and walked on.

As he walked, he felt the warmth of the sun and the sensations of being alive pressing into his flesh. He heard birds singing and spied a picturesque low hanging branch above the sidewalk. He trotted up to it and jumped as high as he could, swatting the branch. *Got it!* But no sooner had he touched back down on the ground his wheezing began to flair up. His mirthful feelings faded as quickly as they had come on. He noticed a woman across the street take a hit from her leopard print inhaler. Could he ask to borrow one? And what, put his mouth all over it then hand it back? *Gross.* As he walked, coughing harder and harder he realized he probably looked like a skid row junkie or something. Just then he noticed another overflowing trashbot. He spied a discarded inhaler amongst its overspill. He stopped and felt so desperate for relief... that he had no choice. It was either this or mug someone for theirs. So he picked it up, taking care so that no one saw, wiped it with his shirt and tried to take a hit. He got the last flecks of medicine into his lungs by sucking as hard as he could manage. And it did provide some relief, if only temporarily. At that moment he noticed his reflection in the window of an office building. Hunched over a trash mound sucking on a discarded inhaler confirmed his earlier suspicions about his appearance. He reckoned, 2163 may have been hotter than hades, but it was still a cold world.

He pocketed the haley and rounded the corner onto South Avenue 57.

***

Witten had joined Owens in the lobby as they tried to diffuse the Getty situation.

"I don't know anyone by that name," she repeated to the inspector with a straight face.

"You're lying. I know that Owens here is a regenerative specialist and all this money," he motioned to the upgraded facilities, "is coming from somewhere, and it's not showing up on the books you gave me. Which tells me you got another set of books around here somewhere. I'm sure George will be able to fill me in."

"I'm sorry I really don't know who this George person is, or who you think he is, but there is no such person as she said, and since this isn't a scheduled inspection… it's private property and I'm going to have to ask you to leave," said Owens standing up straight with his hands on his hips.

"And what are you going to do about it if I don't," said Getty with his slightly unbalanced ex-military swagger.

"I'll report you to your supervisor for harassment," said Owens. Witten rolled her eyes at this, feeling it was the equivalent to threatening to tell the teacher on a bully. A sure way to get your ass beat in her experience. In truth, this was a tried and true intimidation tactic that Owens had had plenty of success with throughout his yuppie life. Threatening to file a harassment complaint was white privilege 101. But that wouldn't work on Getty, because his boss was his brother-in-law.

"Your days of scamming people are numbered. I know he's here. But okay, if you got nothing to hide, you won't mind if I take a look around would you?"

Witten knew she couldn't refuse him. She let out an exhausted sigh and said, "Go ahead." Getty had been so busy lecturing her during his last inspection he didn't even go into the supplies bay. She was betting he was still more interested in playing the righteous hero than being good at his actual job.

As he stalked the halls of Cryonicor, he took out his reader, trying to recall the Flyguy. But this time it didn't show up on his GPS. He stepped out of a back exit, thinking it might have gotten locked out of the facility. The bug was still MIA. Through the sunbleached haze of the midafternoon, a peculiar clearing in the back corner of the compound caught his eye. He approached it, registering the metal markers in neat even rows. After two decades in the military, he recognized the tell-tale signs; the freshly disturbed ground, the nameless nameplates, the attempt to exert control over the chaos of loss with neat little rows.

He began putting the pieces together. He remembered spying on them from his car that day, and losing them as they walked behind the cover of the auxiliary buildings. One of them had a shovel. Then there was something else, on the early footage he had reviewed. Those same two younger techs had wheeled a gurney into the trash incinerator. He was so busy trying to ear hustle their banal conversation for clues, he had failed to notice that they took a body bag into the trash incineration room and left with the gurney but without the body bag.

He charged back into the facility, and set his sights on Owens who was heading straight for him. The Flyguy bug suddenly appeared on the screen. It seemed to be matching Owen's location, keeping pace with his approach.

Before Getty could say anything, Owens opened his palm to reveal the smashed bug. "Did you lose something?"

The two men never broke eye contact. Owens smirked. But Getty just shrugged his shoulders, "I don't know where you picked up that little piece of gadget trash, but you could never trace it back to me. And we both know that." *Disavow all knowledge.*

"We'll see about that."

"How long have y'all been keeping this little cozy crypt out back? Illegally incinerating and dumping human remains, huh? You know what, I don't even need to talk to George, I got what I came for."

***

George soon arrived at 701 South Avenue 57,

or at least what used to be the fourplex where he'd grown up. It had been a modest rent controlled cluster and his Mom had lived there as long as he could remember. It was a terracotta color with peeling paint and a leaky roof. But the two bedrooms were spacious, and it enjoyed phenomenal natural light from two extra large windows in the open concept living room/kitchen. Though the appliances were out of date his mom kept it excessively neat, and was able to keep it looking current thanks to the solid hardwood floors. He had repainted the interior white a handful of times for her over the years, except the bathroom door way. That was where his mom marked his height during his formative years. That bit she never painted over. She was sentimental like that. Julie was an office manager who never had the money to buy her own house in the city and wasn't about to move back home to Louisiana. She loved LA and she considered that unit her forever home. It was built in the 1960's and was rent controlled. When she first moved in it wasn't a good neighborhood but the price was right. As the years wore on the neighborhood around her improved tremendously and she enjoyed a best of both worlds situation. Now it was gone, replaced by pavement and what looked like a kind of gas station. He didn't see any pumps, only stations that read FAST-CHARGE. He sat down on the curb -- unmoored.

He coughed again as his last tiny hit from

the garbage haley wore off. He retrieved it from his pocket, sucking again but to no avail. Embittered, he threw it down. He needed more. Should he wait for Kelley, how could he know to look for him here? He noticed a pharmacy across the street. He wheezed a few more times.

A hand touched his shoulder. Startled, he looked up to see a young woman with an uncanny resemblance to Alison.

"Are you all right? " said Not Alison.

He popped up from the ground wide-eyed, and nodded mutely. She smiled and walked on, grabbing her boyfriend's hand back. George watched the happy couple walking away. His heart broke in slow motion to the sound of their song that played in his head, "By your Side' by Sade. He had big plans for him and Alison. He had his happy ending locked up tight. She had said yes, he reminded himself. *She had said yes*. But it was all stolen away from him, and he didn't know who to be angry at. He checked in with himself and realized he wasn't angry anymore. He was just sad. He wondered which stage of grief this was... he could never keep them straight.

Coughing violently, he scanned the streets for a bopping platinum blonde. The survival instinct would outweigh his melancholia once again, in a dizzying cycle of emotional and physical agony. Then he reached in his pockets and felt the few bills that Kelley had given him. "Walking around money." He made a B-Line for the pharmacy across the street.

Chapter 26

Thanks for Nothing

George walked into the busy pharmacy. At almost 6'4 he towered above the average customer. His stature combined with his dress earned him some hard stares right away. He noticed self check-outs and a smockie checking receipts as people exited. So far, not so different from what he remembered. He started walking the aisles looking for inhalers, trying to swallow his wheezing and coughing to not draw further attention to himself.

Finally, he found the haley aisle and was surprised to find the selection climbed to the ceiling. They came in innumerable colors and patterns. He selected one and compared the price with the bills he had in his pocket. He was short, by a lot. *Thanks for nothing.* He went searching for the nearest restroom. Now he was audibly wheezing.

The restroom needed a code to enter. He couldn't take it anymore. His lungs felt like they were on fire. He ripped open the packaging and took a hit. Relief.

"You okay?" asked the surprisingly empathetic smockie leaning over him.

But he was not okay. Though the medicine helped him breathe easier, overall he was hurting. His headachc had returned with a vengeance. He needed to get to the HBC. He nodded his head anyway, signaling he was fine.

"Good, c'mon let's go pay ki."

The smockie escorted George to the checkout area, where he stood in the line and watched people paying for goods with their watches, phones and occasional cash. Then his ankle bracelet alarm went off, the light was green. He knew he had five minutes.

"Can I use your bathroom?" he asked the smockie, as he was walking away.

"It's out of order."

As he got closer and closer to the terminal he was pondering his very limited choices. He could pretend to not realize he didn't have enough money, and maybe someone else would spot him. But he couldn't count on that. If they didn't at best they would make him leave the haley and he would be out on the streets again with no medicine and no idea if he would be found before he suffocated. At worst, they might call the cops. There was another option of course, one he would normally never consider. But Alison had pegged him with her little astrological birth chart. He had strong convictions… loosely held. He could circumvent his principles if properly motivated. He was at peace with his decision, given his current circumstances. He took another hit and charged the smockie, ricocheting off of him like a running back, spinning out into the street.

The smockie landed on his ass. "Oh my god! Did that happen?!"

***

Getty waited for Owens to return with Witten. He was stashed in George's original recovery room and looked around it with interest. He observed the hospital bed and some second hand equipment for monitoring vital signs. He saw specks of dried purple liquid near an I.V. stand. Perhaps this was a room where patients from their hospice wing were … made comfortable in the moments before their expiration? Then what was with the cameras?

Upstairs in HQ, Owens had diverted the feed from George's current quarters to the original recovery room. He and Witten watched Getty snooping around the room. Gwen joined them, not wanting to intrude but being very interested in the crisis at hand.

"You and your sentimental crap! I should have ripped that crazy cemetery out the first day I got here."

Witten shot a slightly embarrassed look to Gwen who simply stared straight on at the monitors pretending to be invisible. "It's not.. I mean they aren't even marked, how could he know? I never thought—"

"On it's own he probably wouldn't have figured it out to be fair. But he had a spy." Gwen and Witten's jaws both fell to the floor. Someone working there betrayed their confidence? *Who*?! That was when Owens opened the palm of his hand revealing a mangled FlyGuy.

"What the hell? You knew about this?" They leaned in to inspect it closely.

"I neutralized the threat as soon as I discovered it." Owens could lie as well as Witten.

"Still, I should have been informed."

"So you could do what exactly? You had enough on your hands. But whatever footage he may have gotten he doesn't seem to have the full picture."

"He is asking for George though," Gwen reminded them.

"But he doesn't know who George is exactly. He only has bits and pieces it seems. Plus, he clearly doesn't know George is a thaw because he is still reading us the riot act."

Witten's eyes lit up, "You're right!"

"I am?" asked Owens, taken aback by her agreeableness.

"What is Getty's problem?"

"He hates us."

"No. He thinks we are scamming people."

"She's right. In his mind, everything he's doing is virtuous. So his means, though illegal, are justified. It's a hero complex, I've seen this pathology from time to time in combat vets, their PTSD manifests... in an unusual way. I wouldn't be surprised if he was ex-military," noted Gwen. Witten and Owens shrugged.

"So?" Owens asked Witten.

"Hear me out here. What if we come clean to him?"

"Are you out of your mind?"

"Listen, if we can prove to him that we've achieved a successful reanimation, then we're not liars and charlatans anymore."

Gwen gestured with her eureka finger. "A morality paradigm shift. Bad guys become underdog good guys."

"It's pretty risky."

"He's got us dead to rights with the body burning. If he leaves here we'll have an hour tops before they bring the canines in to confirm his theory and shut us down. Then they're gonna find out about George anyway."

The three of them looked at each other with uncertainty.

Moments later Dr. Owens and Witten returned to the recovery room. Getty bolted up from his stool. "I don't appreciate being kept waiting, and I don't know what it is you think you could possibly say to me to convince me not to report what I've seen here."

Owens began, "What if we could prove to you that cryonic reanimation can be realized." Getty arched his eyebrow. He continued, "That it's not a scam, that it is an actual medical reality... "

"How you gonna do that? You admit in your brochures that you've never brought anyone back."

Witten stepped up to him and said in a barely tolerating tone, "Do you still want to meet George?"

***

Meanwhile, Jack was in the back of the cargo pod, scanning every side street and alley for unusually tall men. Suddenly, up ahead he glimpsed the back of the head of a man running or jogging or something. He was tall and he had salt and pepper hair.

"Stop!" shouted Jack at the cargo pod. It pulled over smoothly and the door swooshed open. Jack jumped out and sprinted toward the jogger. He quickly overtook him, grabbed his shoulders and spun him around.

"George Stop!" He pulled the oxy pac mask off the man's face. It wasn't George. Just a leggy startled guy out for a run.

"I'm sorry," said Jack stammering back toward the cargo pod.

***

Priya arrived before Kelley at the intersection where George's mother's apartment should have been. Again she examined the picture on her reader to get her bearings. She was baffled and disappointed by the gas station. She didn't see George anywhere. Kelley rounded the opposite corner in a light jog, he shook his head indicating he'd had no luck.

"Anything?" he asked, panting.

"No." Priya took a hit off her own haley. "Air's bad today."

Kelley took a hit as well. "Yeah, it's special."

"He's probably already experiencing severe respiratory distress. He needs to get to an HBC stat."

Kelley squatted down noticing a discarded inhaler on the street, he picked it up.

"Ew, don't touch that," said mom-Priya as she swatted it out of his hand into traffic.

"Why is it just laying out here in the street when there are trashbots everywhere?"

Their suspicion grew and Priya noticed the pharmacy across the street as peace troopers pulled up outside and went in. "He needs an inhaler, I taught him how to use one," she said, talking mostly to herself.

"You don't think that's about him do you?" Without another word between them, the two jay walked over to the buzzing pharmacy. They entered it mid-commotion. A peace trooper was taking a statement from the unlucky smockie.

"He had on a pair of old work out shorts, flip flops and a shirt like a doctor or a nurse wears.. And he was really tall," testified the smockie.

Overhearing this, Priya and Kelley headed right back out, their heart rate quickening as the adrenaline surged. They scanned the street in both directions. No George. Which way should they go? What if the peace troopers find him first? "George, George!" she called out, hoping he was still in ear shot. Both their watches went off with messages to call into work 911. Then a call came in on her cell. It was Cryonicor. Kelley signaled reluctantly to pick it up.

"Where are you? And where the hell is George?" Witten, Owens and Getty were standing in George's empty quarters, as the sun began setting on SANI.

Chapter 27

R.I.P.

Getty stood arms crossed, shaking his head in disgust. "How convenient."

Owens retorted, "He was just here. You think we build this entire suite for us to use on the weekends?"

"How should I know? Maybe this is all part of the sales pitch, 'imagine yourself waking up in a luxe penthouse in the sky, all your needs attended to..' I admit you guys go all out to swindle people."

Owens looked to Witten for help here, but she was distracted. "We have to find him. If he doesn't get back to the HBC—" she stopped herself, eyeing Getty.

"Enough theatrics," said the inspector. "I've got a report and an injunction to file." He started toward the exit.

"Just wait," said Owens, loudly talking over him without breaking Witten's gaze. "What do you want to do?"

She was pacing the room, brows furrowed searching for the answer. "He was scheduled to get chipped this afternoon, you were right Eli, we should have chipped him day one." She shook her head angry at herself. Dr. Owens noted this was the first time she had called him by his christian name. Then she snapped her fingers triumphantly. "His ankle bracelet! The device to regulate his timed eliminations. It pairs with his watch, and Priya and I have the app on our readers."

"But can you use that to geolocate him?"

"You can if you know what you're doing."

***

George panted furiously in an alleyway after narrowly managing to evade the peace troopers. He took another needed hit off the stolen inhaler, but the medicine was less and less effective. It was because he had spent too much time outside of the HBC already. Nitrogen bubbles were re-forming in his veins as he stood there.

That's when he looked down and realized he had pissed himself during the escapade with the haley. He looked out onto the street nervously as the sun set, no sign of Kelley and no clue where he was. All he saw was the strangeness of the world. He was more than uncertain, he was afraid. Standing there in his own urine soaked oversized shorts, he began to consider his quality of life. His thoughts returned to the question of whether a life like this was worth living at all. He was incontinent, like a helpless old man. He was virtually penniless and would depend on the kindness of Cryonicor for anything from a pod of his own down to a stick of gum. He didn't even have his name, his identity. And of course, lest he forget, he had no loved ones left alive. Even Priya, who he did care for, only wanted to be friends. Sounded like another round of torture.

Again, he beat himself up for the foolish choice he had made back in 2021. If he had just been a man and died like everyone else he wouldn't be in this position. Feeling like a foreign elderly, helpless, idiot. He only had himself to blame. He had been too chicken shit to face up to his own mortality.

But that was before he knew better. He had been sold some bill of goods no doubt, about waking up perfectly healthy in the prime of his life in an idealized utopian future. The devil you know, is better than the devil you don't, as they say. He made a choice with the limited information he had. He knew there was no afterlife, as he had suspected or else he was sure he would remember being there and being pulled back out of it. There was no expression of time or existence beyond our realm. And he found that to be a comfort. And now he knew unequivocally what this life held for him. A life spent hiding, trembling in fear like a cockroach waiting to be discovered in the wrong place. As his freedoms expanded he would get curious and maybe comfortable, used to it even, like Tennyson had become. That is, until a certain day would come when he wouldn't make it back to the HBC in time and he would die a slow horrible death.

A people mover approached a crowd who'd gathered next to the alley where he was lurking. From his position, hidden in shadow, he had a clear view of it all. He tilted his head as he read the smart glass windshield display - #75 - DT SANI. He squinted his eyes across the street and spotted another #75 approaching from the opposite direction, it's destination read: BEACH. He recognized this, though it took him a few extra moments to place it. Had it been in one of his dreams? Or in a story someone else told him? No. It was from that first night, when he had stopped on the road to evade his captors, he must have still been very close to the facility, and that was where he saw his first people mover - #75. That must be the bus to Cryonicor. But even if he did get on the bus heading toward downtown on the North Island, where would he get off? What would his stop be? He slowly emerged from the shadows to look at the route's map posted near the bus stop. He scanned them to see if he recognized something, anything... One stop stood out to him, Ettinger St. He knew that name from somewhere but he couldn't put his finger on it.

He reached into his pockets and he still had his cash. Maybe it wasn't enough for a haley, but surely it would do for a bus ride. He was in pain and he reeked. Slowly stepping into the crowd, trembling, he thought about his many fumbles thus far and how he didn't want to make the same mistake twice. Of course he was afraid, but he felt he had no choice. So he boarded the bus... to the beach.

***

In HQ Witten was furiously trying to hack the ankle bracelet's functionality code. Gwen had never truly seen Witten in action before. She had to admit it was a turn on. It was like rediscovering her wife through the eyes of a stranger. But she was supposed to be getting over Sam, not crushing on her. Gwen had to remind herself why she left Witten in the first place: she was a lying sociopath.

"Got it! This won't give us the same accuracy as a chip, but it should give us a reasonable search radius." In only a few more strokes Witten had a map on the wall reader, with a blinking red dot moving fast down one of the island's main thoroughfares.

"He's moving fast. He's on a vehicle," noted Gwen.

"He's heading toward The Comptons," clarified Dr. Owens. "What in the hell?"

Getty was sequestered for the moment in

an alcove around the corner watching George's highlights from the surveillance footage. It kept the skeptical inspector busy while the doctors quickly informed their team on the ground of George's heading.

Jack had picked up Kelley and Priya. They were rerouting to Compton Beach to intercept George, but they were in a monster traffic jam. The Comptons was a nice part of town. But it wasn't a surf beach, the underwater landscape was too jagged as a result of the quakes. However the gulf had become the home to a new spectacular kelp forest, whose teaming wildlife rivaled those of the Channel Islands. The sunken homes, roadways and landmarks also attracted divers for its haunting museum-like seascapes. It was a favorite spot of local free divers and scuba scavengers alike.

As Owens received Jack's reported progress, he watched them gaining on the lumbering people mover blinking on the screen. Meanwhile Witten's eyes cut to her soon to be ex-wife who was scanning George's database entry for any clue that could help them. In this leaned over position her back was gracefully arched like a leopard. Half in shadow, the light folded around her royal profile giving it a kind of golden lining. Witten caught herself admiring her wife's intellect as well as her form and thought of the re-up papers in her desk drawer for a moment. Was it merely coincidence that had brought them face to face tonight of all nights? She chided herself for letting her thoughts wander off the immediate mission. She loathed her sentimental side. Gwen's presence was already proving to be a big fat distraction. *What was Owen's thinking bringing her here?*

George deboarded in front of the main pier at Compton Beach. The disembarking passengers held their noses as they pushed past him disgusted. He had spent the bus ride steeling himself for the task at hand and was as close to numb as he had ever gotten. The sea held little interest for him especially after he almost drowned on his thirtieth birthday. As a bonafide city boy, he had avoided nature most of his life. He preferred the ground steady and mostly flat under his feet. Never was a big risk taker as Alison loved to point out. He looked out over the sea and could tell through the waning daylight that the water was choppy and the shore was rather rocky, not like the Santa Monica beach he remembered. To his left he noticed a cliffside jutting out over the waves. It was fenced off so no one was up there. He made his way toward it, hopped the fence and began scrambling to the top. *Better get on with it then.*

Meanwhile in HQ, Owens had returned from checking on Getty who was claiming that the footage was faked, some actor pretending to be thawed. "I bought us a few more minutes, but that's it, this asshole is about to walk," said the doctor. He sensed the tension between the Wittens. But he wasn't sure if it was a good tension or a bad tension. "How long have you guys been married?" he asked awkwardly. They both glared at him and remained silent. He held his hands up in surrender and went back to check on Getty again.

"What are you doing here?" asked Witten, keeping her eyes on the vital readings coming from George's bracelet.

"Same thing you are, trying to change the world. It's a once in ten-lifetimes opportunity. I couldn't turn it down."

"Hmmm," she tightened her lips and nodded sarcastically. "Maybe you should have run it by me?"

"Like you run everything you do by me?" Checkmate.

Witten was getting more agitated as the vital stats poured in. "Look at his heart rate, his perspiration, his oxygen saturation is almost down to 80%, even if I could get him back in ten minutes I might have to put him on a ventilator." She picked up the phone and called Jack, "When you do get there, he's gonna be in bad shape, look for someone crawling on the floor or maybe passed out. He looks like he's somewhere by the pier."

At the top of the cliff, just beyond the board-walk, George looked down cautiously over the edge to the crashing waves below. It looked rather unforgiving. He wheezed as he stripped down to nothing but his ankle bracelet. It was magic hour. He noticed there were some folks in the water, snorkeling or free diving, not many but a few. They all wore wetsuits. The water would be freezing, especially this time of year. Of all the ways to die, drowning ranked among the worst of the worst in his book. But he'd heard that when people jump off bridges, it's the fall that usually kills them. They break their necks on impact. That's what he was counting on. A quick, clean, instant death. Instant relief. Instant freedom. If he ran hard enough he could hurl himself past the rocks and land squarely in the water. He reckoned it was easily a hundred foot jump, give or take. He could feel himself starting to lose his nerve as the seconds ticked by. He knew if he delayed any longer he would chicken out, as he had back in 2021. So he assumed his stance, and instead of counting to three, he recited the letters R.I.P. and ran full speed launching himself head first off the cliff, plummeting into the sea below.

Chapter 28

High Tide

At HQ, Witten watched the blinking red dot at the center of the twenty foot radius near the beach disappear and then reappear suddenly out in the water. "What just happened?!" Gwen and Ownes rushed to join her at the reader wall.

"His vitals stopped," noted Owens. The data display for his heart rate etc had all zeroed out.

Gwen looked between the two MD's curiously, "What does that mean?"

Witten tried to rationalize a way out of the obvious. If she said it out loud, it was real. She looked to Owens for help, for some alternative possibility.

But he had none for her. "It means there are no vitals to read. His heart stopped, he's gone."

"Instantly? I thought death was a process?" asked Gwen, parroting what her wife had often repeated over the years.

"Maybe there was a delay in reporting the vitals?" hypothesized Owens.

"Maybe he went for a swim, and it got wet?" asked Gwen hopefully.

"No, the unit is waterproof, designed to be worn in the shower or bath if needed."

"Its geoposition coordinates look like it's still moving but I don't see it going anywhere," noted Owens, his head tilted in confusion.

Witten said, "That's because this image is 2D, he's not moving east or west, he's changing elevation. He's sinking to the bottom."

***

George's body plunged into the icy water. The brunt force of the impact broke his ankle, and busted off the monitor in the process. The fall did not kill him or break his neck as he'd hoped and he immediately panicked. He spun around underwater as the waves held him down. He wanted to give up and just get the damn drowning over with. He tried to stop struggling and went limp, letting the ocean do its will. Alison had often counseled, "catastrophe is only as bad as you let it make you feel." Maybe it would be less horrifying if he just accepted it.

He saw the underwater world begin to reveal itself through the silt. The seaweed forest was dense and thick. The towers of kelp danced around him, illuminated by the last vestiges of daylight above. Schools of colorful fish passed him unaffected by his struggle. For a fleeting moment he was at peace, the pain numbed by the cold waters. The sound of the busy world ceased and all was quiet, as if time itself was frozen, and he could just exist. In this antigravity space he felt at one with himself and with the world around him. The sensation of living pressed down on him as he felt every inch in contact with the environment. He wished he was a fish and could live there all the time, but then he would get used to that too and the anxieties of life would set in once again. This was beautiful because it was temporary.

His insides ached for breath. The fear returned and the adrenaline surge compelled him to surface despite his unwillingness to live. He swam up with a fury, but his bad leg was caught in a winding kelp branch. His vision was blurring and his head was exploding. He didn't think, he just pulled and pulled. The thought of death as a serene timeless non-existence didn't feel quite as comforting anymore. This wasn't working. He needed a new plan. Be. Here. Now. Step one: calm down. Step two: reach down to that ankle and feel for the kelp. Step three: unwrap the branch. And he was free. He quickly surfaced and took three deep life saving breaths before a wave came crashing down holding him under once again. In that moment, he was absolutely clear about why he had chosen to freeze himself in the first place.

There is no preparing yourself for your date with the dark river. How could you judge yourself or anyone else for reaching up for a hand to save them, even if they had no reason to believe anyone was there? As soon as he could surface again he found himself screaming for help.

A diver, done for the day, was lugging his extra long freediving fins out of the water when he heard a call for help and turned back, scanning the water for its source. Soon he spotted George just past the reef flailing. The freediver shouted up to those at the top of the stairs, on the boardwalk, to get help. There was no lifeguard station at this beach, it was 'swim at your own risk.' The man high-stepped it back into the water and dove in. He was an excellent swimmer and reached George in a flash. Another wave was coming. "Hold your breath and dive under it with me. Hold on!" he instructed George, who nodded and grabbed onto the freediver's utility belt. They ducked and dived through a set of waves out of the chop. George had nothing on and got a little cut up by the rocks. Once they were clear of the waves, the freediver put him in a lifeguard hold and pulled him into the beach the rest of the way.

On the rocky beach, George vomited the sea water he had swallowed and rolled over into a fetal position going into shock. He had no more water inside him but was still dry heaving. His face was beat red and he was trembling violently.

The freediver tried speaking to him, "You're okay, you're okay. What are you doing without any clothes on out in this freezing water ki? Are you nuts?" He noticed some scraps of seaweed around his ankle. "Ah, the kelp tried to keep you huh? She's greedy." He rubbed George's back trying to reassure him. "Maybe we should get a medic to check ya out, ki?"

George had the awareness to look around and see the lights of an ambulance parked on the boardwalk above. Two paramedics were scrambling down a long wooden staircase leading from the pier to the rocky beach. He clearly remembered Witten's warning. If officials find out, he could be turned into some kind of government experiment. No hospitals. No ambulances. The friendly diver removed his flashlight from his belt and looked George up and down for any further injuries. He saw the bloody lacerations along his legs and angled his head. George clocked his change in expression. The paramedics were nearing the bottom of the staircase. If they took him to the hospital he was done for.

As George quickly got to his feet, the diver warned, "I don't think you should get up just yet, let them take a look at you, ki."

George stammered backward, thanked the diver and started running down the beach in the opposite direction of the medics. Running barefoot with a busted ankle on the sand and rock wasn't easy. But luckily the medics were slowed down by their bulky boots. His head start gave him enough separation to make a go of it. Even though he was depleted from his near drowning his physical conditioning gave him a shot in hell. Ahead he saw another staircase, but a giant rock formation blocked the far section of the beach. He looked back and saw the bouncing flashlights of the paramedics gaining on him. It reminded him of his first night back, running from Priya and Kelley. He had a choice, he could let them take him or he could go back into the water and try to swim around the rock. He didn't know which option was worse.

***

The traffic jam was finally letting up and the cargo pod was really starting to move. The automated voice over the speaker said, "Nearing destination: Compton Beach." Another call came in from HQ, this time to Priya. Witten gave her the bad news. Their mission was now to do what they could to recover... the body. It would be a mess if the authorities found it first. They would try to identify him, and an autopsy would reveal all his organs were cloned and his blood was synthetic. It would send red flags up across the board and they couldn't have that.

After the call ended, the cryonicists rode with their bobbing heads down and their hearts in their stomachs. In their line of work they were no strangers to icy corpses, but they had never imagined fishing one out of the pacific. No one said a word. They each felt terrible, felt somehow responsible in their own way. He was gone, just like that. No more George. They knew how preservation worked, by the time they reached him, if they reached him, it would be past the critical window, leaving him no chance at reanimation. They were all asking themselves the same question, did he fall or did he jump?

Kelley obviously had brought him out of Cryonicor and foolishly lost track of him while buying condoms. He believed himself fully at fault. Jack and Priya suspected deep down that his accident... wasn't an accident, but perhaps a desperate act. A reaction to either unbearable physical or emotional distress. The latter would have meant that Jack had failed miserably to counsel him when he had the chance. He felt unqualified yet he rolled the dice and play-acted his way through it, and this was the result of his hubris. And Priya had rejected him hadn't she? Sure it wasn't about her in the big scheme of things, but had she done all she could for him?

***

George stared down the fading eastward horizon, he could see the mainland in the distance. He wasn't going to let the paramedics take him. He took a deep breath and dove back into the frigid waters. He was getting pretty cut up as the waves repeatedly slammed him against the rock face. But, he moved himself, good grip by good grip around the tiny cape. Slowly, the stairway returned to his view. He was afraid he was being followed by the paramedics and he needed to lose them. He noticed the entrance to a sea cave on the outermost edge of the rock. Centuries of crashing waves had worn a divot into the side of the monstrous boulder. On pure instinct he ducked inside. A startled pelican brushed up against him as it flew out. It was dark and he was waist deep in ice water. The bottom was covered in algae. Magic hour was over and the last shreds of purply orange daylight were disappearing, as the cave was quickly filling with water. That's when he realized he had made another error in judgement, it was high tide.

***

Witten leaned into the facial scanner and the doors to Tennnyson's clean room whooshed open. Now that George was lost at sea, they only had one other way to prove that reanimation was possible. Witten knew it was a long shot, but she had built a career on long shots.

Tennyson was delighted to get a visitor, his first since the early morning. The trio approached the bed. Getty was visibly disturbed by the ghastly state of Tennyson's condition. He was frail and withered. The computer voice activated, "My name is Tennyson, what's yours?"

Getty was unnerved by the synthetic voice. Quick glances at the MD's signaled him to answer. "I'm inspe-, I'm Jim. I'm with Dr. Witten here and I'd like to... I guess, ask you a few questions if that's okay?"

"I was never that good at tests."

"I'll go easy on you. When were you born?"

"March 3rd, 1986."

Getty rolled his eyes. "Really? Okay, who was the president the year you were born?"

"Ronald Reagan, hey I'm on a roll. LOL."

Getty pulled up a stool. "What year did you graduate high school?"

"Class of '05"

Getty did the math in his head. *Hmmm.* "You married? Have any kids?"

"I was married briefly, to a lady named Saundra. Lasted almost five years. Never had any kids that I know of."

"What religion are you?"

"Card carrying non-believer."

"And you're telling me, you arranged to have your body frozen, died, and you what... came back to life?"

"Well yeah. I was pushing ninety two and I was decaying as you do, but I was lucky in that I had my mind still. But I was also unlucky in a way because I was really facing down my bitter end, and to tell you the truth, I was kinda jealous of my friends who had dementia. Because they had no idea what was going on, you know. It was almost a blessing I had figured. I had been aware of cryonics since I was in my forties and some big time tech wizards had openly signed up for it. I decided what the heck. Lucky I did too, because within a year, I was on my deathbed. Cancer. But knowing I was signed up, made that a little easier too. Still scary as shit mind you."

"What happened after that Tennyson?"

"You're looking at it. These people brought me out of the deep freeze, they tell me I'm the first one, not to brag but, I think that's pretty cool."

"So what exactly is wrong with you now, I mean if this worked, why are you in this bed like this?"

"I really prefer not to focus on the negative, but basically they weren't able to, like, reconnect my nervous system in a way. Some sciency stuff, whatever. So I'm a quadrapaligic. I can't move my arms or legs or anything really below the nose. So I can't speak with my vocal chords."

"What's the plan for you?"

"This is it. I'm just going to pass the rest of my days right here in this bed. But it's not so bad really. It's an adventure in a way. I'm stranded here and I've got to figure out how to get by and make the most of it. I'm working through some pretty intense philosophy at the moment, if Ms. Cayhill will hurry up with those books I requested. Really rewarding stuff. And I am hopeful yet, even if they don't crack this nervous system problem this time, by next go around I think they'll have gotten much better at this and I'll be walking around chasing women again."

"Next go around?"

"Yeah when I die eventually and go back into the freezer, and they pull me out again."

"Okaaaaay… and how long have you been… like this?"

"They brought me out in 2158."

"How do you eat?"

"I don't get to eat, you know that's really what I miss most. I get my vitamins through an I.V."

"How do you go to the bathroom and stuff?"

"Well that's a little personal don't you think Jim?"

Getty was on the edge of his stool, he surveyed the room, the piles of books and the odd machine that turned their pages. Most of all he observed the man in the bed, a poor, duped, freak of nature, isolated in some macabre medical dungeon. The loneliness was palpable. Never in all his years of ground combat had he beheld a more disturbing sight.

***

The water was rapidly filling up the tiny sea cave. George waited for the medics to pass by. But they didn't come. He reasoned that they wisely decided against entering the water to chase after him. He was shaking with the onset of hypothermia. He was going to have to dive back out into the water, directly into the crashing waves. Once the cave filled up with water, he feared he would not be able to get back out again, and he would drown. He imagined plunging himself back into the chaotic ocean, being held under by the waves, struggling. He imagined the sharp pain of being slammed against the rocks by the force of the relentless tide.

He pulled himself together with his mantra. Be. Here. Now. The truth was every second he stood by, his chances of survival diminished. The time to panic was over. He moved himself to the mouth of the cave just as a large wave was about to break onto the cliffside. He ducked back inside in time to miss the burst of water flooding the cave. He was now chest deep. As the tide receded he counted down until the water once again exploded into the cave. Six Mississippis, that's how much time he would have.

As soon as the wave began receding he dove out of the cave into the gulf. He paddled out as hard as he could. As the waves came toward him he remembered his diver friend's technique. Duck and dive. This kept him from being held under against his will, but the tide was so strong that inevitably he was slammed back against the rocks. It was violent. He was cut up badly, bleeding all over now. He no longer planned to make it to the stairs, he was naked and covered in blood. It was almost totally dark out, no one could see him, if he could just get to safety. Though he was suffering from the lacerations, he knew from his recent experience... he could take it. So he grabbed onto the rocks tightly and pulled himself along their side until a foothold appeared. Using his substantial upper body strength and his one good leg he hauled himself up out of the water and scurried to the top of the cliff.

Exhausted and freezing, he realized this was the ledge he had lept from. He was able to locate his clothes. Relieved he put them back on and found the haley in his pocket. He took a hit and sat on top of the cliff, teeth chattering. He looked out over the horizon again, beholding the wondrous light of the early evening. It was the most beautiful night sky he'd ever seen in his life. His heart soared with gratitude to be alive and he relished the imperfect air of 2163.

Chapter 29

Poster Boy

They left the cargo pod under a streetlight next to the boardwalk. Priya, Kelley and Jack began scouring the area with their flashlights. Though they were looking for him, the prospect of actually finding his dead body terrified them. They reluctantly descended the stairs.

Back at Cryonicor, Getty, now convinced that they had reanimated someone, wanted to see where and how they did it. So Owens and Witten led him through the hidden entry to the reanimation chamber. Inwardly, Getty was a tad disappointed with his skills as an inspector. He recognized some of the interior chamber from the drone footage, but had assumed it was a room designed for head dismemberment: part of the neuro-preservation process. He couldn't understand the purpose of their reanimation accouterments even as they explained them, but he did understand the bone saws and scalpels.

As they walked him out Owens asked him, "Do you have any questions?"

"I think I've seen all I need to make a determination."

"And what's that?" asked Witten, getting to the point.

"You think by showing me that man in there, it will convince me that your scam is actually legit, and that will dissipate the venom I have for you. But the problem is, Tennyson's life, however miraculous it may be, is hardly what you advertise." In the lobby he picked up a brochure and pointed to sketches of happy reunited families and healthy younger looking people. He continued, "I don't see the quadriplegics in here, maybe I missed it? Now you say you have another specimen, one who walks and talks and everything. But you can't find him. He went to the beach."

Witten and Owens exchanged a tense glance. They felt no need to share the news of George's tragic fate. Owens pleaded, "He was real, is real, those videos aren't staged, and you saw his charts, his MRI's, his body scans and x-rays since he was thawed—"

"Even if it was true, in the footage I did see of him, he's tearing his room apart, suffering from all kinds of unending medical problems, and seems to feel that this was done to him against his will… you see where I'm going with this?"

Witten rushed to say, "We're just getting started though, you have to allow time to work this all out. I am in here doing it basically by myself. The nature of science is to experiment and to fail, it's trial and error. But if you stop the research then no one makes any progress and we never get to that!" She pointed to the happy people in the brochure.

Getty shook his head in disagreement. "You have no oversight! You're like Dr. Frankenstein, just creating monsters out of your own twisted ambition. I don't care how pure you think your intentions are, you are playing god down here and he clearly doesn't like it or you wouldn't have a graveyard of failures out back or that pitiable freak in your basement."

"But you heard him, he's not suffering, he's happy to be alive, even as he is!"

"I *will* be reporting you for illegal incineration, dumping, and reanimation of human remains. I feel no moral quandary about this. Sometimes people don't know what's best for them, that's why governments exist, to make sure they don't do anything stupid. And if you are telling the truth about George, it sounds like he would agree with me. He'd be better off dead."

The cryonicists' jaws dropped, Getty turned around to see what they were looking at. Jack and Kelley were dragging George through the door. He was beat up pretty good, but not only was he alive, he was smiling.

Priya, pulling up the rear, shouted over the guys, "We need a gurney!" Getty stepped aside as the team burst into action. They wheeled George to the freight elevator and into his luxe quarters where the HBC was being prepared. He moved himself from the gurney into the unit, without any instruction or back talk.

Witten said to him, "It's good to have you back George."

"It's good to be back doc." He winked at her, laid down and sealed himself inside.

***

While George recovered in the HBC, Kelley kept Getty busy with a presentation of the database. George's cryo-records showed his cryostat's provenance from the now defunct company he had originally used for preservation down the chain of custody to Cryonicor, a hundred and fifty years later. He also showed Getty George's FB Legacy page to further confirm his identity. The videos of him from the early aughts were beyond compelling, his hairstyles, dress, and even way of speaking were clearly from another time. Despite the mounting evidence, Getty struggled with his suspicion that it was all somehow a deep fake.

Down the hall, Priya and Jack caught the rest of the team up on what happened at the beach. They searched for a while, but when it got too dark they returned to the cargo pod ready to give up for the night. They found George passed out on the ground right in front of it. "We gave him emergency first aid in the pod on the way back and he came to. He told us he spotted the van under the streetlight from the top of a nearby cliff. But he passed out while he waited for us. He's lucky to be alive. And now I think he finally knows that."

***

A few hours later, George was out of the HBC, showered and getting a physical from Witten in his quarters. Gwen joined them with Kelley's bag of looks.

"How do you feel?" George said, mocking Dr. Witten.

"Very funny. Headache?"

He shook his head no and greeted Gwen, "You again? Finally, I've been wondering where you were, I'm sorry, what is your name again?"

"Dr. Kim, but you can call me Gwen. I believe these are yours," she said, handing him the bag of clothes and haleys.

"Sweet! Uh, I'm George. But you know that already," he was really charming. He pulled a pair of boxer briefs out of the bag triumphantly, "Yes! Undies!" He unboxed the remaining items with the zeal of a kid excited to wear their first day of school outfit. Gwen and Witten were loving his new upbeat attitude. Witten wondered if his walkabout had unearthed his original personality, that had been buried under the bitterness, grief, and pain. "Do you guys mind?" he asked, holding up the clothes. They shook their heads no and encouraged him to change. They hadn't expected him to be so naked under what he was wearing, they quickly averted their eyes.

"You seem in much better spirits than the last time we met," said Gwen.

"I think I've gotten some clarity for sure. Do you like it?" He checked himself out in the mirror. They nodded approvingly. In his extra wide legged linen pants and bamboo knit wide collar tee, he looked indistinguishable from the rest of the citizenry. He continued, "But there are some things that I need and these are non-negotiable." The Wittens looked at each other and nodded for him to go on. "First of all, I do not consent to being chipped. It is my choice and I have made it. Got it?"

"But George, look what happened to you today?" pleaded Witten.

"That brings me to the second thing. You will give me a cell phone. Tomorrow. So if you need me, or you're worried about me, you can call me... just like anybody else. I'm not going to disappear on you, I get that I need you. But I can't be on a leash, I'm not a pet, I'm a fucking human being and this has to be on my terms." He was firm, but not angry or emotional.

"Okay, is that all?" asked Gwen. Witten was pretty irritated that Gwen was telling him 'okay' about any of this, but she would just have to get used to working on a team. At least she respected Gwen, and maybe even Owens to a point these days.

"No, that's not all. This last one is the big one, so brace yourselves ladies." They couldn't help but chuckle at his cheeky side. He continued, "I want to move out. No more cameras. I'll come back as often as you need, maybe even once every couple of days, but I want to live independently, no more Cryonicor cruise ship."

Witten offered, "Well, we do have plans for an outpatient program. We're planning on either building or buying housing and arranging for monthly allowances..."

"That's right," added Gwen enthusiastically, "and we're going to be developing a full complement of both physio and mental health care. There will be support groups, modern history classes, job training and—"

"And how long is that going to take to build?"

"It's hard to say... it could be a year or two once we've gotten more patients out like you we can really—"

"No. That's not good enough. Maybe that'll be okay for them, but not for me. I need a tight timeline to get outta here."

Witten stammered on, "It's just gonna be hard to..."

"Doc, it's not up for discussion. You figured out how to bring people back from the dead. I think you can figure this out for me." Witten's watch went off, it was Owens requesting her presence in HQ. She excused herself.

When she arrived, Owens motioned her to sidebar with him in an alcove away from the others. "Getty wants to talk to George, alone."

"I don't like it," she said after a moment.

"Me neither." Owens craned his neck around to see if Getty was in earshot. "But he's still here, means he hasn't made up his mind yet."

"We know he's convinced the program is legit."

"He knows we've reanimated people, but I think he's still trying to sort out if that's a good thing or a bad thing. If he talks to George, and George's the—"

"—The poster boy you want him to be?" she said mockingly. But as soon as the words escaped her mouth, she understood why he had been pushing so hard for it. He patiently held her stare long enough for her to fully process it. As long as they operated outside the lines, they were vulnerable. They would need testimony to defend them. The law could be bent and broken and recast again around a good story. George's camera ready makeover couldn't come soon enough.

He shrugged his shoulders, graciously skipping the I-told-you-so's. "Sure, he seems to have had some kind of change of heart out there. He's not all doom and gloom and hunger strikes. But is it just the euphoria of escaping a near death experience? Will he be able to stand up to Getty's ethical battering ram... by himself?"

They both knew that no matter how valid their concerns were, they had no choice. It would all come down to how their subject felt about the program. It was the ultimate customer satisfaction survey. Witten nodded her reluctant permission.

"I can't wait for this to be over, one way or the other," said Owens nervously running his fingers through his black hair.

"Let me just talk to him first."

"No. Getty said we can't prep him. No leading the witness or some crap. He's going in hot."

Minutes later, Gwen was recalled to HQ. The team gathered around the monitors to watch the interrogation.

Another light over George's door announced a visitor. Normally he was happy to receive guests, but it was already the middle of the night and he was pretty beat. Enough was enough already. Unless of course, it was Priya. He hadn't seen her since he had gotten out of the HBC. He heaved himself off his couch with a groan and quickly checked himself out in the mirror, making sure his pants were hitting his waist line just right and that his collar was just the right amount of skewed to the left. Kelley was right, it was a perfect fit. He tried to smell his own breath, and was pretty happy with it. "Come."

A man he didn't recognize walked into the room. He was a sizable guy, though not quite as big as George. He noted the man's head was set back in his neck a bit, as if he had a chip on his shoulder too. George didn't care for his energy.

He took a slight step back as the stranger marched up to him. "Who are you?"

The cameras in the ceiling tracked him across the room. Getty didn't say anything, he quickly reached down to his boot and pulled out a switchblade. Then he swiped it swiftly at George's midsection, cutting him. The victim didn't dodge or move out of the way, he wasn't a warrior, he didn't even have the coordination to play basketball. Upstairs in HQ everyone gasped! They didn't know what to expect, but it wasn't that. Priya hit the red alert, and red flashing lights flooded every room in the building accompanied by a dull siren. Owens and Kelley took off down the hall toward George's quarters.

George stammered back and fell down. "Get away from me!" Was this the government coming to take him for the experiments Witten had prophesied?

Getty leaned in and watched George's purple blood seep through his khaki knit wide collar tee. He said, "No way," in a tone of wonder. "You're alright soldier, only nicked ya. Lift your shirt up."

George was starting to calm down as the strange attacker stood up casually and calmly folded his switchblade up. George did as he was asked. Getty leaned in and touched the wound gently, getting the purple blood on his finger. He smelled it, then put it to his tongue and reared his head back. "And I thought real blood tasted bad."

"Why are you tasting people's blood?"

"Touche." He reached his hand out and helped George up to his feet.

Now that George was on guard, and taller and bigger than Getty, he bowed up to him. "I ought to knock you out."

"You're welcome to try it big man. But I'm betting you're a lover not a fighter. Sit down, I won't take much more of your time."

Owens and Kelley plowed into the room almost tripping over each other.

"George, are you okay?!"

As a point of pride, George held up his hand, signaling he was okay and needed no assistance. Kelley and Owens looked around confused. "Touch him again and I'll kick your ass," said the blonde bomber.

"Okay," chuckled Getty. Turning back to George he asked, "How long were you dead for, do you know?"

"Like a hundred and fifty years."

"Wow," nodded Getty looking around the room, noting the giant HBC with a blanket and pillow inside. "Everybody you ever knew gotta be long gone by now. That doesn't tear you up?"

"Of course it does."

"You sleep in that thing every night?"

"Like dracula."

Getty laughed and shook his head, "Forever?"

"Maybe."

"And you're okay with that? Seems like a bad dream, like a never ending torture chamber."

"Have you ever lost anyone you loved before?"

You could hear a pin drop. "More than my share."

"And if they had a shot to live out more of their life, but you would never get to see them again or see how it all turned out, would you want that possibility for them even if it was scary or uncomfortable for them at times? Or would you rather them be dead and gone forever?"

Upstairs in HQ, Priya leaned into the monitors. She recognized her own eternal love for John in George's eloquent hypothetical.

Getty nodded, "the first one."

"So if you can imagine wanting that for someone you love, what's so wrong with wanting that for yourself?"

Witten mumbled to herself, "Preach."

George continued, "Death is unfair. We pretend it's not because it happens to all of us and there is nothing we can do about it, so it's a fair playing field, and that makes us feel better. But it's not fair. It's not okay, there's nothing remotely okay about it. And deep down we all know it. We should be fighting it, not just before it happens, but after it happens too. I'm a gamer, when I was alive before we couldn't pause our online multiplayer games."

"What?"

"I know. Can you even imagine? Every time you had to go take the trash out for your mom, or go to the bathroom, that's it for you. Game over. So the real stars of that world weren't the best or the smartest; they were the ones with the most consecutive free hours on their hands at a time. Isn't that a mind fuck?"

"You lost me."

"It's better if you can pause the game. It's a better game. If there is a way to do it, it's the right thing to do. Just like mainstream medicine, they're trying to save lives - they're not trying to play god or Dr. Frankenstein. These are real doctors! I didn't believe it either at first…"

The men started laughing, unable to continue through the absurdity of it all. Getty collected himself and said, "But we can't just all live forever, we already have an overpopulation problem on this planet."

"I don't think that's a huge concern. I'm so grateful to be alive. I'm just one person, I'm just one story, this isn't going to work for a lot of people, it might not work out for everyone they bring back either, we can't be naive about that. But don't you want to find out what happens next?"

***

Doctors Witten and Owens finally walked Getty out of Cryonicor at three in the morning. "We appreciate you keeping a lid on this for now," said Dr. Owens. Getty wasn't sure exactly how to feel about all of this or what it meant for him, but at least he had resolved to keep it to himself.

Witten added, "If you ever need anyone frozen. It's on the house. We owe you."

"Oh count on it," said Getty as he breezed out into the cool night air. And just like that he was gone, and with him their looming existential threat, at least for now.

Chapter 30

Life is Long

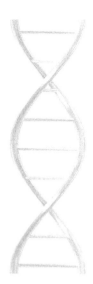

After Getty's exit, Witten returned to her office to find Gwen taking a turn on her speed bag. Her clumsy jabs were cute. "I see why you like this thing."

"What are you doing here?"

"I thought we should talk." They looked at the clock, it flashed 3:14 AM. Witten collapsed in her desk chair and pulled the re-up papers out of her drawer. Gwen picked them up. "You keep a set of these in your desk?"

Witten shrugged, "Just in case you changed your mind at the last minute. What's so funny?"

"I had a set in my desk too."

Witten sat up at attention, "You did?"

Gwen nodded meekly, still smiling. "But neither of us barged into the other's office. And I think we both know why." Witten slumped back in her chair, not sure if she actually did know why. Gwen continued, "Life is long you know, twenty years is a good run. Much better than most people."

"I thought we weren't most people."

"Even knowing how it all ended, I wouldn't trade those years. But there's too much water under the bridge for me anyway. Even though I don't feel like we can really survive that, being here and seeing all this work out like you said it would, I understand why you did what you did. I forgive you."

Witten wasn't especially comforted by her now ex-wife's forgiveness if it didn't come with a reconciliation. "So you left your partners and your practice to work here with me?"

"To work with George and the Alpo's and whoever else is coming out. You know me, I want to be where the action is, I couldn't turn it down. The research we will do here is going to remove the veil of what is possible. We are going to see how questions we dared never to ask ourselves will really play out, about who we truly are, body, mind and soul, and what it is we human beings ultimately want out of life."

"How is this supposed to work, with us, working together like this? I don't know how you do it Gwen. Cause it's tearing me up everytime I see you."

"Yeah. That part sucks, as you Americans say.

It's hard for me too. But it'll get easier... I think. And eventually I hope we can be friends as well as colleagues, because I want you in my life one way or another."

Dr. Witten could have easily gone the rest of her life without seeing a constant reminder of her marital failure. But, Owens hadn't really given her a choice. It's not like she could go work for another cryonic reanimation outfit. Their phone's went off with matching reminders:

Flight to Costa Rica leaves in 24 hours,
you may now check in online.

"Shit. Our re-up trip. What a waste."

Gwen stood up, "You know what? You should still go." Witten raised her eyebrow. "I'm serious. Trade in our coach seats for a first class ticket for yourself. When's the last time you went on a vacation?"

"By myself?"

"Yes! Traveling alone can be one of the most therapeutic experiences one can have. Travel at your own pace. You don't have to compromise with anyone. Wake up when you want, eat what you want, go where you want. Do it for yourself."

"What about Cryonicor, what about George?"

"George is okay right now, let us worry about that stuff. You have me and Dr. Owens and Priya to back you up. Don't you get it Samantha? You've made no secret about your fear of death. But you've spent the last fifty years of your life killing yourself trying to avoid it. You've got to start living and stop being haunted by the end."

Witten took her wife's words to heart. She struggled to imagine what a shock to the system a trip like that would be. She had never traveled much in her life. She was always nervous that an accident would befall her too far from a preservation center and she would slip away into oblivion. But maybe it was time to stop being ruled by precaution, fear, and dread. Was their room inside her for other things?

***

The next morning in the Cryonicor break room, Priya rifled through the fridge. She pulled out a container marked, WITTEN, and opened it out of curiosity. Chopped up celery stalks, raw onion and apple peels. Yumm. She put it back disgusted at the lengths people go to for their wellness. Kelley walked in nervously, his eyes red from a sleepless night.

Priya informed him, "Owens is looking for you."

"Well this day is shot. Do you think they're gonna fire me?"

Priya took a bite out of an apple and talked with her mouthful, "They should. But I don't see how they can. You already know too much, plus they are gonna have a tough time replacing your skill set. But you deserve to be fired, and I am saying that as your friend."

"I just thought..."

"—He's not a toy. He's a person and he almost died. You get that?"

"Yeah."

Their watches lit up. Priya said, "Meeting now."

"Shit."

***

Upstairs in HQ Gwen and Owens were at the head of the class. His black eye was almost gone. Dr. Witten was the last to arrive. She was accustomed to calling meetings, not attending them without warning. But this was her new normal and she was doing her best.

Owens asked Witten, "How's George?"

Owens knew exactly how he was but she appreciated his gesture of deference. She performed in kind. "Physically his wounds are healing, his ankle is broken, but with our nanobone treatments he should be healed in a week or two tops. The HBC has rectified his headaches and his respiratory issue, as long as he does his time everyday. Just like us, he shouldn't be walking around without an inhaler, he has a personal supply now. And he can go out like a normal person for a few hours at a time. He will need a new ankle bracelet for his timed eliminations for a few more weeks."

Gwen raised her hand politely. "He's also made some demands." Owens looked between the Wit-

359

tens confused. "No geochip. He wants a cell phone instead. And he wants to move out of Cryonicor. He is refusing to stay in his quarters on site. And he didn't ask this but, if he has come and go privileges we should give him an allowance, equal to what the state gives all of us. It's good for his independence."

"That's a good idea," said Kelley.

Owens shouted, "you don't get to talk!" The room was chilled. Kelley died inside a little. Dr. Owens stood up for a moment stroking the two day old graying stubble on his chin, he glanced up at Priya who looked away sheepishly. "Well, I plan on converting his quarters to a honeymoon sweet for the Alpos, who we are bringing out by the way so... buckle up. We will need to relocate him, but outside? Sounds risky. I don't think we should leave him alone, he tried to take his own life last night."

The room fell silent. Gwen had learned this from George and confided it only to Owens. But in the back of their minds, they had all suspected it. She added, "It's not ideal, but George is not going to do well if he stays here. He could make another attempt on his life if we treat him like a prisoner."

Witten said, "I agree with Dr. Kim, staying here is not a long-term solution. We need to build an outpatient program that we can use to transition patients, plural, hopefully."

Owens interjected, "And we will. But that's not

gonna happen overnight. What do we do with him in the meantime? Priya, what do you think?" Everyone's heads turned at once, to the raven eyed young cryonicist sitting in the back..

***

Later that afternoon, Witten politely knocked on a closed office door which whooshed open for her instantly. Owens was seated, going over mountains of data at his desk top reader. He pulled down his googles acknowledging her.

"Thanks again for the HBC units," she said.

"You're welcome."

"Look I don't know what kinda mind games you are trying to play with this hiring my wife stuff, but I am not—"

"Let me stop you right there. YOU brought her in here. YOU told her about George. I thought that was incredibly stupid. But I was wrong. She's exactly what we need, and if you could see past your personal feelings, you would agree with that."

"You should have discussed it with me first. We expired last night. How are we supposed to function as a team? How am I supposed to deal with seeing her everyday?"

"You're a big girl, you'll figure it out, cause she's not going anywhere."

"Then maybe I will."

"Oh really?" He sits up straight and leans into her game of chicken.

"I don't need this."

"Please. You think I buy that for one second? With a background in cryonics you might be able to get a gig at a blood bank at best. I don't care how brilliant you are. You're worth a lot, but only here."

She realized she was no different than Jack or Kelley or Priya, being a doctor didn't change anything. She was marooned. She sat down and buried her head in her hands at her wits end. He was surprised to see this kind of vulnerability from the ice queen herself.

After a beat he said, "I'm not a monster, I'm not trying to torture you. The truth is I knew about your marital problems. And I felt like you were distracted, making careless mistakes. I'd love to have this place all to myself except I can't do what you do... yet. So I needed your head in the game, I thought if you and your wife got back together, you could focus on your work and... if she was here, you might be able to work things out."

"You manipulative little prick!"

"I know I tried to save your marriage for my own personal gain, I'm practically Rasmussen."

"Well it backfired, because now we're two exes working together."

"It may have started off that way, but she's a full on rock star and I think this is really a win for me at least, either way."

"We're not ready to thaw the Alpos."

Owens said, "That's what this visit is really

about. Well, it's not your call anymore. I'm sorry."

Witten leaned in, elbows on knees trying to entreat him to see reason. She asked, "What's the rush?"

Owens angled his head in thought for a moment. "What are you afraid of? Failure? That never stopped you before - have you seen that cemetery out back? Your will to thaw at all costs is truly terrifying."

"It's different now."

"Why?"

"Because of George. He's alive. He's real. They're all real. We can't fuck this up."

"I don't think you're afraid of failure, I think you're afraid of success. This is what you wanted right? Now it's here. It's your moment doc. What are you gonna do with it?"

Witten let her guard down a moment, reeling from her loss of control. She said, "It's hard for me to..."

"I know," Owens interjected, nodding his head empathetically.

The corner of her mouth popped up and she said, "But I don't know if you know, like I know."

"Well, I'm a doctor too."

Something in this simple statement put her more at ease. She realized the burden that all of these decisions and secrets had taken on her life. And in Owens she began to see a mysterious ally, maybe even a partner. She announced, "Well it will have to wait until I get back."

"Get back? Where are you going?"

"Costa Rica, I leave in two hours." She had only decided in that moment.

"For how long?"

"Three weeks."

"No way, you can't leave for three weeks! I'm not approving that!"

"And I won't be reachable," she turned around, taking her leave.

"Don't you walk out of here. I am your boss."

"Fire me," she said over her shoulder before disappearing down the corridor.

Owens fell into his chair. What was he going to tell Martinez? He may have been the boss on paper but he would have to get used to making decisions in committee. Witten was his most worthy in-house adversary to date. She was totally irreplaceable and she knew it.

**

"Hello, my name is Mandy, can I get you anything?" asked the perky first class flight attendant. She continued, "Perhaps I could offer you one of our Delta brand Meyers I.V. Cocktails to ensure you are fresh with optimal immunity for your foreign adventure?" The attendant gestured to the couple behind Dr. Witten, who were both enjoying an IV drip and an inflight movie.

Witten dug through her carry-on bag and retrieved the vial of Tiger Blood. "I'm happy to pay for that, but do you mind if I switch it out with my own," she said, handing her the vial. "I'm a doctor."

"Of course doctor. And thank you for flying with Delta." The attendant began swiftly preparing the drip while Witten reclined in her seat and eagerly flipped through the brochure for the rejuvenating thermal hot springs of the Arenal Volcano.

***

As the light from the full moon shimmered onto the water surrounding The Keys, Priya laid in her bed wide awake. But she laid in the center of the bed, sprawled out across it. She stared up at the ceiling uncertain about the choice she'd made or where it would lead. But she was ready for something new.

***

George's long legs dangled out of the side of the open HBC unit. A new ankle bracelet was secured to his wrapped ankle. He petted Priya's black cat sitting in his lap. Her second bedroom had been all cleared out to make space for his HBC which took up half the room. George examined the half painted nursery walls that now made up his new home. He was scrolling through the internet, gorging himself on all that he had missed out on since he'd died. He stopped himself, and turned the phone screen off, resolving not to make the same mistakes he'd made in

365

the past. He put down the cat and laid down in his chamber. He realized there was a lot he didn't know about his new roommate. But at least he didn't feel alone anymore.

***

Meanwhile in the foxhole, two side by side tubes were carefully removed from their row, on their way to the reanimation chamber.

The End

Acknowledgements

This project has been whirling around my head for almost ten years in various formats and several people have been instrumental in its creation. First and foremost I would like to acknowledge my brother Matt Abbott who has been my chief co-conspirator in this effort offering tremendous amounts of his time helping me brainstorm and edit. He is ALWAYS ready without warning to donate entire evenings and days off to play in fantasy worlds with me. My mother Elizabeth Abbott has served as my trusted final proofreader and been an evergreen champion of my writerly pursuits. Brent Kyle contributed the cover art for the book and has been my chief believing mirror. My husband Ken Kabukuru has shared me with this project for ages. I thank him for his understanding and love as well as his shrewd notes and fantastic story ideas. I would also like to thank my beta readers: Bridie, Manny, Jenny, Katy, Gus and Miho whose thoughtful notes were invaluable to me.

THAW 2

For a preview of the first chapter of THAW 2, please visit: https://www.ackabukuru.com/thaw2preview

Printed in Great Britain
by Amazon

79297857R00210